A SERPENT IN ᴛ

CW00470835

A SERPENT IN THE HOUSE

Victoria F. Leffingwell

Translated by the author and R.L. Leffingwell

Original title: La serpiente en casa
Copyright © 2020 Victoria F. Leffingwell
shuinero@icloud.com

ISBN: 9798739566034
Imprint: Independently published

Translated by the author and R.L. Leffingwell
Book Layout & Cover design: Inma P.-Zubizarreta, 2021
Cover photo: David Clode on Unsplash
Author photo: Victoria

For Teresa, who cannot read this story,
but who lived it,
and for Manuela who did not live it,
but can read it.
With love

Do not cry for me,
you who have loved me so much.
I rest in the Lord and ask
that we meet in Heaven.
Saint Ambrose

Early rose death in flight,
early rose the dawn
early you have fallen to ground.
Miguel Hernandez, Elegy

TABLE OF CONTENTS

ACKNOWLEDGMENTS

The great writer García Márquez wrote his novel "Love in the time of cholera" recalling an epidemic. Even being light years away from the teacher, this novel, of loves and heartbreaks, passions and intrigues, has been able to be written thanks to the forced confinement in the times of that monarchical virus, the terrible plague that is hitting the whole world, and it could well have been called "Heartbreak in the times of Corona."

But it is to my magnificent partner and friend Robert, whom I always have to thank for everything I write, for the infinite patience involved in putting up with me, and being by my side when I start to create characters, when they come to life and grow and grow until they end up becoming people, and specially with the translation of this novel. Thank you, friend!

Sarasota, Florida March-May, 2020

PROLOGUE

This novel is pure fiction, but it is based on a true story. The names of the protagonists and certain details have been changed to preserve their anonymity, and circumstances have been fictionalized, but could it all have been like this? Are the events narrated a complete fiction?

All the characters, to a greater or lesser extent, had to live in a turbulent time, too much was happening, not only in our country of Spain but also worldwide. Several of the protagonists endured, directly or indirectly, the consequences of two world conflagrations, and all of them lived through the Spanish civil war, which were added to another series of catastrophes and calamities of the period, such as the unfairly called "Spanish flu," which began in 1918 and devastated the entire world for two years, claiming more than fifty million lives; they also witnessed the establishment of the Dictatorship of Primo de Rivera, the stock market crash of the North American markets of 1929 that sank the world economies, the fall of the monarchy in our country in 1931 and the subsequent establishment of the Second Republic, the so-called National Uprising, the fratricidal struggles during the war, and the loss of the war on the part of the Republican side, which would lead to the omnipresent power of General Franco, with its consequences for the losers; they suffered the times of rationing and black market, the constant threat in the years following the end of the contest due to the actions of the Maquis, a delusional anti-Franco organization, a war-horse of the Civil Guard, which until well into the 1960s were not considered finally exterminated.

Under the putative umbrella threat of the maquis guerrillas, and blaming on them many acts, outrages, misdeeds and murders that the organization had not committed, many people carried out private revenge, seized land and farms that were not theirs and, in the worst cases, committed horrible crimes against people who had no political significance, nor had stood out in any way.

Really to know what actions the members of the maquis carried out in the various Spanish provinces, despite the many documented studies that exist, is an almost impossible task, since in the first years after the end of the war the maquis was a mixed bag into which almost everything that bothered people from the winning side could be spilled, and many took advantage of this circumstance to achieve their particular ends and thus remain unpunished.

In the case of the protagonist of this novel, although there are no certainties or confirmations of the events that are narrated, since all the actors and spectators of the drama are dead, and the living who could contribute some significant data by having heard it from their elders, cannot or will not do so without breaking the fragile balance between conscience and good name, yet, indeed, in recent years it can be affirmed that there are sufficient indications to know that his murder was simply a crime of passion, and that the circumstances of the period in which they found themselves favored the perpetrators, allowing them to escape ordinary justice. Of the other, the divine, only they could know whether they have also been able to outwit it.

But were the facts like this?

Because, as I think Siri Hustvedt has said, and correct me if I'm wrong, the art of fiction is simply to make what is only in the writer's imagination seem real.

1. SUMMER 1967 - CEMETERY

At last it seemed that the long process that had begun twenty-five years before was going to end.

The *sepulturero*, the entomber, with his trowel and mortar, was finishing off the enclosure of the burial niche. The simple black marble tombstone resembled a book open in the middle: on the right hand side were the dates of Juan Carlos's father, whom he had hardly had time to get to know, but whom he always longed for, and on the left his, with an epitaph that read: "Your mother and your sister do not forget you," although neither of them were present that day. The mother had died seven years earlier, with the same grief that had kept her from going to pray at his former tomb; and the sister at this time was in bed suffering from a serious illness.

Only his brother-in-law Jorge, accompanied by a few friends, had gone up to the cemetery, fulfilling a promise made many years before, with the simple and small box containing a few bones, the remains of what he had been, and while the priest said the last prayers, Jorge remembered...

2. JORGE - MAY 1942

"Don Jorge, a couple of Civil Guards have come to look for you," said one of his employees, who hastily entered the office. "They are waiting for you out there. Come out, please!"

Jorge, who despite his relative youth was in all his movements very parsimonious, when he heard who were looking for him, got up immediately, since although the civil war that had devastated the country had ended three years before, there were still many final spasms and debris, and his position at the head of communications in Turgalium put him in direct contact with the authorities almost every day. The latest bands of the maquis and their unwanted incursions continued to worry much of the populace.

"Good morning, Don Jorge, we are sorry to bring you very bad news..." the corporal said as soon as he appeared, for what they were going to tell him this time was personal, and just by seeing the faces of these *Benemérita* he sensed that it was something very serious.

As he had lost his mother seven years before, a victim of peritonitis that snatched her life when she still had a long time and a great desire to live, and without being able to see her greatest dream come true, which was to be able to see her five children established; and as only three years later, in the middle of the war and a few months before his marriage, his father also died, he assumed that something had happened to one of his siblings, who all lived in Madrid. He'd seen his wife and his little daughter shortly before, in their home on the same floor as the offices, when he'd had his eleven o'clock midway meal, a custom he had acquired when he arrived in the city in December 1935.

But it had nothing to do with his siblings.

—Don Jorge, there has been a terrible accident. We need you to accompany us to identify the body of your brother-in-law — the corporal continued — We know it's him, but the head is shattered and someone in the family must do it. We have just communicated the sad news to the wife of the deceased, although we've only told her that there's been an accident and that he was injured, but we don't believe she is in a condition to go there, the sight of the corpse can be very unpleasant.

Jorge felt his legs weaken and he involuntarily began to tremble, his mind had not yet registered what his ears had heard. How was it possible that what they were telling him was true? It must have been a mistake, macabre and sad, but a mistake.

Because only the day before, not even twenty-four hours had passed yet, he and Juan Carlos had been talking in the same place where the Guards were now. His brother-in-law had come to Jorge's home to see his sister and his goddaughter, and then to say goodbye to him as well, since he planned to be away a few days at his hacienda "La Operetta," located in the Badajoz district of Valdecaballeros for although he and his wife, Margarita, lived in Turgalium, they spent long periods in the country, and when they did not, Juan Carlos had the habit of going to the hacienda very frequently to review everything first-hand, although he had a wonderful administrator who even resided there; but he liked to check how the crops were going, talk to his workers and enjoy the Extremadura countryside for a few days.

But there was no mistake. Someone had put several bullets into his head in the early morning, while he was sleeping peacefully, and they had done the job with such cruelty that it was almost impossible to recognize his kind face amidst the mass of bone, blood and flesh.

Once he had recovered a bit, the first thing Jorge thought was how to communicate this to his wife and mother-in-law, imagining their reaction, because the blow would be huge for both of them, and he knew that it was he who would have to do it.

At that moment and as if out of the blue, his friend Manuel arrived at the offices, and he saw a ray of hope: he would not be alone for the shattering statement.

Manolo had not gone there fortuitously. A few minutes before he had learned by chance of the misfortune, and the gruesome details, and with good judgment he thought that perhaps his knowledge as the dentist of the deceased would be necessary for the identification and removal of the corpse.

The two went through to the flat, not knowing exactly how they would attack the matter, but hoping that some inspiration would come to them that might mitigate the blow a bit.

This home, located in the city's Plaza Mayor, was accessed from the street by going up a short flight of stairs; the door at the top of the stairs opened into a long corridor that had two other doors at its extremities: one into the family residence and the other into the Telegraph Center.

They turned right down the corridor, and when they reached the apartment, Teresa, Jorge's wife, who was preparing her daughter for a walk, was a little surprised to see them appear at such an unusual time. But she was immediately delighted that they were there, since the visit would give her the opportunity to chat for a while with adults, and take a break in that way from the incessant chatter of her little daughter Manuela, which (although she found it very funny) on many occasions exhausted her, as usually happens when with children, although you adore them; and she ended up feeling a bit beat. The girl, at almost three years old, was in that beautiful and amusing but terrible time, when everything is questions, discoveries and continuous movement.

Her pregnancy with her second child was in the sixth month and she was already feeling heavy and tired; nor did the still incipient but constant heart ailment contribute to her well-being: as a child, one day when she was going to school, it suddenly started to rain and her clothes and shoes got soaked. But rather than tell the nun, perhaps out of shyness or embarrassment, she remained silent and spent several hours in wet shoes, uniform, and even underwear.

When she returned home her head and throat ached and she had a high fever. Her mother and her aunt Tomasa (who lived with them since before her father had passed away and was a second mother to her) were scared when they saw the state she was in: she was shivering with cold, her eyes were red and watery, her forehead was burning, and her general appearance was pitiful, so after putting her to bed and forcing her to have a hot drink, they immediately called the GP, who came and simply diagnosed tonsillitis.

But many days passed and little Teresa did not improve; her general decline had them very worried, she spent hours asleep or delirious, and seeing that with the medicines that had been prescribed for her she did not improve, they decided to do something that was customary at that time in serious cases: a consultation with three famous doctors from another city, who, after examining and listening to the girl, gave a unanimous verdict: the tonsillitis had degenerated into rheumatic fever and great care would have to be taken in the future so that the heart did not suffer. But her heart did suffer. Since then her health was seriously affected because in addition to painful periodic outbreaks of rheumatism, she had ended up with a significant decompensation of the heart, which, although it did not prevent her from functioning normally and performing many tasks, did decrease her stamina when she felt discontented or was forced to go to any extraordinary effort.

With that second pregnancy her health seemed much weaker, perhaps because unlike the first in which she could rest and relax whenever she felt like it, with little Manuela around that luxury was no longer allowed, although she was very lucky to have fantastic domestic help that freed her from most chores. But knowing that in a few months the new offspring would completely absorb her and she would be able to enjoy Manuela less, she was now trying to spend as much time with her child as possible.

Although at first she was delighted by the visit, as soon as she observed the faces of her husband and her friend, she knew that something had happened. She insisted that they sit down and tell her, fearing that something had happened to Gabrielle, her friend and Manolo's wife, who had gone to Paris to visit her family, or to her mother, who, although she was in very good health, would turn fifty four years very soon.

—I'm going to tell Juliana the cook to get you a coffee, but first of all I want you to tell me where those faces come from. Tell me what's wrong, Jorge, don't keep me in suspense.

Jorge approached his wife, pretending a tranquility that he did not feel, and hugging her said:

—Teresa, there has been an accident. We do not yet know the details, but by all indications it seems that Juan Carlos is injured. I just wanted to tell you before going to the hacienda and make sure it was me who was telling you. Manolo has to see some patients in that area and has offered to accompany me.

Upon hearing those words, Teresa's sixth sense told her that they were deceiving her, that her brother, her only brother as well as her friend and confidant, had disappeared forever. A thick black curtain came between her and the outside world, and she was just short of falling to the ground. The pain that gripped her belly and locked her heart in a tight grip was the strongest she had ever felt; not even when she gave birth to her daughter, after a slow and painful delivery, had she felt like she did at this moment; but drawing strength from where she did not have it, and not wanting to believe what her instinct was whispering to her, she sat up and told them:

—I'm going with you too! We must notify Margarita immediately in case she wants to come with us, and tell mother not to leave the house until we return. Tell her to inform the doctor in the meantime, so that everything is ready for our return.

Before Jorge could speak, Manolo came forward and said:

—Margarita already knows. Now we will go to see her for a moment and we will also see your mother. You'd better stay here. As soon as we see him and know something we will phone you or send you a telegram. Let's not do crazy things because we will need all our strength later to take care of him. You try to be as calm as you can and leave everything in our hands. We are leaving now, the sooner we do it, the sooner we will return.

Teresa, although her spirit was far from being calm, agreed to their proposal and let them go, but not before insisting that they keep her informed of the news they found.

As a next step, they went to the house of Teresa's mother and sister-in-law which luckily was very close to where they were, as they did not want to delay more than strictly necessary before leaving for the hacienda.

That house, a magnificent three-story building, was where Teresa had lived until her marriage and there, on the first floor, her mother, Edelmira, continued to reside, and on the second floor the wedded couple formed by Juan Carlos and Margarita.

Edelmira was not at home. According to a servant, she had not yet returned from her usual round of churches and convents where she went each day, an occupation that consumed much of the morning and which she was unable to renounce, only failing that self-imposed obligation when she was ill (fortunately on very few occasions), or traveling.

After insisting to the girl not to let her mistress leave the house under any circumstances, once she arrived, they went up to see Margarita, who was in. They were both surprised by the fortitude with which she received them, for they both knew that she was aware of the terrible news, although not that he was dead. Finding her as smiling, painted and groomed as she usually was, seemed a bit strange, but they blamed it on the impact of the news. You never know how someone is going to react to bad news, whether with tears or with laughter, but they were both extremely shocked that she was so calm and relaxed, as if the matter did not touch her; the two left the flat with a strange feeling, but neither commented on their thoughts. A difficult task awaited them and they set out for the hacienda.

When they spoke with Margarita, even though they did not know how much of what they said registered, they insisted that in case she said something to Edelmira she should downplay the accident, and of course that she shouldn't think of telling her that it seemed serious, and that she do the same with Teresa. She did not have to tell them the whole truth so as not to worry them unnecessarily, which she agreed to without any problems, and told them not to worry, that she would control the situation and would take care of notifying the doctor.

The trip was anything but pleasant. Although the distance between Turgalium and Cañamero was not many kilometers, the road was bad, with many potholes and curves and it took them a long time to arrive. In addition, the circumstances of those moments prevented their enjoying the beautiful, flower-covered landscape of the Extremadura countryside in spring, as they had done on other occasions. Even though anticipating what they were going to see, the horror that awaited them went beyond their worst imaginings.

La Operetta, although registered and judicially belonging to the Valdecaballeros district, was located between this town and Cañamero, so when they reached the latter city they took a dirt back road to shorten the trip as much as possible. During the drive from Turgalium, Manolo had been telling Jorge about another terrible event that had occurred in 1928, another crime that had shocked the entire region in which a 25-year-old woman, nicknamed "La Molinera," had been murdered and mutilated cruelly by a former suitor, unable to bear that she lived happily with her husband. Manolo, although he had read it at the time, had forgotten all about it, but it so happened that not a week before he found an old newspaper in which the events were narrated with sundry details.

Not that it was the most suitable subject at that time, but it served to make Jorge's mind forget a little where they were, and what they were going to do.

When they finally arrived at the hacienda, another pair of civil guards were waiting for them at the door of the house, plus Antonio the administrator, the judge, the forensic doctor and several workers; a little further away were crowded numerous onlookers, who, although they had no access to the interior, did not want to move from the spot so as to learn everything that was happening.

The house on the estate, where the two friends had been frequently in the last year, both in get togethers and in a large hunt the previous fall, resembled an Andalusian cortijo: with only one floor, it consisted of several bedrooms and a bathroom with the latest and best facilities. All the rooms were large and very sunny. Passing through the entrance hall, you came to a beautiful living room with large windows from which you looked upon the garden and orchard. Around a huge fireplace there were four armchairs, and scattered around the room were various side tables. A large dining table with six chairs and two armchairs sat further away opposite the fireplace, before a sliding glass door that led to the back veranda. A three-seater sofa, upholstered in green velvet, with two matching armchairs, and a long table in front invited the visitor to sit down. Paintings, tapestries, lamps and soft rugs completed the pleasant room, in which they had had such good times, but Jorge and Manolo, accompanied by the others, did not stop there for even a moment, but went directly to the main bedroom.

Like the living room, this room was usually a cheerful and bright place, very large and decorated with exquisite taste, but that day the windows were closed, the curtains were drawn and the only light that illuminated it was the one coming from the ceiling lamp .

The scene they faced was terrifying: with its blue and white striped pajamas the body looked like that of a person asleep and relaxed, but the head, or what little was left of it, was a bloody mass, and seeing that horror Jorge felt a painful surging in his belly. He stumbled closer to the least visible corner and scarcely reached it when his stomach emptied everything he had ingested in the last hours.

Although the state of the corpse's head made identification very difficult, Manolo's expertise confirmed the victim was Juan Carlos, and once that was done, everyone left the room as quickly as possible.

Jorge was beside himself. It was the first time he had seen a person in those circumstances, and although he tried to remain lucid, only one thought filled his mind: Why? Why? His friend, more experienced in these types of scenes since he had been at the front during the war, and therefore had faced similar cases, held him tightly, since he feared that at any moment he would fall to the ground.

Once in the living room, and after forcing Jorge to have a strong drink that would make him react, having previously observed how the bedroom was, Manolo, not clearly realizing several shots had been fired, said to all present:

—The windows are closed and I have not seen any sign that the door has been forced. Do you have any idea what could have happened here at dawn? Because I knew him well and that is why I can assure you without any doubt that Juan Carlos has never been prone to suicide. Besides, the murder weapon is not there either. This looks like the work of a bloody madman.

Before the pair from the Civil Guard, present along with the judge during the entire time that the examination lasted, could answer, Antonio the administrator, spoke:

—Don Juan Carlos never closed his bedroom if he was alone. Only when the *señora* of the house was here did they close that door. Anyone who knew their customs could have come in and commit this atrocity.

—But was there no one in the house, not even a servant or someone to do the chores? Manolo kept asking.

—No —replied the administrator— usually, when the boss came, only one of the servants would take care of his meals, or any other need he had. When he came with Doña Margarita it was different, because she always brought her maid and her cook, but as you know, Don Juan Carlos was very easygoing and did not want any fuss. What he liked was enjoying the countryside, everything else didn't matter to him.

At these words, Manolo, who had the judge on his right and was a few steps from the doctor, with a strong and forceful voice rebuked the administrator:

—Antonio, your house is there next door. How is it possible that you didn't hear anything? I can't believe you didn't get woken up by the noise that the murderer necessarily had to make. And the rest of those who live on the farm? There are many people around, it doesn't make any sense that nobody heard anything, and that you didn't find the body till this morning....

Antonio, his face red as if he were going to have a stroke, giving a step towards the outside door answered:

—Yesterday afternoon I went to have some wine with several friends. We over did it, and when I finally fell into bed I was in no condition to hear or know anything. If the gentlemen no longer need me for the moment, I will retire.

Manolo was dumbfounded, but did not comment.

After the inspection of the deceased by the forensic doctor, with the approximate establishment of the time at which the death had occurred (midnight on the same day they were still in), the Judge ordered the removal of the body and the coroner arranged what was needed for its transfer and subsequent autopsy, which would be carried out in another location. As they did not yet know how long the entire process would take, they suggested that once it was finished he should be buried in the same location.

Although Jorge had recovered a bit, his head still did not rule as usual, and hence he agreed to the proposal, signed the necessary documents for this purpose, and after saying goodbye to those present, the two friends went to the car that would take them back to their city, even without knowing how they would tell Teresa, Edelmira and Margarita the bad news.

They stopped in Cañamero, not to drink wines as they usually did when they went to the farm, but to calm their stomachs and minds a bit, decide how they would present the facts to the three women, and comment on what was on their minds.

The first to speak, anticipating the words that were about to come out of his friend's mouth, was Jorge, who, forcing back the tears that were already fogging up his glasses, said:

—Did you notice that Antonio always referred to Juan Carlos in the past tense? Didn't you find something strange? And even more, living as he does on the farm for his convenience, so as not to pay rent elsewhere, does it seem normal to you that the same day that Juan Carlos arrived at La Operetta he would go "to have wines"? Doesn't he have all the time in the world to do it when he is alone? I would suppose that an administrator, even if he is as atypical as he is, would spend the first hours when his employer arrives, informing him of the news.... Even being in the state of shock I was in, it sounded strange to me. And neither did I see any sign of pity, or at least sympathy or feeling in him. Man, something here doesn't fit.

Manolo nodded and also commented on everything that seemed strange to him, which was quite a lot, because they were talking about an hacienda where almost fifty people lived. Were they all deaf or drunk? Or had they made themselves deaf by covering up something they knew? The civil guards had suggested that the atrocity could be the work of the Maquis, and the judge and the forensic doctor had shared that same feeling, perhaps because they all lived in the area and had information unknown to them. Perhaps the administrator, as well as all the other families that lived on the farm, had heard something, and were silent for fear of future reprisals. But now they had a tough task ahead of them, so they resumed their journey.

Coming home was like lifting the lid of Pandora's box. They did not have a planned script, they had preferred to leave everything up in the air and just see how they could get through the moment, although the two agreed to spare Teresa, Edelmira and Margarita the maximum possible details, to be concise in the exposition of the facts as much as they could, and to insinuate that the outrage had been the work of either poachers or the Maquis. Jorge had asked Manolo to accompany him in that ordeal, something his friend planned to do anyway.

They arrived at Teresa and Jorge's house. Although it was quite late, she and her mother were waiting as would be supposed; not so Margarita, who had passed by there but who told them she was very tired and was going to sleep and to let her know when they knew something; those two were so nervous and restless that they were not even shocked by her statement. Each one reacts to adversity in a certain way, Teresa told herself, repeating the phrase that Jorge used often....

There was no choice but to speak and deliver the tragic news: Juan Carlos had died. The two women, who still harbored certain hopes, and who, when they saw them arrive without the wounded man, thought he might be in a hospital, fell as if struck down and it was a long time before they came to their senses.

3. JUAN CARLOS - NOVEMBER 1935

The day had dawned cold and foggy. At that hour, however, almost eleven in the morning, the monastery shone in all its splendor. In a room at the Hosteria, the groom, helped by his three best friends, put the finishing touches on his outfit, still without believing his luck: in a few minutes his betrothed, his precious Margarita whom he had met only a few months before, would become his wife until the end of his days.

It had all been fortuitous, for he was naturally shy and calm and not very fond of revelries and celebrations, but on the last day of the preceding year a few of his friends from the city had insisted so much that he had no choice but to accompany them to a great fiesta that was celebrated in his city's Casino —an elegant combination of gambling lounges, social hall, restaurant and ballroom.

The very select of Turgalium society had congregated there: the women displayed their best finery and the men did not lag behind, with formal dark suits, immaculate white shirts and even, the most daring, showing in the upper pocket of the jacket a flower, instead of the usual handkerchief to match the tie.

The dresses of the women might be the envy of a fashion parade: precious and vaporous, each and every one of them contributed to enhancing the youth and beauty of their wearers.

It had been a difficult year and the general strike known as the October Revolution of 1934, during the second biennium of the Second Republic, encouraged by broad sectors and leaders of the Socialist Party, the Workers General Union, the Workers National Confederation, the Communist Party of Spain, and the Anarchist Federation, although carried out mainly in Catalonia and Asturias, had made its impact felt in the rest of the country, and it had even been noticed in such a small city, far from the spotlight, and conservative, like Turgalium, so that the desire to have fun and forget, even if only for a few hours, was in everyone's mind, and the fiestas this time were much more impressive than in previous years.

In the Casino, a large orchestra and vocalists enlivened the atmosphere with their songs, and numerous couples danced to fashionable rhythms on the central dance floor. In addition, the new Charleston dance allowed women to dance alone without the need for a male companion, so when the orchestra attacked any of these songs all the attendees threw themselves into demonstrating their expertise, giving the event even more charm.

Juan Carlos and his friends were in the ambigu, tasting a selection of canapés and drinks, when he saw her: she stood out among all those dancing, with her mid-leg ivory-colored dress, wide neckline at the back, a long pearl necklace that swayed rhythmically with each step, shoes that melded with her skin and, above all, a beautiful smile that made thousands of stars appear in her green eyes.

—Do you know who that girl is?" he asked.

His friend Manolo, one of the city's dentists, replied:

—Yes, it's Margarita. She's just arrived from Argentina after spending a few months with relatives. She's from Guadalupe and that's why you don't know her, but you do know her brother Francisco. We're going to tell him to introduce her to us.

The two of them went over to Francisco. The piece had ended and Margarita had joined the group around her brother, who at that moment must have been telling something very funny, since everyone was laughing.

—Good evening everyone, it seems we're having a good time, Manolo said. —And who is this beauty we have here, if it may be known?

—Well, nothing more and nothing less than my sister Margarita, who has just returned to us after her long journey through the Pampas, Francisco replied. —Look sister, these are my good friends Manolo and Juan Carlos, be good, don't break their hearts!

Margarita came forward, and with the greatest naturalness, before either could react, she planted a kiss on each cheek, a custom that she had acquired where she recently resided, which they both loved, as it was different from what they were used to. Women then, when they were introduced, extended a hand timidly and only the "fresh" or "loose" woman (or of light behavior, as they were euphemistically described), and those from other countries, dared such behavior.

At that moment the orchestra began to play a tango, and Margarita, taking Juan Carlos by the arm, said to him:

—Let's dance! If you don't know how to do it well, don't worry, I'll show you the steps.

But he, in addition to having an exquisite education, was a good dancer, something his mother had insisted on, knowing his shy character, as a key to open doors to future relationships, and he knew that dancing that tango with someone like her would be a wonderful experience.

Juan Carlos followed her, mentally wondering which gods were favoring him that night to make such luck possible, because by his side and without any effort on his part, was the most beautiful girl he had seen in his life.

They danced, they laughed, and he, who was generally of few words except with people he knew well, was eloquent, friendly and charming, showing off his knowledge but without pedantry.

I have already made a small sketch of Margarita's physical charms, but these were not the most important once she was known. The words that most defined her and her most characteristic trait were "a charming creature," she was very lively and witty, she made jokes about anything (sometimes a little risqué, by the standards of the moment) and being in her company ensured that one would not be left without entertainment even for a second.

Quite the opposite of Juan Carlos, who was serious, shy and reserved, and who had always dedicated most of the hours of the day to study, reading and another of his passions: listening to music.

The night passed happily and from the moment of the tango until he left her at her brother's house in the early hours of the morning, they did not separate.

Juan Carlos was in a cloud. So much so that he did not close an eye that night, and as soon as his sister Teresa (with whom he had an unbeatable relationship) got up, while the two of them had their customary breakfast of hot chocolate with churros and sponge cake, he told her everything that had happened, the accumulation of sensations that he had experienced and, very seriously and putting great emphasis on his words, he said:

—Teresita! If I don't marry Margarita, I won't marry anyone!

Teresa was quite surprised, because she knew her brother and knew that he was not prone to outbursts or sudden crushes, but as she continued to listen to the narration of how the previous night had passed, she was infected with his enthusiasm and was happy for him. For once, the first time in his life, Juan Carlos departed from his role as a super responsible person and acted freely.

She had seen Margarita only for a moment at the Casino, but as she was occupied with her friends and some suitors who were hovering around her, she had no chance to see what her brother was doing.

Teresa had not known her father, as he had died when she was only nine months old, leaving behind a young inconsolable widow, then only twenty-six years old, and the two children. Although Juan Carlos was only a six-year-old at the time of his father death, his serious and responsible character made him adopt the role of protector, not only of his little sister but also of his mother, and this had increased over time, so that in that house no decision was ever made, no matter how small, without first consulting him. In addition, as he was very cultivated and had studied law, he was the right person to solve any problem that arose, from the most trivial to the most important.

The two siblings talked about Margarita for hours and hours; to tell the truth, it was Juan Carlos who spoke, while Teresa listened to the torrent of words, the praises and the panegyric, surprised at the turnaround that her brother had experienced in so few hours, until he exclaimed:

—I have to get ready quickly. I'm meeting Margarita for an aperitif. I'll eat with you today, but tell mother not to worry if I'm a little late. Margarita returns to Guadalupe tomorrow and I want to be with her as much as possible. I'll tell you everything later.

Teresa was still sitting at the *mesa camilla* (a round table draped nearly to the floor with a heavy velvet, and supporting underneath a brazier of glowing oakwood charcoal), mentally reviewing the conversation, when her mother and Aunt Tomasa came in from their usual morning rounds visiting convents and churches, where they prayed for the whole family and conversed with the nuns and novices, many of them their goddaughters.

—Do you know what gives with your brother? He's running like the Devil's after him. — commented Edelmira, who was very given to saws and similes, and normally used some such idiom every time she spoke.

Teresa, was not sure how much she could tell them without betraying her brother's confidence, and she replied:

—Well, last night he met a girl, he liked her quite a bit and they have arranged to have an aperitif together, but he told me that he will have lunch with us, although perhaps a little later. I'm going out too, for a stroll with cousin Piluca, so if you get tired of waiting for us, you can start.

Aunt Tomasa, who had been silent the entire time that the mother-daughter exchange lasted, commented:

—As long as she's not a gold digger.... You know that Juan Carlos is terrific, but when it comes to women, he's a dodo. And he's a fine match. Any girl would be more than happy if she caught him....

At that comment, Edelmira could not help bursting out:

—What do you say? A dodo? What Juan Carlos is, is the best and most responsible son that any mother could have! The thing is, is that as you've not had children, you don't know the kind of offspring that are out there; look, I will tell you....

Teresa smiled, as she always did when the two sisters-in-law were engrossed in one of their endless conversations — where the two, and each in her own way, tried to affirm her point of view — knowing the deep love they possessed for each other and that they could not live the one without the other, and that the discussion would not get out of hand, or, in her mother's expression, that "the blood would not run to the river." She got up, went to fix herself up, and left them to themselves.

When Teresa and Piluca were walking through the square they saw Juan Carlos coming out of one of the bars accompanied by Margarita. They approached them and after he made the expected introductions and invited them to have a drink with them, Margarita said:

—Teresa, you can't imagine how much I wanted to meet you, and also you, Piluca. I know that the three of us are going to be very good friends and I would like you to come soon to see me in my town. Look, on January sixth they have a very beautiful festival there and the Three Wise Men present an offering to the Virgin. I'll expect you without fail that day!

Faced with such vehemence and taken by surprise, the two cousins were delighted to accept and said goodbye, but not before assuring their new acquaintance that they would go on that date.

In the afternoon, after the great New Year's meal, in which the four members of the family tasted the favorite viands of the man of the house (a menu that he had tried in Madrid for the first time on a trip in his student years and which he said brought back very good memories, and insisted that they eat each New Year, although with some slight variations of certain dishes), and which consisted of a magnificent mincemeat soup, followed by over-roasted split sea bream and an excellent leg of suckling lamb, washed down with a good homegrown wine and culminating in sweet liqueurs with the desserts, Juan Carlos went out again, something he usually did not do, because on Sundays and holidays when they ate together, after a long after-dinner chat with his family he retired to his library to read and listen to music until a cousin or friend came to pick him up and they went for a walk.

The three women were speechless at this unusual behavior, but before the two ladies said anything, Teresa spoke up:

—This afternoon my cousin and I met Margarita. She is very pretty and very nice. She has invited us to her house on Three Kings Day, and Juan Carlos later told me that he will notify a chauffeur to take and bring the three of us. Aunt Tomasa, you don't have to worry: she's from a very good family and she's not looking for money. It seems to me that the two have fitted in very well and they look very happy together. At least, I've never seen my brother laugh and smile as much as in the last few hours.

As the two trusted her good judgment, they calmed down and dedicated themselves to their prayers, interspersing comments about Juan Carlos's new friend.

January sixth threatened rain. It was a cold, unpleasant day, but the spirits of the travelers were high and the low temperature did not matter to them. Well equipped with coats, gloves and scarves, carrying as a detail a tray of cakes in their hands, the three of them stepped from the rental sedan at Margarita's door. As soon as she saw them in the hallway she started giving them kisses and hugs as if they were family members she hadn't seen in a long time.

—Come in, come in, she told them —Today it's extremely cold, somebody told me it's snowing in the mountains, but the house is very warm. Now you sit in front of the fireplace for a while and as soon as you warm up we'll go to the Monastery to see everything, you'll see how much you will like the ceremony.

And without further ado, she took the two girls by the arm, and led the group to the living room, where a large fire was crackling, giving the whole room a cozy atmosphere. Her father, Don Rosendo, got up when he saw them enter and kindly invited them to sit in the armchairs that were in front of the fireplace, but not before ringing a small bell that he had within reach. Immediately, a servant girl appeared, well uniformed in black, wearing a white lace apron and an immaculate cap on her head, and making a small bow as she entered. She asked:

—What would the *señores* like to have?

Teresa and Piluca looked at each other puzzled and almost began to laugh. Despite the efforts that both they and their mothers put into trying to "civilize" and polish the successive servants who passed through their houses, they never achieved more than one tasteless and graceless "you," or even "yous," far from the finesse and charm of the maid in front of them.

When she left, while the two men chatted amiably about the haciendas, the laborers, and the crops, the two girls almost in unison asked:

—Where, how, and when did you get that jewel?

Margarita, watching the door in case the object of their inquiry came in, told them:

—You can't even imagine what Eulogia was like when she entered in service here. She knew absolutely nothing about anything, worse even than the worst we had ever had before, She ate with her hands, wiped her nose with the edge of the dress, well I could be telling you how she was until night falls, and it wouldn't end, although I realized right away that the poor thing was very clever, but she lacked instruction and a hand to teach and direct her. Her parents are our guards at one of the farms and they were not capable of teaching her even the most basic things, so I took her to the terrace one day and asked her if what she wanted was to be a rustic all her life. Imagine, she didn't even know what the word "rustic" meant! When I explained it to her in simple words, she said "No, missus, what I wants is 'bein' sos fine-uz at least like you", so, as soon as I recovered from the fit of laughter, I took as my main obligation every day to teach her to behave and be a good maid, and I seem to have succeeded because there is no one who sees how she behaves now who does not praise her manners.

At that moment Eulogia returned with some sarsaparillas and a good plate of cold cuts, and the lady of the house discreetly fell silent. After placing the food and drinks on a side table and holding out to each of them a starched white linen napkin with a tatting in the center, she asked whether anything else was wanted and with another little bow she left the room.

Once the travelers had warmed up a bit and had had their aperitif, leaving the owner of the house ensconced before the fire, the four of them walked to the Monastery to watch the festivities. Not only had the vast majority of the inhabitants of the town gathered there, but since it was a well-known festival throughout the province, numerous outsiders and riders with decorated horses flocked to the square, increasing the splendor of the spectacle.

It took them a long time to access the huge monastic precinct, because Margarita was well known and loved by her townsfolk, and at every step they had to stop to greet this one or that one; and when they finally arrived inside the building, what surprised them the most was the immense luminosity, and the crowd that pressed and jostled into the most recondite corners.

Although they knew the interior very well, they had never seen anything like it: the small and dark Virgin was almost hidden among the multitude of flowers of the most diverse colors, also surrounded by the Prior and the rest of the friars; and a constant movement of the censers perfumed the entire church. The three Magi appeared and made procession through the excited crowd, which happily applauded in unison.

Francisco, Margarita's older brother was one of the kings, and when he saw them on a bench he made a sign indicating that they would meet later in a bar in the square. The ceremony was magnificent and both Juan Carlos and his three companions enjoyed the spectacle; the three from Turgalium were very happy to have been present at it. When it was all over, they went to the agreed upon spot; and there awaited them not only Francisco, still dressed in his regalia, but a cohort of friends with whom they immediately merged in a friendly chat. They all decided to have lunch right there, and it was after eight o'clock when the banquet was finally over. The day as a whole could not have been more pleasant, and when they said goodbye it was already clear that visits between the inhabitants of the two cities would be frequent.

When brother and sister got home, after dropping off their cousin, although it was very late and normally mother and aunt would already have retired to their rooms, they found them waiting up, eager to know all the details, not only of the celebration but more precisely of the new friend.

Teresa told them:

—I would have liked very much for you two to be there. The ceremony was beautiful. Next year we will all go together and you'll see how you will love it ....

But Tomasa, less diplomatic than Edelmira, interrupted her:

—Yes, yes, Teresita, very well, we imagine that, but what we want you to tell us (that's why we're still up), is Margarita's stuff; the other can wait. Let's see, tell us everything, and don't forget any details about her house, or how she was dressed, how they treated you, well we want to know everything, so get started.

The two young folk looked at each other and burst out laughing at the vehemence of their aunt, and Teresa, helped by Juan Carlos, gave them a long description of what they had experienced that day with their new friend. It was far into the night when everyone finally went off to sleep, each with their own thoughts about the day, but all happy.

Events unfolded much faster than what was commonplace in a place as slow and peaceful as the one they lived in: in the following month Juan Carlos's trips to the city of Margarita, and also some of her visits to Turgalium, were very frequent and at the end of January, one night when he was having dinner with his mother, his sister, and his aunt, he laid aside his napkin, got up, and announced very seriously:

—Today Margarita and I have become formally engaged. On Tuesday I will bring her to you so that you two can meet her. I know you are going to like her very much and all I ask is that you do not pester her with questions. There will be time for everything because I'm going to marry her, so don't come down too heavy. And you sister, please watch out so these two behave well.

And with a big smile on his face he sat down again.

The three were left with their mouths open. Everything went so fast, and above all, the decisive tone of Juan Carlos's words was so unusual, that for the moment none of them reacted, until Edelmira, getting up, also declared:

—Well, we're very happy for you, my son! And I believe that I speak on behalf of the three of us: do not doubt, son, that everything will be ready and we will receive her with the greatest affection that we can — an affirmation to which the other two nodded agreement.

As the visit was only four days away, the two sisters-in-law decided that all the rooms would be thoroughly cleaned, a good snack would be prepared, and they would all dress in their best clothes.

Of this house, a stately three-story building on a street near the square, which the grandfather of the brother and sister had built and to which Edelmira and her husband had moved a month after Teresa was born, becoming the home of the couple and their children (plus the aunt who was already living with them at that time), only the middle floor, called the main one, was inhabited, since it was ample enough to permit the four (with all the swarm of servants who accompanied them) to live with great ease and even to allocate a couple of rooms for the exclusive use of Juan Carlos (what he called "my office and my library," a common practice of the time, when men enjoyed certain privileges still denied to women). The upper floor, even though it was the most beautiful and bright of the three, was practically empty, and its most important use had been as a place for games and hiding places for the two siblings and their friends when they were little; on the ground floor, as well as a large patio, stables for the horses and equestrian paraphernalia, and closed rooms in which were piled furniture and odds and ends, there were several rooms destined to store products from the vineyards and the family farms. In one of them were crowded sacks of walnuts and dried figs coated in flour and ready for consumption. Potatoes, cabbages and dried fruits among other things; large jars of preserves; jams made with the fruit collected in the summer; cans with quince paste; jars with tea, chamomile and linden, which were collected from the bushes that grew next to a spring and had an unbeatable quality... were all placed on wooden shelves. And bags of chickpeas, white beans and other legumes were found on the floor, but resting atop wooden duckboards that kept them dry.

In a separate room, closer to the patio and with large openings left from the replacement of French doors by grille work to allow the air to pass through, were the products of the slaughter: on large hooks hung slabs of bacon, from which a good piece was cut every week for household consumption; the hams, loins, sausages and potato sausages were hung from the ceiling to facilitate their ventilation; the pieces of pork cut and marinated to make the Extremenean specialty called *prueba* were in a trough, and in a large basin filled to the brim and covered with gauze to prevent any bugs from touching it, was the lard.

In the next room, sitting on a sturdy, squat table, a five-foot high capacious tin receptacle, with a tap near the bottom, stored the oil necessary for annual consumption, a product also derived from the thousands of olive trees that were interspersed within the Santa Teresa vineyard, property that the family owned in the Madroñera district. This was an oil of great purity and fine flavor, highly appreciated by all who tried it. Every month a couple of tin carafes were drawn from this storage tank, and their content was in turn poured into green glass bottles, for daily use or for gifts to convents or friends. In that same room were also the demijohns (thick green glass containers encased in cane wickerwork to keep out light and with large cork stoppers to preserve the color and flavor), most of them filled with wine and some few with vinegar from the same place.

This wine, of an intense and very pure red color, had a graduation of almost twenty degrees — forty proof. It had a very rich flavor with a fruity touch, and perhaps its best characteristic was its permitting one to enjoy a couple of glasses (even for non-drinkers), savoring a delicious aftertaste, without suffering the dreaded hangover of inferior wines, all of which made it very suitable to drink almost at any time of day.

The cheeses were also stored there: from the mildest to the most cured, they all rested on a large board, near the window, also covered with gauze that allowed them to air but prevented unwanted incursions of bugs, ready for consumption, since to all the members of the family it was a delicacy that they always craved.

In another smaller room, but also with very good ventilation, the hunting products were stored. Juan Carlos was not too fond of this sport; however, he invited his friends at least half a dozen times a year, whether for elegant organized hunts of large game, which could last for days, or shorter hunts in season for turtledoves and partridges, or with beaters for rabbits and hares. Since both at his beautiful estate "El Azuqueque", and in the other popularly called "Los Aldeanos" there were large hunting grounds, where you could hunt game from wild boar to deer (much appreciated by all his friends and cousins every time he organized a hunt there), after each expedition he returned home with numerous kills that a butcher was in charge of preparing and making ready for consumption.

The small pieces, such as partridges and turtle doves, after being plucked, and having the viscera extracted, were placed in clay jars filled with oil and stoppered for better conservation.

The ground floor was accessed from the street through a door that led to the first hall, small and secluded, adorned simply by a couple of plants with large green leaves, always bright because their care was one of the maid's tasks. After passing a second door, one reached the proper entrance of the house. A granite staircase with a wrought iron balustrade and a carved and polished wooden banister communicated this floor with the upper ones, but the three were totally independent.

The morning after Juan Carlos's statement, the two ladies, captaining three maids armed with straw brooms, rags, buckets and everything necessary for a good cleaning, and having drafted the two older daughters of the so called "Aunt" Ana and "Uncle" Joaquín (resident guards at the vineyard), who always came when there was a big and important cleaning at the house, began the attack. Only the cook was spared the battle, locked in her domains with the mission of preparing sandwiches, exquisite cakes and everything necessary for a posh snack.

Cobwebs were annihilated, windows and doors were cleaned, the upstairs floor thoroughly mopped; the same was done with the ground floor, the two entrance halls and the stone staircase, leaving the level where the family lived for the end, as it was the one that least needed it, although neither the curtains nor the lamps and tapestries escaped the severe scrutiny of the sisters-in-law.

Tuesday afternoon the house was bright as the midday sun. Seated at the *mesa camilla* in the parlor, with a glowing brazier under the velvet table-skirt, and a large fire in the fireplace at the other end of the room, Teresa, her mother, and her aunt waited a little nervously for the arrival of Margarita, who, accompanied by her fiancé Juan Carlos, arrived at the scheduled time, five thirty in the afternoon.

In a simple but elegant brown cloth coat, which had a light fur collar and buttons of the same color, and wearing silk stockings, low-heeled shoes also brown, hair tied in a small bow at the nape of the neck and with two tiny pearls on her ears as her only adornment, save a wide smile, her appearance was picture perfect.

Once the coat was removed, the three of them saw her in a green dress, simple but of a superb cut, admirably setting off her figure and constituting an exact counterpoint to her green eyes, lending them even more brilliance and expression if that were possible.

Once the pertinent introductions had been made, and all were seated and in conversation, Tomasa, unable to hold back any longer and with a wide smile on her normally grim face, blurted out:

—Margarita my child, can you believe that today my sister-in-law and I were very nervous thinking about what you would be like and whether you would like us and we would like you? And look, Teresita had told us how beautiful and charming you are.... You know, old woman things....

To this spontaneous declaration, Margarita laughingly replied:

—Well, Aunt Tomasa, I was just the same. During the whole trip to get here I kept wondering, not if I would like you both, that I was sure of, but whether you would like me, and although Juan Carlos told me not to worry, I couldn't chase the butterflies out of my stomach....

At that moment a well-uniformed maid entered with a silver tray bearing a sugar bowl, milk in a creamer, and a large pitcher of steaming chocolate. She was followed by another maid, also dressed for the occasion, with several platters full of a variety of cakes, biscuits and an appetizing chocolate mousse, which they placed on another table where the plates, cups and cutlery were already located and, once the table they were sitting at was covered with a beautiful richelieu lace tablecloth, they proceeded to serve them the "high tea."

The encounter could not have been pleasanter. Margarita put everyone in her pocket with her grace and spontaneity, adapting herself at every moment to the person she was talking to, telling stories of her trip to Argentina, displaying wit about anything she commented upon, and when, late in the afternoon, she said goodbye to them and they were left alone, Teresa could not help exclaiming:

—What did I tell you? Isn't she lovely? No wonder my brother is mad about her, because the truth is that she's stupendous.

And the two sisters-in-law fully agreed with that comment.

After this formal presentation, thus consolidating the courtship, which proceeded in the best possible way, the couple set the date for the traditional "petition for the hand" of the bride-to-be for the beginning of September, making it coincide with the Feast of the Virgin of Guadalupe, patroness not only of the city of the bride, the enclave where it would take place, but of the entire Extremadura region; and since it would be a holiday, when no one would have work obligations, they could be accompanied by all their friends.

September 8th arrived. After Juan Carlos and his family (who had spent the night at the Hostería del Monasterio) had breakfast they went to Margarita's home located in the town square, a few steps from where they had slept, where she was waiting for them, along with her father and his two sisters and two brothers; the bride's four siblings were also there. The house, of one story but very large, had an impressive yet welcoming appearance, and Don Rosendo, its owner, like his five children, smiled from ear to ear when he received them.

Juan Carlos had bought a beautiful platinum and emerald bracelet for his betrothed, since although the traditional gift was diamonds, he thought, with good judgment, that the green of those gems harmonized better with the color of her eyes, and she gave him a watch with chain, to carry in the left pocket of his jacket.

Although it left little time, they set the wedding date for November, even knowing that those weeks would be dizzying and extremely tiring with the preparations. After the exchange of gifts, several friends of the couple and other members of the families joined the celebration, tasting a selection of local produce as an aperitif, followed by a splendid meal held in the back garden of the house, where everyone ate, drank, chatted and had fun all afternoon; and to end the day, the young people went out, leaving the older people entertained by their conversation.

Margarita wanted to order her trousseau in Madrid, and Juan Carlos' favorite tailor also had his shop in the capital, so the trips of the two families were very frequent in the two months preceding the wedding. They had chosen that date in order to be able to enjoy a long honeymoon and arrive in time to celebrate Christmas with the family, but as Tomasa used to say to her nephew:

—My son, I don't know what the rush is all about. It's not like there was something on the way.... You're going to kill us with so much fuss.

To which he smiled placidly, gave her a hug and left her with her comments, knowing that she was talking for the sake of talking since his intended bride had charmed not only him, but everyone else.

There was indeed quite a fuss, as Tomasa put it, because in addition to clothes and personal effects, everyone had another important task: despite the fact that the family owned other properties in Turgalium, as the couple had decided to live in the family home, it was necessary to equip and furnish the upper floor, empty until that date and still missing things more than necessary to make it pleasant, but a team of masons, carpenters, painters, and various other workers were in charge of modernizing the old kitchen, bathroom, and toilets and service rooms, as well as painting the entire flat.

Margarita, helped by her sisters and Teresa, commissioned beautiful curtains and sheers for the entire "noble" part (that is, the parts inhabited by the family as contrasted to the service) and she brought the very highest quality furnishings for the home which would be hers. It was the custom in that epoch among families with means that the parents of the bride give her the trousseau consisting of sheets, tablecloths, towels and all the clothes necessary for ordinary or extraordinary use, plus utensils, crockery, glassware and cutlery, as well as the complete furniture for the future home, and that the groom's provide furnishings and the furniture for two rooms: the office or library and what was called "the bachelor's room," a bedroom with twin beds, a side table, a comfortable armchair, a table for reading and writing, a three-section wardrobe and another piece of furniture with a ceramic pitcher and basin for the first morning ablutions, as well as a set of clothes for that room and all the suits, shirts, coats and personal clothes necessary to his status. Local nuns had lovingly embroidered his initials on all his shirts and handkerchiefs, and the initials of the future spouses had also been intertwined on the bedding sets; nothing was missing and the smallest details were covered.

Juan Carlos, who already had a magnificent office and a large library on the middle floor, limited himself to moving everything upstairs — to the great satisfaction of his mother and aunt, who found a couple of extra rooms and began to speculate how they would use them in the future.

The two ladies, mindful of the cold weather that was approaching, gave Margarita a lovely coat made of astrakhan, soft and warm, so that she could wear it on her honeymoon, and this present filled her with joy and, according to her custom, which the two ladies were getting used to, showered them with kisses, laughter and hugs.

Although Margarita planned to come to her new home accompanied by her personal maid plus a maid for everything else, Edelmira, assuming that the new bride would not know how to cook, as often happens with many other young girls, and knowing well how finicky and fussy her son was about his meals, in the time between the wedding announcement and the day before the ceremony, with the help of her cook had been training a girl, the daughter of the vineyard keepers, to prepare their food. The new cook was already skilled enough in her duties, and in addition, for the first year, all she would have to do was prepare the couple's breakfasts and high-teas, since another of the customs for newly married couples was that the bride and groom went for a year or more to their parents' homes for lunch and dinner: to the family of one for lunch and to dine with the family of the other. As Margarita's father did not reside in the same town, it was decided, with great joy on the part of everyone, especially Teresa and the two sisters-in-law, that they would take all their meals in the family home.

At last all was ready, and although everyone ended up very tired, the experience had been good and the results were visible: the new apartment was beautiful, the closets were full of suits, the furniture, curtains and rugs lent a very elegant air to the rooms, the kitchen was replete with copper pots hanging from hooks; and a sideboard painted in a light tone for daily table service, as well as a large marble table, with four wicker chairs, in the center, were relucent. A hall closet held neat stacks of all the linens.

The day before the ceremony, the groom with his mother, sister and aunt, plus some close relatives and his school pals from El Escorial, close friends who would not have missed the ceremony for anything in the world, stayed at the Hostería del Monasterio, where they tried to rest as much as possible, anticipating a day full of emotions that surely awaited them. They had decided that the person to walk the groom to the altar would be Teresa instead of Edelmira, since the latter feared that her nerves would betray her and she would "make a spectacle of myself" and diminish the prominence of the couple.

The groom's father would of course be missing, as he had been missed at all the major events in the little family; and that day they also would feel the absence of Margarita's mother, who had died three years before. But no one wanted to cloud the joy that everyone felt with sad thoughts, and although each one privately ruminated on the absences, none of them voiced these thoughts, lest they sadden the listener.

The night before the wedding, another of the local customs would have been for the groom to celebrate a bachelor party by going out with his friends and all his old school mates from El Escorial who had traveled to accompany him at his wedding, to drink and fool around with loose women until well into the wee hours, but Juan Carlos refused to do so: he wanted to be fresh and awake and no woman who offered herself would be able to outshine his beloved; he had already had a few years of fooling around in Madrid with Petra, a Theatre Eslava chorus girl, so he convinced his friends that they would all enjoy a quiet dinner and retreat to their respective rooms at a reasonable hour.

The day had come and he still couldn't believe his luck! When he left the room to join his sister, who was also fully prepared, he gave her a big hug and the two admired each other: Juan Carlos, with his impeccable charcoal gray morning coat, matching tie, a white linen shirt and shoes shining like patent leather, had a very elegant air, and his height and carriage enhanced the outfit; and Teresa, in a jacket suit with a long skirt of dark navy blue, black high heels, a single-loop pearl necklace around her neck, and a Chantilly mantilla on her head, which left her face clear and allowed her perfect features to be appreciated, was the living image of beauty and serenity.

The two sisters-in-law, dressed soberly in black suits and coats of the same color, completed the small family party and all of them, accompanied by friends and cousins who would be the witnesses for the groom, left for the Monastery.

Shortly after their arrival, the bride appeared accompanied by her father and godfather and all her closest relatives. The church was beautiful, illuminated and full of flowers, and the guests of the groom sitting in the right side pews and those of the bride on the left, all decked out for the occasion, filled them completely.

When Margarita entered a murmur of admiration ran through the assembly, for although they always say that no bride is ugly on her wedding day — or rather, every bride is beautiful — in this case the statement corresponded to one particular reality: she was a beautiful bride! With a firm step and without any hint of nerves, she walked down the aisle between the rows of pews, smiling at everyone and talking to her father at the same time. She had chosen for the occasion a simple ivory white dress, with a box neckline and long sleeves, and on the edges of both, pink stones softened the severity of the ensemble. Her hair was parted and pulled back from her face; a discreet bouquet of orchids and a large tulle veil that reached to the floor completed her toilette.

The emotional and long ceremony went according to plan, and just as she had predicted, Edelmira spent it crying: there were many emotions that crowded inside her and the tears did not stop flowing, although Tomasa tried unsuccessfully to stop them. Once the witnesses had signed and the couple had been congratulated by all the invitees to the wedding, as well as by locals who had gathered outside, the procession headed towards the place of the wedding banquet, and there, all seated at tables sumptuously prepared for the occasion, the celebrations and toasts soon began.

The newlyweds had chosen an excellent menu: abundant hot and cold appetizers which in themselves satiated the hunger of the attendees, followed by an exquisite almond soup, regional trout and suckling lamb stew. At the end of the whole feast, many delicious desserts followed, one upon another.

Finally, the seven-story wedding cake. When it appeared, everyone applauded. This beautiful tower of sponge cake, covered in whipped cream and decorated with strawberries, and served with a good champagne, delighted everyone, perfectly topping off their dinner.

After more toasts and congratulations, the newlyweds left for their trip, while all the rest continued dancing and celebrating for hours. After so much food, drink and emotions, it was not advisable for those who had traveled here to return to their homes at night, so everyone except the newly married couple decided to sleep again in Guadalupe and avoid the narrow, curving and dark roads.

For the three women, there had been too many emotions in too short a time. Now back in Turgalium and having resumed their daily habits, after the turmoil and hustle and bustle of the past weeks, everything seemed to be quiet and lifeless; Teresa, her mother, and her aunt missed Juan Carlos terribly, they yearned for the happy couple to return and be integrated into a life that seemed to them perfect and wonderful, for they had everything needed to lead an enviable existence. Although currently many things in the country were in turmoil and it was even feared that this unrest would lead to war, for them, far from the large urban centers, life was good and tranquil. Little by little, as the days and weeks passed, things returned to their normal course and the three women resumed their routine.

The couple had chosen Galicia as the honeymoon destination, and for over a month they enjoyed everything that this beautiful region offered, from wonderful seafood meals, to unmatched sunsets duplicated by their reflections in the sea, to visits to small villages (where Margarita, with her proverbial ease, had gotten along wonderfully with those who lived there). Juan Carlos, a good connoisseur of the area, which he had visited many times with his mother, who used to take the waters at the Mondariz Spa, had reserved rooms in the best hotels and pensions in the various cities and towns they would visit, and although the atmosphere was already becoming a bit unsettled and hectic in anticipation of what would unfold only months later, nowhere did they have problems. They left until the last full week of their trip their visit to Santiago, to the city and to the eponymous saint at whose image behind the altar in the cathedral they knelt, and which, following the custom, they kissed.

Meanwhile, at the family home, the three women and their servants were preparing for their arrival and the imminent coming of the Christmas holidays. Five days before Christmas Eve, laden with suitcases and gifts, smiling and happy, the travelers arrived.

They all wanted to ask and know, but it was Aunt Tomasa who came forward:

—Children, we already know that you will be tired, but there is nothing that cannot be cured by a good bowl of hot chocolate with freshly made croutons. I say I won't let you go up to your apartment until you tell us everything.

Margarita, winking, replied at once:

—But Aunt, everything, everything?

To which the old woman, with her cheeks redder than a ripe tomato, said:

—You can skip the rough details, your mother-in-law and I are no longer up to such adventures; and Teresita here shouldn't hear them either, but the rest we want, without even a comma missing! — and covering herself with a shawl and gesturing to the rest to sit, she sat down.

The remainder of the evening passed peacefully; anecdotes of the trip, the description of hotels, places, and everything they had experienced took hours, but everyone was happy at the end of the narrative, told with grace by Margarita while her husband limited himself to smile or nod according to what she related, and when Teresa realized the time that had elapsed she urged the two older women to leave them alone. At last the newly married pair was allowed to ascend the stairs to their domains to rest.

Married life began. The night of the 24th they all celebrated together in great harmony and after a copious dinner the five went to the church to hear the traditional midnight mass. As the couple had not yet visited her family, Margarita wanted to see them and be with them for a few days, but not before assuring her sister-in-law that they would be in Turgalium without fail for the big party at the Casino, reminding her that it was there she met her husband. Taking hold of Teresa's arm, she put her face close to hers and whispered into her ear:

—Who knows? Maybe that will be the night you will meet yours....

Little did the two of them imagine that her words would be prophetic.

4. JORGE - DECEMBER 31, 1935

The year 1934 had ended differently from all previous ones. He was in Gijón; it was a beautiful coastal city in the north of Spain, but far from his beloved Madrid, where he had always lived with his family, surrounded at all times by his siblings and friends. Now he was working, and his work obligations had not even allowed him to spend the Christmas holidays with them as he would have wished. But he did like the job very much, and also his new colleagues, as well as the city in which he lived now. And although he had arrived in the city shortly after the so-called Revolution of 1934, and its repressive effects were still being felt, the posting had, among other far from negligible incentives, a Cantabrian Sea where he could swim as he wished when free from work, even though the days were cool and the water was cold. Swimming was one of his favorite hobbies and a sport that he and his siblings had practiced every day at the Canoe Center swimming pools while living in the capital, or in different seas when their parents took them on summer vacation to localities on the coasts. Personally, his father did not like the sea, because it reminded him of how his own father had died in distant Cuba, but he wanted all his children to learn from a very young age to be confident in the water.

Jorge had not chosen that destination, but was sent there for internship after passing the Telecommunication Officer exams a few months earlier. He was a good mathematician, had always had a great head for numbers and when he finished high school, unlike other kids who were undecided and fluctuated between opposing careers, he knew exactly what he wanted to do: he would become a telecommunications engineer, a field that attracted him enormously. He wrote a brilliant entrance exam at Superior Engineering School, and was equally outstanding in the first year, but things would not continue the way he had chosen.

His father, a highly accomplished artist who had been a chamber painter to King Alfonso XIII and therefore received a regular fixed salary, was, since the fall and subsequent exile of the monarch in 1931, going through financial hard times in a politically uncertain time — for he was also looked upon with distrust by the Republicans who viewed with suspicion the access he had had to the close circle of the exiled king. Now lacking the royal remuneration, only his new-found collaboration as Artistic Director in Kaulak Photographic Studios and some portrait commissions from individuals, allowed him to maintain a house with a wife and five children, plus a relative of his wife who had lived with them for years, and the service people who helped with household chores. It was a populous house therefore, and the family had for some time been used to living well, attending renowned private schools and rubbing shoulders with the best strata of society.

But things were no longer as they had been and money was scarce; every day the children were growing older and therefore had more needs. Debts accumulated, and although the father was optimistic and believed that it was but a bad streak, and insisted that they would soon again ride the crest of the wave, the political and economic situation of the country did not conduce to verisimilitude in his asseverations. Late in the afternoon of an early summer day, as the brothers and sisters and their friends were getting ready to go out to celebrate Jorge's grades at Engineering School, his mother, Manuela, commented:

—This morning, when I was talking to Carlota she told me that some positions have been opened for Telegraph Officers. You have to be over eighteen years old and pass an exam. Once approved, it's a permanent, lifetime position, whether the government are Monarchists or Republicans. Jorge, you meet all the requirements, why don't you go and find out?

Her son answered that he would do it without fail the next day, and then he went with the group to have fun. Things were not good in Madrid at that time. Unemployment was severe, street riots abounded, and the various political factions constantly fought verbally, when not physically, but for the young people none of this prevented their desire to have a pleasant evening; what they wanted was a bit of fun. The gang was made up of his two little brothers, aged sixteen and seventeen and with whom he was very close, his intimate friends the four Fuentellanas, and two other brothers, the Rocaduras, also high school classmates plus cousin Ricardo, who never missed a celebration. There were ten boys willing to have a good time and eat up the world that night if necessary.

But the uncertain climate weighed heavily, and although the general slogan was to have fun, they soon began to talk about politics, and debates also quickly followed.

Most of the group were conservative in their political feelings; one of the brothers Fuentellana, however, had recently joined the Communist Party, another of the friends had strong sympathies for the Anarchists and some of the rest, like Jorge, had drawn close to the ideology of Ramiro Ledesma Ramos, founder of the JONS, a militant Right group, and each and every one of them tried to defend their positions, explaining vehemently what had brought them to that point.

They spent the first hour talking, or better said, arguing, and when things started getting too hot, Demetrio, one of the Fuentellana brothers, who in addition to being a great friend of Jorge was his sister Marisa's boyfriend, put an end to the discussions telling everyone that the objective of that night was to have fun, and that they had better leave the confrontations for another occasion, so in the end they stopped politicking and bickering and went to a festival in a nearby neighborhood, where they danced, drank and met pretty and friendly girls, so the night ended wonderfully for everyone.

The next day, as he had told his mother, Jorge went to find out about the announced exams, picked up the printed details, with the necessary requirements, the date of examinations and everything pertinent, and went home to study whether he should apply.

The family lived on Calle del Espíritu Santo, in a spacious flat with more than enough room to be comfortable; the two girls shared a room with Lala, their mother's aunt who had always served as a stand-in grandmother; the two younger brothers also shared a room. Only Jorge, being the oldest of the boys, had his own bedroom, where he often secluded himself to flee the noise in the house, either to study or to listen to music without annoying and unwanted interruptions.

At noon, while everyone was waiting for his father in order to begin lunch, he commented:

—Look, here I have everything related to those exams and I've decided that I'm going to take them. I like the program and as mother said, once inside, the civil service job will be forever. I don't think I will have any problems passing them, and as soon as I pass the exam and the internship period, I'll be able to choose a destination, which although at first it might not be Madrid, I'll be able to get closer as time goes by. I will have a secure civil servant job, and here there will be one less mouth and one less problem.

His two brothers and his older sister Marisa agreed with his decision. Not at home for lunch was the eldest of the five offspring of the marriage formed by Manuela and Guillermo, Carolina, who was already a functionary in one of the government ministries, and her income, in addition to contributing to the family economy, was employed to accumulate her trousseau, as she planned soon to marry her life-long boyfriend, Enrique.

When Guillermo arrived, Jorge explained what he had already said to the rest of the family. His father brightened up with joy and caught Jorge in an affectionate hug, exclaiming:

—I know you will pass the tests with no problems, son, and I will be very happy for you. What I want for my children is the stability that I have not had. You will always have my full support!

From that moment on, Jorge studied tirelessly, and when the exam date arrived he passed it without any difficulty, since for the practical part he had mastered the Morse telegraphic system to perfection (a language invented by the American Samuel Morse, and which was based on a combination of sounds conceived of as dots and dashes which represented the letters, numbers and signs necessary for writing); also, he reached seventy words per minute on the new Siemens teletypes brought from Germany, and in terms of theory, based on the knowledge acquired in the School of Engineers, he was able to make a brilliant oral presentation that won him the praises of the panel of examiners.

A new door opened in his life. It opened into Gijón, the city he had been posted to for internship in order to become a good telegrapher and where, once he had completed that period, he could stay with a fixed position or opt for other destinations. On that New Year's Day, which opened 1935, after a lively night with his companions at the Ateneo Casino Obrero in the city, he walked along the San Lorenzo beach, missing his family, but knowing that his professional decision had been correct.

And so time passed, unfolded, opened up, and continued. The weeks and months did hold frequent communication with the family, especially on his part, since telegraphers could send free telegrams (the so-called "notes" in their argot) to whomever they wanted. He also used these times for excursions, walks, hiking routes and frequent visits to the beach with his friend Daniel and other colleagues. In July he got very bad news: his mother had fallen victim to peritonitis and everything suggested that the outcome would be rapid, as indeed happened on the

18th, despite the many attempts that one of the brothers Fuentellana and his team of doctors made to prevent it.

Jorge was devastated and in great pain. The rapidity of her death, and the demands of his work in the growing political turbulence, did not even permit his traveling to Madrid to give his beloved mother a last kiss, nor to accompany her body on her final trip to the cemetery.

Another new stage was opening in his life, as well as for the rest of his family. For in addition, a few months before that loss, the brother who followed him, Ramón, just turned seventeen, had gotten a girl pregnant and, following the customs prevailing at the time for those who had any honor or sense of shame, his father had forced him to marry her. Being a minor, he had no choice but to abide by the verdict. The family dispersed.

In Gijón the political situation was boiling. The miners in the coal basins were up in arms with their demands, every day a military intervention was feared, and soon it came. As work piled up for Jorge and his colleagues, freedoms were restricted. As soon as the internship ended, he decided to ask for another destination. It would be something temporary, a few months, maybe a little more, perhaps a year, and then he would go back to Madrid, where his life really was. Little did he imagine then what the future would hold for him.

He applied for a position in Extremadura, in a city which he knew only by name, but which was an essential hub for communications with the neighboring country, Portugal. It had the great advantage of being closer to Madrid than was Gijón. He did not know anyone in that town, but neither did he in any of the others on the list of posts, so he said goodbye to his bosses and colleagues from the Asturian city and returned home with a fifteen-day leave before reporting to his new destination.

It was Christmas time, but at the flat on Espíritu Santo there was sadness, despite the preparations for the wedding of Carolina and her boyfriend Enrique, which would take place the day before Christmas. Their mother was gone, his brother

Ramón was gone, since he had married and no longer lived with them, his father was so beaten down since losing his companion that he could hardly even paint, and painting was what had always saved him, even in the past, even in other very difficult times when all seemed lost. The only one who seemed a bit normal was his sister Marisa, who with her good spirit and energy tried to rebuild the family, although without much success, so Jorge found himself in a very different and diminished environment from the one he had left.

And outside his home, the Madrid that awaited him was not the same one that he had left a little more than a year before: the general discontent had sharpened, positions had radicalized, and it was no longer safe to walk aimlessly hither and yon, as his gang of chums liked to do. Everyone was worried. Too much uncertainty.

The wedding passed with more pain than glory, Christmas Eve and Christmas too, and he said goodbye to his family and friends, since on December 28 he had to report to his new destination, Turgalium. It looked like a prank, like an *inocentada*, as his friends told him, but it was the date that he got. (As December 28 commemorates the day of The Innocents, it is used, like April Fools Day in America, to play practical jokes, called *inocentadas*.). He would never see his father again, and it would be many years before he would meet again with those who had survived, and by then they all had many scars on their souls. He took formal possession of his position and settled in his new city.

~. ~. ~. ~. ~.

He had luck with the lodging recommended to him: a good inn run by a married couple and their daughters, very close to his work and where from the day he arrived until he left them to start his married life, he was treated with great affection .

And the food was unbeatable! Guillermo, his father, had suffered hunger at certain times in his life, so when he was flush with money he inculcated in his offspring the love of good food; and Jorge, although he looked very thin, could "really put it away" as people commented. The establishment's kitchen fulfilled his best expectations: good quality, excellent preparation and quantities sufficient to feed not merely one diner, but several. So from the first day, having the basic points of accommodation and meals resolved, he found himself comfortable in his new destination.

On New Year's Eve a very important party was celebrated at the Casino and his second in command encouraged him to attend, as an easy way to meet the most representative people of the city and some girls. And there he went. The atmosphere was very pleasant, the music was good, he met the Mayor, doctors, lawyers, the city notary, the captain of the Civil Guard... He was introduced to various beautiful and charming women, but for him the significance of the night was when he met Teresa. She was the most beautiful and elegant woman he had ever seen. And he knew that their paths would always be united.

5. TOMASA - 1914

The screams penetrated the walls of the flat and reached the neighboring homes. Edelmira, clinging to the already cold corpse of what had been her husband, cried, screamed and convulsed, and having tried to revive Florencio with kisses and hugs, now was shaking him with force, seeking with that action to infuse in him the breath of life and awaken him.

Because as she had roused herself from sleep, she noticed that something strange was happening, for although she was a very early riser, her husband always rose first, and normally when she opened her eyes, Florencio was already dressed and ready to have breakfast and start on his way to his warehouse.

But that morning when she opened her eyes, her dear Floro, as she always affectionately called him, was still in bed, with eyelids half-open and a half smile on his mouth, as if recalling a pleasant dream; and when she neared she noticed a coldness and stiffness that alarmed her.

She called him. He did not answer. She snatched up her nine-month-old daughter Teresa from the crib, and still wearing only her nightgown, ran from the bedroom to find her sister-in-law Tomasa, who lived with them.

Seeing Edelmira's frantic state, who said only "Your brother, your brother," Tomasa without a word lay the little girl in her bed, and surrounding her with a barrier of pillows, followed

Edelmira, already fearing the worst. When the two of them got to the bedroom, Tomasa took his pulse and saw instantly that her brother had left them forever, but she sent one of the maids running for the doctor, even though she knew there was nothing they could do to bring him back to life. The wait for the doctor, though minutes, seemed like hours; Edelmira could not believe what was happening. And knowing what she did not want to believe, started screaming, shaking and kissing the corpse.

They heard a small noise behind them, and turning, they saw six-year-old Juan Carlos, the other of the couple's two children, watching the scene without comprehension. Tomasa, while very affected, was more whole in her judgment than her sister-in-law, and taking the child's hand led him from the bedroom.

—Aunt Tomasa, why is my father still in bed? And why is Mother crying so much? Is Teresita sick and is she going to die like Carmencita too?

—No, no, Teresita was in her crib and she wasn't even awake when your mama got up, but I took her to my room to keep her sleeping because you know she doesn't like noises. Don't worry, she's sound asleep. But your father isn't feeling well this morning and we've sent for the doctor, just like we do for you when your throat or tummy hurts, right? We'll get you ready, you will have breakfast, and then the maid will take you to play with Cousin Sebastián. Don't you remember that yesterday he told you that he had a brand new spinning top and that today you were going to have a championship tournament?

—Yes, yes, and I'm sure I will win! —the little one answered — Because I'm older than him, although Sebas is a bit taller.

After the child was washed and dressed, aunt and nephew went to the living room where there was already prepared a little pitcher of steaming chocolate and a plate full of croutons, as was usual every morning for breakfast in that family, and leaving him in the charge of a servant girl, with precise instructions to take him out of the house as soon as possible, she returned to her sister-in-law's bedroom, first entering her own room to dress and check that the baby girl was still sleeping.

Edelmira had stopped screaming and now her crying and hiccups were subdued; it seemed that she too was going to fade away, she looked about her without seeing, beside herself, but Tomasa, who was now in charge of the situation, ordered her:

—Please, get dressed as quickly as possible. The doctor must be about to arrive and I don't want him to see you like this. Don't worry about a thing, I'll talk to the doctor when he arrives. In the meantime I'm going to tidy up a bit around here.

Edelmira, still in a state of shock, obeyed her sister-in-law and went to dress and groom herself.

Tomasa was the youngest of Florencio's siblings — he had a brother and two sisters — and the one most loved by him. In one way or another he had always protected and cared for her; and when she was left without means of subsistence, he took her in.

Against the good judgment of her parents and also of Florencio, who was the eldest of the siblings and more than fifteen years her senior, when she was over thirty and already formed part of the group known as "the spinsters," she had happened to meet and fall madly in love with a cattle trader. This man, nice looking and with fine manners, which concealed his real character, had arrived in Turgalium the day before the start of the annual regional cattle fair that was held in the city at the beginning of June. He was lodged at a good inn, where gathered the cream of the travelers who attended the event. The two daughters of the inn owners were very close friends of Tomasa; the three got together every day, either to do needlework, stroll, go to the church to say their prayers, or to read some serialized fascicles that they bought every week, with which they lived and relived the adventures or misadventures of some poor women to whom the most terrible things happened, but for whom everything worked out, for after much suffering, in the end the heroines lived happily ever after.

Fate determined, or it merely fell out by chance, that when this dealer dismounted in the inn's large horse corral, while a groom was taking charge of his mount and he removed the saddlebags holding his belongings, Tomasa appeared there in search of her friends. The trader smiled at her as only he knew how to do, and at that very moment she felt her legs buckle and fell in love like a schoolgirl.

Raised in a rather retired, even repressed, environment, where her mother's only diversion was to go to church and her father's to work, and born into a family that enjoyed a very healthy economy, the youngest child, Tomasa, had not had many opportunities to find an adequate husband; those who approached her in her youth were all from the social class known as "craftsmen," good boys but without much economic means and also without polish, who would not have been accepted by her parents anyway. Furthermore, Tomasa was not what we could call a beauty but quite the opposite: she was ugly, short and stocky, unlike her two brothers and her only sister Celestine, who were very tall and lanky. The only thing that stood out on her flat-featured face was a very pleasant smile and beautiful curly black hair. She also had very lovely hands and feet, but who was going to notice those particular details? Only her family and friends saw them, and none of those features were sufficient to make a wedding.

Amadeo, which was the name of our cattle trader, smiled at everyone and that always opened doors for him, but his beguiling and charming character hid a coldness of feelings and a great contempt for anything that did not benefit him. When he entered the premises of the inn and before going to his room, with a smile he asked a servant girl:

—You don't happen to know the name of the friend of your mistresses?

—Yes, she is Miss Tomasa. She's loaded. I'd be happy with just a little piece of her dough...

A bachelor on the lookout for good pickings to free him from his travels and hassles now that his youth was passing, and without professional skills other than what he'd learned from his father (that is, going from fair to fair and turning a small profit brokering cattle sales), he perked up and prepared for the siege. That afternoon, while the three friends were strolling, he approached them, and doffing the green felt hat that he always wore when on business, introduced himself and kindly asked if they would allow him to accompany them, even for a few minutes, upon which, at first surprised, they happily accepted. So began the assault.

From the beginning of this stroll together, it was clear to the three young ladies that Tomasa was the objective he aimed to conquer, and not only did the sisters not mind acting as the obligatory chaperones, but they later fostered in Tomasa the dreams that they all had but did not dare voice. When the fair passed and Amadeo disappeared with it, all their conversations revolved around the same topic: how handsome and well groomed he was, how pleasant he was, how knowledgeable, how interested he was in Tomasa; the hours they used to spend in prayer, sewing, and serials, now flew by talking about this man who had so impressed them.

And Amadeo returned. And he came back well informed. He had a plan: he would face all the impediments that might present themselves and he would marry her. His days would then be assured, and of course he could always corral a better piece of tail, beautiful and accommodating, when the occasion arose. Putting everything on one card, and using his sharpest technique, he asked the owner of the inn, a good man who was also well set up, to accompany him to the lumberyard that her family had, to introduce him to Tomasa's father and thus be able to ask permission to see his daughter. The innkeeper agreed, not divining what the other was up to, believing his assurances that since he had met her he could not live without her, and that he needed her father to approve their relationship.

Tomasa's father was sitting in his warehouse office when they arrived and received them with the kindness and courtesy that characterized him, but as soon as he heard the trader's request, he put him off, claiming that everything seemed very hasty, although, like the good merchant that he was, he did not close the door completely but instead accompanied his rejection with the suggestion that perhaps in the future, once informed whether his intentions were serious, and he was who he claimed to be, they would talk about the matter again. Amadeo did not give up his efforts, for the visit to the warehouse had confirmed that the one he wanted as a future wife was good prey, the best he had flushed so far. The maid had informed him well: there was a lot of dough there.

The warehouse was an immense one, almost on the outskirts of the city and in it all kinds of wood were piled up, not only national but also many exotic woods from different countries. Large boards of cedar, walnut, pine, palo de santo and mahogany among others, were placed and classified next to the walls, ready for sale and use.

It also housed a cabinet-making workshop, where many carpenters under the orders of the owner's two sons, Florencio and Nicasio, made precious tables inlaid with mother-of-pearl or with other woods, contrasting in intricate designs; wardrobes, turned chairs and with their seats covered in soft leather or velvet, sideboards with leaded glass display cabinets, simple or very elaborate headboards... Everything that came from there had the stamp of elegance and good taste in addition to the great solidity and wonderful construction. Thanks to the popularity that they had acquired, not only for the quality of the woods but also the perfect workmanship of their furniture, Tomasa's father had amassed a good fortune which he had wisely invested in rural and urban properties, and all this real estate and land yielded him huge benefits.

The cattle trader did not give up his efforts to secure a family alliance, but seeing that his plans were not going to be carried out as easily as he had originally supposed, he took the bull by the horns — in his own expression, which, like many of his, referred to animals — and he devised the next step: they would elope. Tomasa was initially scared by the plan, but he, with practiced cajolery and telling her that it was the best and simplest way, since once everything happened, the father would have no choice but to swallow the facts — and he himself expecting it to be true — said they could live together happily ever after without her having to renounce her family. To this passionate logic, she surrendered.

With the connivance of her maid and the two sister friends, she sequestered at the latter's house the clothes necessary for the first days, and put all the money she owned in her pouch, a few hundred pesetas (a very tidy sum in that epoch) proceeding from gifts from her father, and that she had been accumulating and saving for many years.

When the day came, she went out in the afternoon accompanied by her maid as she always did, saying goodbye to her mother and her sister Celestina (already married and living in another town, but who, having a difficult pregnancy, spent some time at the family house to be better cared for), and they went to the inn where Amadeo awaited her.

They remained there till night finally fell, sheltered from prying eyes, and when only the stars illuminated the sky they managed to mount a good horse and set out for Jaraichico, the pretender's town that was about five leagues distant from Turgalium, arriving as dawn began to lighten the summer sky. They went directly to the small church of the place, where, as Amadeo had arranged, the priest and two friends who would serve as witnesses for the wedding were waiting for them, as well as his parents, whom he had forced to be best man and maid of honor. The ceremony was lackluster, simple and ugly, far removed from what Tomasa had dreamed and imagined for herself when she'd read her fascicled novelettes and made herself the heroine.

In the bride's city, the night before, when the maid had come home alone without her *señorita*, the mother and sister inquired as to her whereabouts, but the female, following the instructions she had been given along with a good tip, answered evasively and went into her room. Hours passed. Tomasa was not coming home. The father and the two brothers decided to go looking for her at the last place they knew she had been, the inn. The good innkeeper, oblivious to the goings-on that the others had brought upon his head, made the two sisters, who pretended sleep, to get up and they, between weeping and hiccups, confessed the truth.

When Tomasa's father heard this news, twenty years suddenly seemed to fall upon him; he took hold of his sons' arms for support and murmured sadly:

—Let's go home. There's nothing else to do here.

In the hallway of the large house, their mother and Celestina were waiting for them, and just by seeing their faces they knew that something serious had happened. When Florencio began briefly to explain what they had been told, the two became faint, and the efforts of the three men and the groom, as well as a maid who brought a pot of linden tea, were required to revive and calm them and help them into the house. A great tragedy had befallen them and their lives would no longer be the same.

Tomasa and her now husband, lacking their own home, settled in the house of his parents, a shack where they lived with dogs, cats, chickens, a goat and two sheep, in three small bedrooms without doors, separated by tacked up rags from what the family pompously called the salon: a square habitation with sooty walls engendered by a corner fireplace that served both to heat the room and do the cooking. At the two ends of said fireplace were a pair of trivets, and on top of one of them a large pot full of water bubbled awaiting its use, while the other trivet served to hold the frying pans or pots where the meals were made, blackened cooking utensils of repugnant aspect, which had long escaped any encounter with soap and water.

Instead of the modern bathrooms such as her father had ordered installed on two of the floors of her house, equipped with the greatest comforts and with hot and cold running water, in the humble home of her in-laws one's necessities had to be relieved in a privy situated in the garden, covered only by some badly joined wooden boards that did not prevent air or rain from entering through the cracks.

Tomasa was a proper young lady and as such she had been raised. Every morning and every night her maid brushed her precious hair with fifty strokes, she did not know how to cook since at her parents' house they had always had a cook, nor did she know how to do any other domestic work. She had never even made her own bed. In every moment of her existence, other people had done everything for her, so finding herself faced with such a humble and miserable life was a tremendous blow.

But she loved her husband and believed that love was mutual. Given that fact, she could bear all the discomforts and endure living with his in-laws, who were quite crude.

Her hands, the greatest treasure that she possessed, next to her hair, in a short time were covered with chilblains, because in her new house she had to wash the few dishes that there were, scrub the clothes they used, and sweep or badly clean the rooms. But she loved her husband. Or believed she loved him.

Amadeo covered the distance between the two towns several times, trying to speak again with his father-in-law, or at least with the brothers, but his efforts were in vain. Because in his wife's family home things had turned upside down, and not exactly for the better. The father and mother gave up going out; their only departure from the house came later, inside a coffin. Such was the sadness and shame they felt, that the mere thought of meeting friends or acquaintances stopped them, so the two brothers were, from the unfortunate day, the ones in charge of the warehouse and cabinetmaking workshop.

The months passed and the situation did not change. The trafficker, seeing and understanding that the approach to his father-in-law was impossible, tried to get news of how the situation was through the two sister friends of his wife, but they too were denied access to the house, since the Tomasa's parents considered them an important part of the whole disaster, for without their connivance and aid the events would not have been possible. Realizing that these ways were closed, he went several times to the warehouse to speak with his brothers-in-law, but when, after repeated attempts, he managed to speak with Florencio, what he told him was a blow to his plans: Celestina had died.

After giving birth prematurely to a son, she could not recover from the postpartum hemorrhages, and when they were finally stopped, her general condition was very weakened. The sad atmosphere that reigned in the house did not help her mood to improve either: she missed her sister with whom she had always had a great complicity, the house seemed in permanent mourning, and only a few cousins visited them from time to time. The conversations, when the parents were not present, revolved around the absence of Tomasa and the death of her baby. In a matter of a few months, her life faded until one day all ended for her, plunging her family into a double sorrow.

In a very short time the two sisters had disappeared ....

But Amadeo, trying to turn his situation around, and always with the aim of achieving his own benefit, invited the two sisters to visit his wife, in order to let them be the ones to communicate the news to her, feigning ignorance of everything, since he did not know how she was going to react.

At this point in the trader's history, the mask that usually disguised his true character began to slip. Because he saw that unless everything turned around soon, he had made a bad deal. He had burdened himself with a useless woman who was neither pretty nor had money, and his evil nature was struggling to get out. When the sister friends finally came to visit they were horrified to see what in just over two years their friend had become. And they hadn't even entered the house!

Amadeo had prepared a light meal in the garden to prevent their seeing his dwelling, and there the two sisters told her everything that had happened to her beloved Celestina, and the great sorrow in which the family was mired. Tomasa said she had to go to her city immediately, and Amadeo, who saw a great opportunity to restore relations, hurried and prepared what was necessary for the departure. In less than half an hour the carriage that had brought her friends there headed back with the three women inside. The husband rode at a trot alongside.

They arrived at what had been her house, she knocked on the door several times, no one answered.

For the father, alerted by the noise in the street and having cautiously peered from one of the balconies without being seen by the travelers, despite the pleas of his wife, forbade them to admit her. For him both his daughters were dead, although one of them was still breathing.

Amedeo tried to see her brother Florencio, but the business was closed for the mourning period, although he learned that his brother-in-law and his young wife were expecting offspring.

As it was now twilight, the couple decided to stay overnight at the inn, thinking that if they returned the next day the father would have softened and everything would return to normal.

That morning was the day of the weekly market, whither many people from the region came to stock up on the products that the peasants brought: freshly made white cheeses, chickens, tench and trout still slapping their tails in the clay pots filled with water, pork ribs, as well as all kinds of fruits and vegetables, butter puffs, lupins, olives and pickled gherkins, all products that would fill pantries with fresh foods for the week, and Amadeo decided to stroll through the market while the other three returned to the house, believing that if he was not with them it would facilitate matters.

One of the maids was leaving the house when the three of them arrived, and Tomasa, who had known her for years, rushed over to her asking about her mother, her brothers and even her father, but the maid turned around and quickly re-entered the house, closing the huge door with a sharp bang.

Tomasa did not know what to do. She sank down onto one of the granite steps at the entrance and cried and cried until the two sisters almost dragged her away. Everything was lost. She no longer had a family.

Months later, the news reached Jaraichico that her mother had died. Tomasa, filled with pain and remorse, returned to Turgalium, but again her father did not let her into the house, nor could she, therefore, see her dead mother so that she could bend over the body and give her a last embrace. Her despair grew with each passing hour, because the love or infatuation that had led her into such a dreadful life was also dissolving; her husband treated her badly, every day was worse than the previous one, he insulted her constantly without reason, the treatment she received was more horrible than that which might be given to any stray cur, and she had to work from sunrise to sunset. How distant were the happy days when such things only happened in the novelettes she read with her friends. And now it was happening to her. Not in a novel, but in sad reality.

And more months and more years passed.

One day when her husband had gone to a fair, a ray of hope appeared: it was Florencio, her dearest brother, whom she had not seen for years, on the threshold of the humble home. She approached him, not even knowing if he would allow her to hug him; when her brother took her hands in his and drew her to his chest, she sobbed and moaned, feeling what she had lost and what her life had become. Florencio, calming her down with affectionate words, said:

—I don't think you knew, but I married a good girl a few years ago. Her name is Edelmira and until we got married she was a seamstress. She is very young, since she is thirty-something years younger than I, but she is very sensible. God has blessed us, we have a beautiful child, a son, and we are already expecting our second. I hope it will be a girl this time, but what we really want is for it to be born well and healthy.

My wife Edelmira is the one who has insisted that I come to visit you and assure you that you will always have a place in our house, that you will be well received there and that you will not lack anything. Our father is very old, but still sticks to his fixed idea of not wanting to know anything about you, and I do not even know if you heard that a few days after your disappearance he signed a new will in which you were disowned and repudiated forever. He forbade Nicasio and me, and mother (may she be in glory), even to name you, but we have all missed you. If one day you decide to leave here, the doors of my house will be open.

Faced with this statement, Tomasa, instead of redoubling her tears as anyone would have thought, wiped away the ones still on her face with a corner of her apron and grabbing his hands with all the strength she had, replied:

—The mistake I made I'm paying for, but I'll never forget what you came to tell me. Tell Edelmira that from today I consider her my dear sister and that she will always be in my prayers. And I hope that one day I can hold her in my arms, as well as your son, whom I already love, even though I have not yet been able to see him, and I can tell you the same about the child on the way. And now go in peace and calmly because your offer did not fall on deaf ears, but my husband must be about to arrive and I don't want him to see you here.

Florencio heeded his sister and left very saddened. The little he had seen of the house, the condition of his sister, and the dignity with which she was handling the situation, impressed him vividly. Gone was the vivacious, graceful and carefree girl he knew and remembered. His sister had now grown into a woman aged beyond her years, dressed practically in rags, with leathery and damaged hands and hair. Her once beautiful hair, now badly tied up in a low bun! But still, from the brief conversation they'd had, he realized that her spirits were still intact and that if her circumstances changed, she could still go back to being what she had been. But her circumstances did not change, or rather, they did — for the worse.

The parents of the cattle trader had died, victims of an influenza that devastated the region, so there were now only two who lived in the shack. Every moment of every day Tomasa thanked all the saints she could remember, for not having children, and at the same time she asked them to return Amadeo to the way he was at the beginning, without yet realizing that everything had been a masquerade on his part, and she prayed that the violent and aggressive character he had developed over the years would calm down and they could live in peace, because for a while now, when she put food in front of him and something displeased him, he would break out swearing like a mule driver, throw the content of the plate at her face, get up and loudly scream:

—Useless, you're useless, Miss Piece-of-shit! You could at least learn to make soups, like the ones my mother made.... You don't even serve for cooking.... One of these days you'll see what is good.... I'm going to tan your ugly hide. Then you'll learn...

And he'd leave the room, kicking everything in his path.

She was silent and endured. Until the verbal harassment became physical. At first it was a push. Later, kicks. And when it seemed to her that her husband could not humiliate her and hurt her any worse, one day for no special reason, he grabbed her by the hair gathered in a bun, threw her to the ground, dragged her across the yard and began to kick her. Alerted by her screams, the neighbors ran over and saw with terror everything that occurred; they barely managed to separate him from his victim and so saved her from becoming a corpse on the spot. She ended up with a bruised face, a burst eardrum, a shattered body and two broken ribs.

After that day and enduring the terrible pain resulting from the brutal and bestial beating, although apparently nothing had changed in her, her decision had been made and she was only guided by one objective: to leave that house and never see that animal again in her lifetime. She could not prepare anything because she had nothing to prepare, only a couple of bills out of all the hundreds she had brought when she arrived in that dismal town. And escape from there without help was not possible, because except for those neighbors who had come to her aid, she didn't know anyone. She, who had formerly always been so sociable, was now isolated, since Amadeo had taken good care of that from the beginning and had not wanted her to interact with anyone, claiming that the people of the town were bumpkins and not like the ones she was accustomed to, that they didn't even know how to read, much less talk like educated folks, that she would get bored with them, and all the stories that occurred to him at the time, and fool that she was, in love to her very core and thinking that he really didn't want to share her with anyone, believed him. It even thrilled her.

Now she finally comprehended his ill will and evil, too late. For once, though, fortune smiled on her: One day Amadeo appeared at the hovel with an old dealer whom he intended to swindle by his cunning arts, and while she was present it came out in the conversation that he knew her brothers; she apologized for absenting the room for a moment, and while the two men drank a glass of wine, she took the opportunity to look in the other room for one of the few five-pesetas bills that she still had, and wrote these words on the edge:

"Tell my brother to come and get me. I only ask you this."

When her husband left the other alone for a moment, she surreptitiously handed the visitor the paper bill and repeated the message in a whisper, to which the good man nodded wordlessly. It was done. It was now only a matter of waiting. Two days passed and she had no news. But she did not despair. On the third, when she was hanging her humble clothes in the yard that adjoined the neighbor's garden, she heard her brother's voice! Although her husband was not at home, she nevertheless used caution in approaching the wall that separated the two houses, where she now beheld Florencio and with a grateful sigh said in a low voice:

—Thank you brother! Thanks for coming. In five minutes I'm back.

She retrieved her shawl, put on her shoes, took one last look at what had been her home for years, and went out. Florencio had a recently purchased carriage, and when his sister appeared on the road urged their departure without delay.

After a smooth journey the two reached Turgalium. It was late afternoon, she was exhausted but happy to have escaped the hell that had been her life. Edelmira was waiting for them at the house on the main square with her two little ones, Juan Carlos and Carmencita. With profound emotion the two women merged in a long hug while the children took them by the legs, also wanting to hug and kiss the newcomer.

From that day on, and until Tomasa recovered, Edelmira was more a mother than a sister to her sister-in-law: in the morning and at night she first dipped the damaged hands of the other in warm oil, then went on to massage the palms and fingers; when the oil was well introduced, she applied petroleum jelly, and finally covered both hands with soft cloth gloves that she had sewn herself. She also devoted herself to restoring Tomasa's erstwhile beautiful hair.

Little by little, with a lot of patience and a lot of love, Tomasa's mood, like her external appearance, was changing and after a few months it was almost what it had been before. She would never be separated from her young sister-in-law, whom she adored, until her death.

~. ~. ~. ~. ~. ~.

And now, when it seemed that with the birth of Teresita they had overcome, although never forgotten, the death of little Carmencita, when they had moved to what had been their childhood home, when she had no financial problems because her brother had taken care that she would always have clothing, food, maid service and someone to look after her, and now when her sister-in-law, or better said her beloved sister, while caring for all, kept an especially loving eye on her... now, they were struck down by the unimaginable: Florencio had left them forever.

6. JUAN CARLOS - SUMMER 1931

The King has fled his royal residence and I have returned to mine — not to a palace, but I have returned home, which to me is the best place in the world, witness to my childhood and my whole life. I have the law degree in my pocket and passed the bar exam, although I do not think I will practice for the time being, if I ever do. Now what I do have to do is unburden mother of all her tasks, handling the assets that we still have, which could have been bigger with better administration; but mother has done more than expected, and that, for a person like her, with no formal education, is commendable. Furthermore, because she is so good and charitable, so aware of the realities and miseries of others, many have taken advantage of her and forgotten about the large sums she lent them. They cannot be sued in court, and she would never do that either, but let's see whether with a little tact and working behind the scenes I can achieve something, because in reality I have been the great beneficiary and large sums have also gone to my education. Sometimes during these eight years, especially in the last few, when I was fully aware of how the family finances were going, I have told her and Aunt Tomasa it would surely be better if I left El Escorial and finished my degree at a public university. But each time I brought up the subject they both raised their voices to high heaven and told me to be quiet, insisting that I stop talking nonsense. Anyway, I'm home. We will see what I can do.

At the moment I am acclimatizing, it is a big change of habits, I miss my friends and Petra, but here I have the usual ones: My cousin Sebastián and his brothers, my great friends Emilio and Manolo... and being at home is always so nice.... I feel so loved and protected by my three ladies that the political situation we have now seems to me an unreal reality, and the chaos and riots that are taking place in the country contrast greatly with the calm of our small circle. I do not know whether the Republic will be the solution to all the ills that afflict our nation. Time will tell.

At the age of sixteen I left my home and went to study at El Escorial. It was a great change in my life then, but I have always been happy to have had that opportunity, not only on an intellectual level but because of the good friends and colleagues I forged there, plus the support and understanding of the Augustinian priests, who although lovers of order and rules always taught us so many things, not only academics but also a lifestyle, and that has been the most important thing.

The El Escorial school when I entered, in the fall of the year '23, was what was called a School of Lineages, a place where the students were few and the attention was total. It was, together with Deusto (run by the Jesuits), a very elitist school and few were able to study there. It had been founded by His Majesty King Alfonso XII in 1875, and when I began my studies there, there were almost a hundred students, distributed in different classes, mine being the Class of '23. It was run by the Augustinian Fathers who had adopted the ideology proposed by the monarch, and the whole institution was based on two principles: it was Catholic and liberal, and it had the Most Pure Virgin as its Patron, to whom both the Augustinians and ourselves prayed with fervor.

When I arrived at El Escorial I knew that my mother had chosen the perfect place for me: not only because of the grandeur of the architectural complex, but because all the surroundings instilled an indescribable peace and tranquility. The complex itself included the basilica, the royal palace, the pantheon (final abode of so many Kings of our country), a large library, the Monastery, and our college, which was located in the front half of the left wing of the Monastery. And the environment surrounding this marvelous ensemble did not lag behind, either in beauty or in serenity for the spirit: strolling through the Jardines del Príncipe, or the Garden of the Friars, visiting the Casita de Arriba, or basking in the sound of the water from the Arenitas fountains, the Batán or the seminary fountain, was something we did often when our studies allowed us to, as well as climbing the slopes to what they call the Chair of Felipe II and from there contemplating the landscape in all its extension... Talking about the beauty of El Escorial would take me years, not for nothing is it considered the eighth wonder of the world since the sixteenth century. I had better focus on my school!

Within the college the atmosphere that I found could not have been better. The Augustinians have always been a liberal clergy, who aimed to instill in their pupils unconditional love for God and for freedom, and their maxim when I joined, which continued during all the years I was there, was: The Free Church in The Free State. With this doctrine we already knew the guidelines and I have always been grateful to be so privileged and to have had the opportunity to learn to think for myself, outside the partisan slogans of the moment; as the vast majority of our educators were graduates and doctors of Letters and Sciences, their intellectual level was far above what existed in other centers, and they urged us constantly to exercise our own judgment, even though sometimes it differed from the one who provoked the debate.

We were twenty-one in my class, and we all became friends as well as classmates, but it was three of them, Paco, Josetxu and Adrià, with whom I became intimate from almost the first day, and that very special relationship that began then was strengthened during the eight years we stayed there, and it will continue for the rest of our lives, regardless of any geographical distance.

The organization in the school was simple and Spartan: those of our class did not even have individual dormitories, while even the advanced classes at best had a dormitory for two or four people; because we were the younger, our dormitory was a large room for all, with the beds aligned perpendicularly against two of the walls, leaving a large central corridor whence the father in charge of keeping an eye on us could do it without much effort. There was a door at each end, one that led to the shower room and toilets, and the other to a large room with stand-alone closets, one per student, where we kept our clothes and personal effects. Both these rooms had their respective doors that opened into other rooms.

In our boarding school there were not, as in some other centers, students who helped the "young men" in exchange for free education, no. In ours we were all the same and we were supposed to do some tasks, like make our own bed, which most of us had not done in our life and which we had to learn urgently. When I told Teresa about it she laughed, imagining my consternation.... We had a bad time of it, but after the first week my bed turned out perfect, and since then I got used to doing it. In fact, when I returned home on vacation, although I always had service, I liked to prepare it myself, or at least review how it was made, because I like the sheets well tucked in, so my feet do not slip out. I learned to adjust the bed clothes perfectly to my liking.

At six thirty in the morning our day began. The father in charge of the bedroom would appear with a bell, and even if you tried to continue sleeping for a minute longer, even by putting the pillow over your head, the noise was so persistent that even the most indolent gave up. From there, half asleep and adorned with sleepy seeds, we went to the daily ablutions, got dressed, and at quarter past seven were ready in the school chapel for confessions and mass; as soon as it finished, at eight-fifteen, we headed to breakfast like ravening wolves. They only allowed us three-quarters of an hour for breakfast. During that time, despite the cold showers, we were still so sleepy that the person in charge of watching us did not need to exercise his discipline; we talked little and responded in monosyllables, knowing there would be plenty of hours during the day to talk and comment. The friars had the theory that the day should start with a good breakfast and they served us potato omelette, coldcut sandwiches, cheese and sausages, coffee and milk with some kind of pastries, which we relished like wild beasts. Had it not been for the bell that called to class we would have continued eating for hours.

Our school had magnificent facilities, not only for learning but also for sports. The first four years were preparatory, and from there on we would study the career that each had chosen, but in my class the vast majority of us chose Law, and the four of us had it clear from the beginning, so we never had to part. In those early years, classes lasted almost an hour, leaving the last few minutes for a short break, while the father who was going to teach us the next subject came to the room. We dedicated the whole morning to various subjects: literature, biology, chemistry, geography, philosophy, grammar, composition, art, music history, Latin and Greek as dead languages and French as the necessary modern language in case someone decided to pursue a diplomatic career. The teachers were very good, intellectually speaking, and they constantly encouraged us to debate, to learn to question things, and we had a lot of material at our disposal to be able to inform ourselves well about everything.

We spent those morning hours (relieved only by a paltry twenty-minute recess) in class, and at two o'clock we entered the dining room where, unlike at breakfast with only my class, we met with all those who studied at El Escorial, in total almost one hundred people, plus the laymen who served us meals, the reader at the raised lectern, who read passages from Saint Augustine, and those who were in charge of watching us. The atmosphere there, despite the fact that in principle we had to behave and be silent, was relaxed, and jokes and wisecracks were the order of the day, especially those made by the older fellows, supplemented by some of the bolder younger ones.

As I have always been rather shy, at first I was a little scared, afraid of the punishments that could befall, but little by little and with Paco's influence, I let myself go, or as he always said, "wake up," and the truth is that within a few months I found our lunchtime a source of fun and relaxation. The menu during the week, was always the same: our multi-plate *cocido*, just like what most of us also ate at home, although the school's was more watery, and the following, unrelated dishes, the *principios* (it always seemed funny to me that the last part was called the first, or principal); nothing was as rich or delicious as at home, but we didn't care, because the company of other students more than made up for the loss in culinary quality. At night and on weekends there was more variety, but also nothing like what a normal good kitchen would turn out. When hunger nagged you had no recourse but to swallow that hogwash, and although we protested, our complaints fell on deaf ears.

For the first years, during which according to our families we were still "growing up", although to tell the truth we were as tall as we were going to be, we ate everything you tossed at us, and even I, who in my house was said to be "a finicky eater," ate everything without complaining, much. Of course I also have to confess that the packages that arrived from Turgalium, lovingly prepared by my aunt Tomasa, helped a lot. And they arrived very frequently.

We four, armed with jackknives and some hunks of bread, gathered away from prying eyes and with great care unwrapped the precious gift until we got to the heart: a box full of ham, loins, sausages and cheeses and, wrapped separately, a good tablet of quince paste. In a trice the content was reduced to half, and on those days we even allowed ourselves the luxury of passing up the meager snack that the friars gave in the afternoon to some of our less fortunate companions. But it was not only I to whom they sent packages. From the north, and thanks to Josetxu, we tasted all kinds of canned fish; from Catalonia, exquisite pastries, *ensaimadas*, stuffed with sweet pumpkin purée, sent by an aunt of Adrià residing in Mallorca to his family and that they forwarded to him, to which were added the sausages *butifarras*, *fuet* and *longanizas*; and from Paco's farmhouse everything came to us: even on one occasion they sent us some pickled partridges in glass jars that arrived without problems. What did we care then about the meal the friars had cooked? If that day a package had arrived for any of the four of us, we passed our lunch plate to somebody else and went hungry for a while until we could open the loot and voilà, fine and dandy. The most important thing, although the gifts were, consisted in the camaraderie with which we shared everything, and the good times we had thanks to the celebrated packages.

In the early years we had to wear a uniform: from the waist down we wore black merino wool baggy pants with socks of the same color, and boots most of the year. When spring came we would change our boots for shoes with laces, and on top we would wear gray shirts and jackets of the same material and color as the pants. If we went outside the premises because a family member had come to visit us, they let us put on our "regular" clothes, but sometimes it was not worth making the change to spend a few hours outside; we were so used to our school clothes that we did not miss the variety and colors of ordinary clothing. As I have always liked to wear dark clothes, the lack of color did not bother me at all, but some of my companions, including my friend Adrià who was very particular in that regard and had a wardrobe like that of a marquis, frequently protested about how boring it was to dress the same every day and exactly the same as everyone else, "like school kids." Little by little, Adrià adapted to the uniform, or at least he stopped nattering about it.

To protect ourselves from the cold, which was intense in winter, we had long coats, also black and, although we were provided blankets for the beds, more than one of us used these coats when the chill was worse at dawn. Coming home on vacation and finding a warm bedroom was one of those pleasures that cannot be expressed in words, but the friars seem to have wanted us to be strong, even at the cost of catching pneumonia.

The rest of our school trousseau consisted of our "linens," and gloves, scarves, and two hats. All very sparse and far from what were our usual clothes. We learned to be frugal in that respect too, since we had no choice.

The afternoons were devoted to what we called "experiments" and sports. In the Physics Lab we had all sorts of artifacts to learn mechanics, to do chemistry experiments (with the occasional fright when mixing substances); we experimented with animal remains to learn anatomy (I still remember, as if I had done it yesterday, the first time we faced a ruminant's stomach and its four parts: *rumen, reticulum, omasum and abomasum*), we dissected eyes, we studied the four-stroke engine, we did experiments as if we were Mendel's disciples, with yellow peas/smooth and green/rough. In short, we put into practice many of the lessons we had learned in theory in the morning and when things sometimes turned out the way they were supposed to, our joy was limitless.

Another of the afternoon subjects to which great importance was given was gymnastics, because the Augustinians strictly adhered to that principle "*mens sana in corpore sano,*" and made us repeat endless exercises, from skipping rope, climbing ropes, vaulting the horse, etc., to sprinting and long-distance races, going through all the gymnastic varieties that the person in charge of the lesson came up with that day. I had never been interested in the least in sports except as an spectator, so it was quite an uphill climb for me. Furthermore, as I must wear glasses due to my myopia, any exercise was much more difficult and painful for me than it was for my classmates, but gritting my teeth, I did like the rest. Besides, I wasn't fat, but I was what we could call a little fleshy, and that physical peculiarity also worked to my disadvantage. When a few months passed and I lost weight, the kilos that I took off helped a lot, and things were not so bad, because the crude reality is that at the beginning the whole thing was an ordeal; I did, however, like to attend the gymnastic competitions that were often held there.

In the Lonja of the Monastery, soccer fields had been laid out where up to ten simultaneous matches could be played. It was the first school in Spain to have soccer fields and great games were played there, not only between our and other school teams, but between professional teams. Sometimes on Sundays we had visitor students from other schools that did not have their own soccer field, and that was always a reason for fun and partying, because we would cheer on our mates with great shouts of support and, if we won, we would spend the following hours commenting even the slightest incidents. When we lost, we did not allow such a mishap to discourage us in the slightest: we found more than a thousand reasons to justify the result, and in most cases it was in our considered judgment the referees or the linemen who were to blame for the untoward event. I have hardly ever played soccer, being a bit clumsy for that sport, but as a fan, few can top me, and the support for my team has been unwavering. Following soccer matches is one of my favorite hobbies, far above other games like basketball, for example, so having the opportunity to see different competitors in our own center filled me with joy.

Another of the sports practiced at school was tennis, and in that I did stand out from the first moment. After a few lessons to learn all the rudiments of the game, Juan Carlos was always there, ready with his racket for whatever turned up. I played singles, doubles, whatever they put in front of me, and could spend hours whacking the ball; sometimes our encounters lasted so long that we ended up tired and sweaty, but after a good shower and a change of clothes the feeling was always very comforting.

At school the first four years we also studied Latin and Greek, and we had to do direct and reverse translations of the two dead languages. Those subjects were two that I liked very much, and in particular Latin was very useful to me later when I started on my law degree, since I could translate entire passages of Roman Law, the basis of all our civil and criminal law, with the greatest ease; that is why I was able to obtain the best grades of all the students. Unlike classmates who were bored with Latin, I didn't mind spending hours until I deciphered the meaning of a paragraph, or put into that language what the teacher had given us to translate, and little by little I even had the pleasure to be helping colleagues, even from higher classes than ours, with their translations. Sometimes, when we were at lunch, they would send me some folded papers with a request for their immediate translation, something I did delighted to be helpful, and which created a magnificent reputation for me and gave me the option to meet older colleagues.

Another subject that we studied in depth was philosophy: from the pre-Socratics to the latest world philosophical trends. We were fortunate to have a magnificent library at our fingertips, and by mastering Greek and Latin we could read directly from the classics, without having to resort to translations that were sometimes not as reliable as they should be. From the first time I was lucky enough to encounter his writings, the few that were still preserved, it was Heraclitus of Ephesus, who from ancient times was already called "the dark one" with his work "On Nature," who attracted me greatly, with his overwhelming maxims and his vision of the world that is always in an eternal process of birth and destruction. We did not have access to the original papyrus on which, according to Diogenes, he wrote his book on a single scroll; the fragments that were within our reach were those cited by other authors, but despite that, in the more than one hundred that we had there was enough material to occupy a whole life, and I still spend hours studying, dissecting his maxims and trying to apply his principles to facts of everyday life. When sometimes, being in the Vineyard on vacation, I lean over the stream that passes in front of the house and put a hand in the water, all the light that its reflections bring suddenly enraptures my mind, and more than one time my family has had to shake me and make me return to the present from the depths of myself.

Other philosophers have also marked me, but none like him, with whom I fully identify, whose teachings have been one of the most valuable things in my existence and whom I have tried, without much success by the way, to make others value. Curiously, my mother, who never had access to a formal education, has so much common sense that she often surprises me with a comment that is a faithful transcript of the teachings of my dear teacher, and that leads me to think that sometimes people on the street are the true philosophers, as is the case with country people, who, being in direct contact with nature and its cycles, know more about the earth and the reactions of animals than many of the so-called erudite experts, and they give us constant lessons every day.

The Language and Literature classes were also wonderful and full of discovery: first we read the classics, then we were introduced to all the other authors, we got to the romantics, we met and commented on the most contemporary works of European and Spanish writers, including the so-called "Generation of 98" and our literary training was vast. We always looked forward to the literature class with great enthusiasm because we knew that the time spent there would reveal new horizons for us, and the Father in charge of that subject taught us to dissect and make textual commentary on everything we read. It was not about learning like parrots, which we already did in geography classes, but about studying in depth and learning to have our own criteria and think about everything we read, regardless of how much or how little we liked the author.

Reading has always been my passion. Those classes, that opening of my mind and the knowledge I acquired in them, were the great foundation on which I have later been able to cement much of what I know. Every time I discovered a new author (new to me, even though his work had been read for hundreds of years), it was like entering a fabulous world that was waiting to offer me so much that many times, as soon as I finished a work, I would go back to the beginning, because now knowing the outcome I could savor and relish the words, the style, the ideas.... I have continued reading voraciously, and increasing my library, and today I can boast of having a very good and well-stocked one, of which I am prouder than of any other material thing that I possess, which continues to increase every year and I hope that in the time to come it will grow even more. Buying books is one of my vices and an expense I have never spared. I read and reread and I always find something new that I had not grasped in a first reading. Aunt Tomasa, when I was little, used to scold me many times, telling me that I was going to go blind, but in that I have never paid attention to her.

I like many authors, many, and choosing is difficult, because you are excluding others who seem essential to you, such as Russian writers, but if I had to choose between all of them I think I would choose three, two French and one Spaniard: Don Benito Pérez Galdós and Honorato de Balzac, as faithful representatives of the realist novel, who have given me such enormous knowledge of life, that I can never stop thanking the Father who encouraged us to read them the day he decided that it was time to know them, and as a third favorite I would undoubtedly choose Marcel Proust, who knew Balzac's work well and who, following in his footsteps, although with a more current approach, I believe, revolutionized the way of writing and after him nothing that is written will be the same. Perhaps a personal circumstance of the latter author was what brought me closer to him: his mother belonged to Parisian high society, while his father was the son of a shopkeeper, something similar but contrary to what happened to me, since my dear mother's origins were also humble, while my father's relatives were among the wealthiest and most prominent in my hometown. Other aspects of his life were opposite to mine, especially his attraction to people of the same sex and perhaps his indolence, but that has never prevented him from being one of my favorite authors, that I read and reread and always enjoy.

The friars did not neglect our religious training and so, once a week, they gave us classes on religion and ethical principles, which most of the time in the best of cases we merely endured, and while we were physically present our minds would fly to other sites. We also had to attend more masses and religious functions than most of us cared to, and our desire was to slip out, or not go, despite the fact that we all came from religious backgrounds, or even very religious I could say, as in my specific case in the fact that prayers of the holy rosary were a daily practice in my house, and that I continue to do because it gives me a lot of inner strength (although I know that my sister sometimes finds it a repetitive and meaningless action, and tries to escape from that routine daily), but all of us at school, and this without exception, had great attachment and devotion to our Patron the Virgin and we entrusted ourselves to Her when there appeared any problem on the horizon, for example exams.

We were also lucky in those preparatory years to have excellent teachers who guided us towards the world of art, first teaching us the different architectural styles and their different techniques and influences, as well as sculpture and painting, and later on the specific study of painters, sculptors, architects and representative buildings of each trend. Those classes, which were complemented by trips destined to show us what we had learned in theory, looking at buildings, paintings and sculptures live, both within the monastery grounds, and in museums or on excursions to different cities, gave us a plus, since they meant leaving the enclosure where we lived and thinking about other possible adventures.

We had the enormous privilege of residing in El Escorial and that in itself was like living inside a museum, so the first thing we studied live was the magnificent complex where we were, because, as our art teacher told us, few buildings, to say the least, had played as important a role in the history of Spain as the one we lived in, explaining without reservation that while the majority considered it from the beginning as a "wonder of the world," for others it was the faithful reflection of the somber identity of its creator, Felipe II.

Architecturally speaking, the building (which began as a Herrerian style and ended as a Renaissance style), is so incredibly fabulous and magnificent that it impresses anyone who sees it, and the immensity of the complex, with its 2,673 windows, its 4,000 rooms spread over three floors, 1,250 doors, 16 inner courtyards, 88 fountains, 45,000 books, 5,000 codices, 1,600 paintings and 540 frescoes is something to which nothing can compare, because the objective of the monarch, who died there at the age of seventy-one, after a long agony of more than fifty-three days afflicted with all kinds of ailments and diseases, was, as many historians have pointed out, to create a European building in Spain and he succeeded.

The Escorial, like Felipe II, has been the victim of many black legends, some true and most of them false, started in the 19th century by the Liberals (and the Liberals were by definition anti-Catholic, so their opinions were very one-sided), although even in the king's time the building of his palace-monastery received sharp criticism from a friar at the same monastery, who complained about the gigantic and expensive work... but I was talking about last century: the first legend is that it is a gloomy building as lugubrious as its promoter, and there I have to admit that what they say is true, although the king, before infirmities took their toll on his body and spirit, was not as many think he was, but on the contrary he enjoyed life, the open spaces of the country air, and in his many trips to other countries a constant in his conversations was how intensely he longed for the sun of Spain. But we have to remember that the Complex, even though multifunctional, is a Monastery, and monasteries always have that aspect. Gloomy and sometimes even more than gloomy.

Another legend our teacher told us asserted that behind its construction some secret idea was hidden, and this, he explained, apart from being ridiculous, was totally false since everything about the erection of the building is documented, as all the papers still in the Library testified, which tell us that the monarch before even thinking of laying the first stone, had first to consult the monks, as it was basically built as a monastery, not as a royal residence (although later it was also), and only after approval by said monks was it possible to undertake its construction.

As for statements that the king collected books on occultism and magic, that corresponds exactly to the truth, because the monarch was very given to learn about these matters, as well as to collect relics, which at the end of his life exceeded seven thousand items, kept in very luxurious receptacles and which belonged to the monastery.

Being resident students we had access to most of the Library's books, which we consulted right there or borrowed when we needed them for a specific job, always with great control by the friar in charge, who noted all the student's data and prescribed a specific period of time for their reading, which generally seemed short to us, and to all this he added a disquisition about how to take care of the book in question while it was in our hands. Over the years, as we got to know each other, little by little his pestering became a little less rigid and with me particularly, whom he appreciated very much; he let me consult even the oldest codices, always forbidden to others, without problem, and moreover, when I mentioned very dark or difficult passages, he helped me to focus them historically.

Another of the many legends refers to the Pantheon and why they built it. At no time did the monarch want to make a royal pantheon, his intention was to erect it to give thanks to God for battles won. And what corroborates this is his vision of what the family is, because in the Pantheon that we know, kings and queens are separated from their children, something that was unthinkable for Felipe II, since he believed that children should not be separated from parents even after death.

One item that gave us hours of debate, not only in class but later on in private chats, was the subject of the Inquisition, one of the legends circulating out there. Some authors and historians have tried to link the Monastery with the *Autos de fe*, which is totally wrong since, although the monarch was a great supporter of the Inquisition, he was not so much a supporter of the autos de fe; in all his long life he gave only four, and none took place in the monastery.

But leaving these legends and studies, what Felipe II wanted and achieved was to create a magnificent library there, where he could keep all his books and relics and we, the students, were the ones who most benefited from it by having access to documents that only scholars with special permits could see. And the same could be said of all the paintings and frescoes that adorned its walls and ceilings, something so grandiose and precious that I looked at them ecstatically for hours.

Before living there I had visited the odd museum, not many by the way, and certainly without having someone by my side to explain what I was seeing, so when we began to discover the wonders that the monastery contained and, while admiring the painting in itself learned about the technique employed, it was so revealing that when we found in a book some of "our" pictures we were so proud that anyone would think the paintings really were ours.

As difficult as it is for me to choose a single writer as my favorite, when we talk about painters the matter becomes even more complicated and I, Paco, Adrià and Josetxu (the drudge-quartet, as the older chaps jokingly called us, but who many times descended their Alpine heights to consult us about something they needed for some project — to which requests we acceded without rancor), each spent many hours explaining to the remaining three the reason for his choice. I had my doubts at first and it didn't seem fair to have to stay with just one artist, but we had instituted that rule to avoid getting lost in the weeds. Fortunately, the paintings chosen by the other three were those that came after my great favorite: The Garden of

Earthly Delights, by Bosch, a work that we had on the premises and to which I dedicated many stolen hours, for it so attracted me that I used study breaks or free hours to continue studying it and to analyze all its content. Felipe II had acquired it from the friar who owned it when he died in 1593. The king was a great admirer of Bosch and decided the work should be added to the pictorial collection at El Escorial. The monarch was always very attracted to the esoteric, and in the Garden there were so many allegorical elements that a whole lifetime would not have unmasked them.

The Garden of Delights was first called El Madroño (arbutus or tassel fruit), alluding to the fruits that appear in it, and as the friar who named it pointed out ... "just like the pleasures of life, its sweetness passes as soon as you taste it." But it soon became known by the name that has survived to this day. The painting is a large triptych in which, when closed, the first thing that stands out is a large globe that is supposed to represent the third day of creation. Once opened, the panel on the left represents Paradise, the one in the center represents Lust, and the one on the right represents Hell, and in the three panels there are so many elements to analyze that we could almost say that not a centimeter of the painting remains without a meaning. For some scholars, the panel on the right is the most famous and shocking scene of Hell in Western art, and it is clear that the suffering of the souls who have fallen there is not only physical but also psychological: they are crazed by fear, anxiety and anguish, and the chaos that reigns in the place increases their pain. The scenes are gripping, overwhelming, far more intense than all other representations dealing with the subject.

In the other two panels there are so many symbolic elements that describing them here would take me too long, but as an example I mention the music written on the rear ends of characters, the flying birds, many animals from Africa such as lions and giraffes (which although they were not known at the time of the painting, we must suppose that its author saw them in bestiaries), shells (which are supposed to be venereal symbols), pigs dressed in nuns' habits... A whole world inhabited by strange beings... And all subject to so many interpretations, depending on who analyzes it... Because the truth is that although the work was dedicated to representing a condemnation and a rejection of many things, in reality it is a playful work. An impressive painting of which I was able to get a copy, and which on many occasions, armed with a magnifying glass the better to capture the details, I continue to study and write about.

Paco had chosen a painter and some works which we had not seen in the original, just the plates that came in an art book in the monastery Library: George de La Tour and his Magdalenas. His other works did not interest him so much, but the light that emanated from the candles in the pictures of the Madelines fascinated him, and "lecturing" us on the reason for his choice he delivered such a complete eulogy that we were left with our mouths open, listening to the depth of his thoughts, the precision of his words to describe them, and the knowledge he had managed to gather about a painter relatively unknown to most, although not to us. I supported his exposition in every nuance, since La Tour was also one of my great favorites, and hearing all that Paco explained was very enriching. In fact, we told him that he should write down everything he had told us, so that we would not forget anything over time, and here in my office I still have the pages that he wrote. Even realizing the failures due to the early age in which he did it, I must admit that it is an excellent work, and I have reread it so many times that I could almost recite it from memory.

José María, my great Basque friend Josetxu, had a passion for Velázquez and Titian and although we insisted that he limit himself to one of them for the "game" that we were playing, there was no way, and as we also liked those two painters a lot, we let him be, but obliging him also to put in writing all the wonders that he told us, something he did some time later and which I also keep.

Finally, Adrià, the Catalan, opted for Pieter Brueghel the Elder, in particular he chose as his favorite work the "Flemish proverbs," and we all applauded the choice, for although at the time we still hadn't seen many of his original works, we had studied his paintings in the art books in our library; he too gave us a kind of lecture telling us many things that the rest of us did not know, such as that Ernesto de Habsburg, nephew of Felipe II, who had grown up in his uncle's court in El Escorial, was, like the king, a great admirer of Bosch, but being short of funds and therefore unable to acquire works by that Flemish master, bought from his competitor, that is to say, from Brueghel. He also told us about a peculiarity of the Flemish painter which consisted of painting on very thin boards, a practice which later caused serious conservation problems; these and many other interesting anecdotes he also included in his written work.

The Proverbs are a study in human stupidity. At the same time, it is a painting one can spend hours analyzing, not only for its excellent pictorial technique in being able to include so many elements and characters in a reduced space, but also for its depiction of absurd behaviors, weaknesses and human follies, continuing thus the most pure tradition of Bosch.

It was an enriching experiment for the four of us, and when we had committed our expositions to paper, all those who read them applauded and congratulated us for having done it, and so the whole process that I have summarized here, which took us hours, days and weeks, had a very happy result for all four of us.

After many and varied "excursions" in our monastery, Father Jacobo, our art teacher, finally decided that he could now venture to take us to Madrid to see other museums.

The first time we went to the Prado Museum, which none of my class knew in person, at the moment was actually a kind of shock in its impact: there was too much to absorb in a visit of a few hours. Succeeding times, and they were many, we could now enjoy all the beauty that its rooms contain. Standing before a painting "that you see in books," as my friend Paco always said, gave us a mixture of joy and disenchantment, perhaps because we did not have it as close to hand as "ours," but all these classes and excursions left us with an indelible taste for painting, and later, every time I have had the opportunity to visit a museum or contemplate a work in an art treatise, I have continued to enjoy it, every day more and more.

In those four years that they called preparatory before beginning university studies, the Fathers tried to instill in us a love and knowledge of music such as was unthinkable in other centers, and we all, without exception, enjoyed those classes. First we studied the entire history of Music, as a primordial base and necessary background, and then, when faced with music itself, we had a sure frame of reference; our learning focused primarily on ancient, classical and religious music, although the divers professors of the subject did not let their condition of religious blind them, and they exposed us to other types of more current music. According to their ideology, it was a question of being fully trained, and for that purpose, to ignore so-called modern rhythms meant leaving the chair without a leg, and we totally agreed, especially when the last two years arrived and we were already beginning to have a little more freedom; we could go out a lot more and they even allowed us to go to some dances once we started university courses. Continuing with our customs, the four of us decided to do some work independent of general course work, expounding why we preferred a certain composer and a certain work above all others. Such was the success of that initiative that many others decided to do the same, fomenting such interest and thought that the teacher in charge of the subject finally included this exercise as an exam, and also gave us the highest possible grade and his congratulations for being creative students.

My group was already seasoned in these struggles, we had the experience of having done it with painters, writers and in many other cases, but deciding which musician and piece were the ones that could be saved, in case you had to choose, was very difficult, because there is music for different hours and what moves you or makes you happy at one moment can afflict you at another; but the rules that we had imposed upon ourselves were clear: a composer and a work. The advantage was that since we were four, the choices opened up a little, although not as much as we wanted, so we decided to be a bit more generous and "allow" two composers and two works, which did not necessarily have to be by the same ones. Josetxu thought that we were opening up too much, and that such an opening would make us spend too much time in preparing an exposition, would incite confusion, and in the end we would not be clear about anything, so after hours of debate we returned to the initial premise a little modified: we would choose one work and two composers and would see what happened.

We spent many hours lucubrating over our respective elections; and to play at being democratic, since we were immersed in a political dictatorship, we agreed that the oldest of the four would begin the presentations. The age difference was tiny, but I was the oldest, if only by weeks, so I got the task. Being the first would not be an easy thing, because the rest would be very expectant and attentive to those first words that would fall on virgin ground, so all the judgments could be more negative; but then I thought better of it and saw it as an advantage, since it wasn't really about judging, but listening, so by my words I had to convey my feelings to others. And then wrap up with a compelling conclusion and on to a discussion.

I spent many hours listening to my favorites, and in the end, as a work for my presentation, I opted for the *Dies Irae*, the Day of Wrath, a magnificent 13th-century Latin song, which was attributed to the Franciscan monk Tomás de Celano, who was a friend as well as a biographer of Saint Francis de Assisi, a figure that had always attracted me a lot because it seemed to me that his life was an example to follow.

Dies Irae is usually considered the best medieval Latin poem, thus differentiating itself from Classical Latin, not only for its accentuation but also for its rhyming lines. The poem describes the day of the Last Judgment, with the Angel blowing the last trumpet calling the dead before the throne of God, and there the elect will be saved for ever and the damned will be thrown into the flames of eternal fire. This hymn was used as a sequence in the Requiem Mass, and the first time I heard it, as a six-year-old boy during my father's funeral, something definite was recorded in my mind, and when as a teenager I found that music again, the memories of that day crowded together and I decided to study and get to know the poem in depth. The inspiration for this hymn seems to come from the Latin Vulgate Bible, and one of the most surprising things is that already in the first stanza a mention is made of the Sibyl, announcing the end of the world —*"Dies Irae, Dies illa, solvet saeclum in favilla, Teste David cum Sibylla"*— and that in its fifty-seven lines it presents us with all the fear and anguish of the soul when it finally has to appear before its Creator. Even knowing the poem by heart in Latin and Spanish, I can't reread it without a chill running through my body. And putting words and music together sometimes make my eyes water.

I explained as best I could why I had chosen that composition, and spoke of my father's death, how it had marked my existence, some of the facts and circumstances of his life, and expressed for the first time out loud my wish that he were one of those chosen to be on the right hand of the Father. I must not have done it badly, since my three companions decided that we should stop there, as although everyone knew the composition, that day they were feeling it in a different way and wanted to immerse in it fully. So as the majority ruled, I had to leave my composers for a better occasion.

We had another meeting and as a result we agreed that it was better for the remaining three to deal with the piece or musical passage they liked the most, and leave the composers for later. The next on the list was our Catalan colleague, Adrià, who began by apologizing because he said that after my presentation, which had moved him a lot, his would seem thin and poor to us, words the three of us vigorously opposed and we urged him to start. He started humming and at once we all knew what he had chosen: Beethoven's Hymn to Joy. What a great pleasure to hear something so festive after something so gloomy and threatening! The choice could not have been more on target, musically speaking, and when he began to explain the reasons for his election we all applauded.

It turns out he was born the same year that the Palace of Catalan Music was inaugurated (1908, like all of us), and his father, who was a great music lover and a personal friend of the architect who had designed the entire auditorium, Lluis Domènech i Muntaner, decided to take him to the Palau for the first time on his tenth birthday. That day the program was dedicated to Beethoven, specifically to his Ninth Symphony and it was there, in the fourth movement, that Adrià first met the beautiful Ode, written by Schiller. In 1793 the great composer, only 23 years old, had encountered the poem of the German writer, and from that moment he wanted to put it to music. It would be some thirty years later that the work was composed.

Beethoven conceived his last and fourth movement to be performed by a chorus and soloists, and thus the Hymn to Joy has its place as the first choral movement inserted in a symphony. Beethoven added the first strophes to the original poem, which give strength to the whole composition:

O Freunde, nicht diese Tone!
Sondern lasst uns angenehmere anstimmen,
Und freudenvollere,
Freude! Freude!

When Beethoven composed his Ninth Symphony he was already totally deaf and although we knew that detail, when Adrià reminded us of it, our admiration for the beauty of the work grew, if that were possible, the four of us marveling at such a feat. We deemed our study mate's presentation totally charming and fully enjoyed it.

The one in charge of the next "musical session without music", as we called our expositions, was Paco, and we were all expectantly waiting for him to delight us with some of his Andalusian wit, but following his custom he surprised us: he was very clear about it: his favorite work was "The Brandenburg Concertos," the six concertos that Johann Sebastian Bach presented in 1721 to the Marquis of Brandenburg, although it is more than likely that he composed them over several years, while he was *Kapelmeister* in Kothen. These marvelous concertos, in which Bach used the widest spectrum of orchestral instruments in totally audacious combinations, were very loved by all four of us, who knew them by heart, so that choice was also very welcome. Each of the six concertos establishes a precedent in musical writing, and curiously, the required number of instruments coincides with the seventeen musicians that the maestro had at his disposal in the Kothen chapel. Paco, like the rest of us, liked all six concertos, but it was the second that in his words made him "touch the absolute," and as proof of his knowledge he whistled, after his manner, the thirteen minutes of the concerto. We spontaneously burst out clapping, and as we were sitting outside, at a stone table under some leafy trees, several onlookers approached at the sound of our applause, and our companion had to repeat the feat.

The great surprise came from the hand of Josetxu. Because while the three of us had chosen classic works as favorites, and deciding on a specific one had been difficult and painful, our friend surprised us with something different. His choice was clear and forceful: the zarzuela "La Verbena de la Paloma," a work by Tomás Bretón, also subtitled The Apothecary and the Chulapas and Badly Repressed Jealousy, an operetta with libretto by Ricardo de la Vega, which debuted in Madrid in 1894 and which reflected very typical, characteristic and endearing inhabitants of old Madrid. The four of us knew the play, we could sing its songs and together we had seen it performed on one of our school excursions to Madrid, but what we didn't know was that it was the first zarzuela our friend had heard live. It turns out that his father, a Basque shipping company mogul, traveled to Madrid very frequently, and on one of those trips he decided that Josetxu should accompany him, and also to the theater where zarzuelas were performed. For a boy from the north, it was an authentic discovery to behold those stylized characters that embodied what Madrid was, or had been, and at that very moment he adopted La Verbena as his favorite among his favorites.

He told us all the impressions he had had that day, how from that moment on he had memorized the three scenes that make up the work, had gotten all the songs by heart, and could sing and perform them all, whether it was the role of Don Hilarión, or those of Casta or Susana. At that, we divided up the roles and the four of us began heartily to sing out, but we must have sounded a bit out of tune because the older students who were nearby, instead of clapping, urged us to shut up!

It had been a grand experience to share our musical preferences and we decided to leave them there, not to continue with the initial project of also choosing composers. Exam periods were approaching and those scholarly games were stealing too much time, but we decided to put everything in a small booklet for glory in posterity, and so that when we had children they could read it and see how their parents entertained themselves when they were teenagers.

Those and thousands of other memories come to mind now that I'm sorting papers in my office. Those eight years gave us much, for although it may seem a cliché, they were all a time of great discoveries, and even the simplest things represented a great adventure for us. When we got a little older and the friars let us go out alone, the simple act of going to see a movie was something so wonderful that the previous hours already seemed like a gift, anticipating what we were going to do and we were not going to do, and when we returned to our confinement, our comments afterwards filled hours, although they also made us more aware of how trapped we were in that almost ideal world in which we lived, because while we were in the bubble of El Escorial, many things were happening in the country, too many.

In 1928, the dictatorship of Primo de Rivera had reformed Article 53 of the University Statute, and recognized the right of the private universities of the Church to title their own graduates. Until then that privilege only corresponded to public universities. Therefore, the religious universities could issue official titles, and the major beneficiaries were the universities of Deusto and El Escorial, run respectively by the Jesuits and the Augustinians, and therefore us.

This reform caused a great commotion among teachers and students. A fight that would last months broke out between the private and the public school. In an Assembly held in Madrid, and which was attended by representatives of all the Universities, the repeal of said article 53 was demanded, and a general strike was threatened if there was no positive response within eight days. Such a strike, called at the state level and in a coordinated manner, was a powerful weapon in the hands of the students, since it was the first time that this had happened, for until that moment the strikes had been local, uncoordinated and almost spontaneous.

In the following months, in addition to the repeal of Article 53, the students expanded their demands. With the refusal of the Regime to make concessions and not reach any agreement, in March 1929 the strike was called. Only the day before, Primo de Rivera had issued a statement threatening the loss of enrollment for those who did not enter class. In Madrid and other large cities there were major clashes between the strikers and the police, and in the end the Government suspended the Decanate and all academic authorities from their functions, as well as ordering the loss of the paid enrollment of the strikers.

All this, although it affected us directly, did not affect our academic life, which continued as if nothing that was happening a few kilometers away had anything to do with us, despite being the directly benefited or harmed. But without wanting to be pedantic, I can say that our academic training was so far superior to what was taught in public universities, that the fact of having to revalidate our degrees in one of them did not worry us. For us it was a clear example of the Spanish sin, par excellence, Envy; and therefore, although we followed the news that reached us, we were not worried about that particular. Everything was in turmoil, not just the students, and you see how the picture is right now.

At the moment, none of the four of us have been in the least interested in thinking about pursuing any political career, although by training and knowledge we could be the ideal candidates to hold public office, and get to occupy the highest positions in that field. It may be that we are too much the humanists, too "philosophical," and that is why we are not attracted to entering a world that, with very few and rare exceptions, is plagued by careerists and individuals who not only do not look out for the common good but, in the expression of my mother "are out to feather their own nests." Now we are without the King. Excesses produce these consequences, but who am I to judge the behavior of another? I live and let live.

7. EDELMIRA - OCTOBER 1938

Monologue.

Yesterday my Teresita got married.

The house has been left empty, because she filled everything, thank goodness that Juan Carlos and Margarita are still living upstairs, and that Teresa is going to stay in Turgalium. Look what a coincidence, in the house next door to where she was born twenty-four years ago. My beloved home on the Main square.... How often I think of it, and the dopey thing I did when I sold it for four bits, but I always needed cash, and look for what, in many cases people did not pay back the loans I made to them.... Selling that house was one of my biggest mistakes and I'm sure that until my dying day I will be regretting it, even if there is no longer a remedy for it, but thinking of how comfortable I would be there now, instead of in this big house where I have so many rooms left over... And, for the life I live now I could get by with a smaller one.

So since today I am alone here with wet nurse Justa, and I got up earlier than usual, I don't know if because yesterday I ended up too tired, or because this morning I started to think and turn over in imagination how life is going to be for me from now on, I am going to take advantage and tell you my story, which is not a novel, to see if it does you any good and when you know it, do not make the mistakes that I have made.

I am fifty years old and I am neither tall nor short, as you can see, very common.

Neither fat nor thin, common too, although I tend more towards thinness than fat. My daughter always says it's because I'm very irregular with my meals, but I don't know what to tell you, I eat when I'm hungry and I don't pay attention to the hours. Starting today I have to be careful because none of them will be with me, neither Tomasa, or Juan Carlos, or Teresita, and without any of those who were here before, it will be more difficult to think about lunch or dinner at a specific hour....

Everybody always said that I am very pretty, but the truth is that I have never paid attention to them, because when I look at myself, or looked, because I don't even do it anymore, except on some special occasion like yesterday for the wedding, I don't see myself as they say. I have green eyes, like many of my beloved cats, and blonde hair that is already filling with gray, for all the troubles that life has given me, but that does not matter to me. My faithful Maria, my lifelong hairdresser, continues to come here every day and style my hair the same way she's done for many years: she pulls all my hair up to the crown of the head, ties it with a small ribbon and then makes a braid that twists and fixes it with hairpins. I don't like having hair on my face or neck, so with the bun I am well combed throughout the day.

Also, every morning when she comes she takes the opportunity to tell me the stories that pass through the city, and it's not that I'm interested in knowing them, but I don't know how to cut her off and tell her to shut up. We'd be better off using the time praying the rosary, but once we did, and she complained about this and that, and in the end I had to stop because she was getting impossible, and that was no way to carry on.

As I was telling you now, I have no family at home, except for the maids who have been with me for so long now that they are like family, but Juan Carlos got married, Tomasa has gone forever and now my daughter is married too.

My life has been marked by losses, many and ever since I remember, it's not that I complain, but it is what has been.

I got married very young, I wasn't even eighteen years old, and no one could have felt a greater love than the one I had, and still have, for my dear Floro and look, when he passed away I got many suitors, but the thing of putting another man in my house and in my bed was something that never crossed my mind, although others have done it and it does not occur to me to criticize them, but each one is each one, and I did not think of giving another father to my children. It seemed good to me, you never know what he would be like with the children or myself, and after the husband that I had, none of them was going to reach the bottom of his shoes, because a kinder, more affectionate and better man, it seems to me there cannot be another like him in the whole world.

My father was a butcher, hardworking and honest to the core, and he only thought of getting the best for us, my two sisters, my brother and yours truly. My mother was dedicated to taking care of us and the whole household, and she wanted me, who was the oldest, to learn a good trade so I could earn a few bucks for myself, so when I was almost fifteen she put me in a tailor shop so that I could learn to sew and make pants and jackets for men.

None of the four of us were able to have much education, because neither my mother nor my father knew much about letters, but they both had a lot of common sense and they wanted us to have more than they'd had, and we all learned to read and write well, the four math rules and whatever was most necessary to be able to develop ourselves through life.

My brother, who was big and strong, learned the butcher trade, and he has done very well because he is a formal and serious person, who always does what he promises.

I could not say so much about my two sisters, because the one who follows me, Jacinta, was lazy and indolent since she was born, she has never wanted to learn any trade, and even to give a little help with housework, mother had to chase her through the rooms, and never managed to set her on a good path. And then, when she was a young teenager and should have had a little more knowledge, she got in with bad company that led her astray. I have tried for many years to get her straightened up, giving her good advice and helping her where I can, but the only thing that interests her from me is the money she can get to buy a liter of wine.... I didn't even want to invite her to Teresita's wedding because I knew that she was going to make a spectacle, and with all the fine people who were going to come it was not acceptable, it's been pity enough not to be able to do it in the church, and thank goodness that Don Rafael was able to celebrate it in home, but this war is consuming us all. I do not understand politics, but it seems to me that they should be a little more reasonable and not make the population suffer like that, but if you want we can talk about that later, my mind is wandering, and I just want to tell you my story.

Well, Jacinta, as I was saying, is a hopeless case and it won't be fixed anymore easily. Any day now someone will tell me that she has been in an accident or something, and she will die... Less than a week ago I found her in the doorway in a mess, lying on the floor and she had even vomited on herself. Between Cross-eyed Juana, Nurse Justa and me, we raised her as best we could, sat her in the kitchen and the cook made her a good coffee to see if she would wake up, but it cost us God only knows until we got her in condition, and that's just talking to talk, because the condition she was in was the worst, the worst.

As soon as she came to a bit, the first thing she did was ask me for a peseta for wine. Oh! If my parents were raised from the dead they would die again to see how she is, thank goodness that the Blessed Virgin has spared them this suffering, because raising a daughter who turned out like that is a bitter herb, because she never saw those examples with my parents, never, who never had much, but who always gave us a good upbringing, respect and fear of God.

The youngest one, Eusebia, at least has no vices, but she is a slippery fish and always has been. She married a good boy and they had only one daughter, Consolation, who is good as gold, and without all the slipperiness of her mother, who you never know how she's going to come at you. As my sister is also quite envious, I try and always have done since we lived with our parents, not to give her any reason to believe that I think I am better than her, or that I have more, but the reality is the reality, and we both know what there is and although I treat her like I'm walking on egg shells, always being very careful of what I say and what I keep quiet, I like to see her every day, even if sometimes we end up daggers drawn, or not on very good terms, it seems such childish behavior, being the two as old and widowed as we are, that we continue fighting over silly things, it must be that we do not have much education.

After all these intermissions I will continue with my story, and since I am not in a hurry I can tell you all of it till I finish.

So I became a seamstress and I liked the trade very much. Taking a piece of fabric and then turning it into pants or a jacket or any other garment gave me a lot of pleasure. I was lucky that the tailor who taught me everything, Mr. Macario, had no other apprentices when I entered his workshop, so he was able to teach me the entire trade calmly and without skipping any steps.

I learned to cut, sew and finish off, and when two years had passed I could do the same as my employer, even if looks like it is wrong to say it and without being presumptuous, but he even told me so.

Because since the best of the city used to go to his tailor shop, and all the gentlemen we made suits for, in addition to repeating, recommended us to their friends, we could not cope with all the work we had for the whole year, and the two of us worked side by side all the hours it took to serve them, not caring about staying up late sometimes if we had to deliver a cape, a suit or whatever they had ordered.

Mr. Macario and his wife Mrs. Pepa did not have children, so I was like a daughter to them, and I owe them a lot because they were second parents to me who taught me not only to sew and earn a living, but also to behave.

At first I took a lunch box with food from my house, because I was there from morning to night, but Mrs. Pepa spoke with mother and told her that I didn't need to bring anything, that I could stay to eat with them, and that's when my education began, because both of them taught me to use silverware well, not to talk while I had food in my mouth, to clean myself with a napkin before and after drinking water, to say please when asking for things and to say thanks.

In the tailor shop, as important people came, I also learned to treat them properly, with a lot of education and respect, but always keeping my distance.

I wasn't much for going out like my sisters did. When I returned home I was tired, after working with the needle for many hours and standing also as many hours, and the only thing I wanted, as soon as all the family finished praying the holy rosary, was to go to sleep, and on Sundays, the day that I did not go to the workshop, I took advantage of any scrap that Mr. Macario had given to me and made my brother some pants, a doublet for my mother or any other piece, instead of going to the Plaza to fool around with Jacinta and Eusebia; the two of them were always trying to get me to go out together, because when I went more young men would come, but I preferred to stay at home with my housework, talk to mother, tell her what I had learned that week and help her a little, because the poor thing never had a minute to sit or rest.

At seventeen I hadn't had a serious boyfriend or suitor, but I didn't have time to think about it either. If one of them came one day, it would be well all right, and if not, I would stay with my mother.

As the business continued to prosper, my boss took three more apprentices and I was promoted in category, because despite my youth, he said, I could run the business with my eyes closed.

One morning, when I was putting some hot coals in the iron and had prepared the pants that someone would come to pick up and which I wanted to put the finishing touches on, a very elegant gentleman entered, wearing a brown suit and a good cape of the same color around his shoulders, and greeted me very politely.

Immediately, Mr. Macario came out and I saw from how he treated him that he must be someone posh, but after returning the greeting I stayed where I was.

Don Florencio, that was his name, came to order a suit because he had to attend the wedding of a cousin, who was the one who recommended our tailor shop to him.

My boss took his measurements, they chose the cloth to make a three-piece suit, in a good merino wool fabric, and asked us if we could also make him half a dozen dress shirts, and two jackets to wear in his warehouse when he was there with his carpenters, to which my employer nodded happily at such an important request.

As time ran a bit rushed, especially for the suit for the wedding, Mr. Macario told the other three and me to stop what we were doing, and dedicate ourselves to baste and sew what he with my help was cutting and preparing; we spent the whole day working on that, and at night we almost had the suit ready for the first fitting.

When I left the workshop with my companions, Don Florencio was at the door, as if waiting for us, but he limited himself to saying good night and we continued on our way. It was a pretty good night for the month we were in, but we went quickly because we all wanted to get home soon.

The next day, Don Florencio returned to the tailor's shop for the first try on of his new suit, and as soon as he left Mr. Macario called me to the room we used for accounts, papers, and such things, which was a hovel where two people couldn't stir, but we managed to keep it as orderly as possible, and since I understood the accounts when he couldn't, I was the one in charge of doing it.

I thought he would have to go out and that he wanted me to write something down, so look at my surprise when he told me that Don Florencio had liked me very much, that he was very impressed with me and had asked him to accompany him to go see my father, in order to get permission to be allowed to see me. I didn't know what to say or think, so I went back to my chair to continue sewing, and keep doing whatever I was doing.

My father, who was even younger than Don Florencio, although he had not had dealings with him before, liked him a lot, he thought he was a very thorough and serious man, not one of those who are going to take advantage of those in the classes with fewer possibilities, and he agreed to let us see each other if I agreed, because although he had no studies, he was a very sensible man, and he saw the difference in age and position between us, and he was not sure if the romance was going to flourish.

So three days after seeing each other for the first time we entered into courtship. I was a bit shocked at first, when he started to come to pick me up at the tailor shop, but my parents always sent one of my sisters or my brother to accompany us, and in a few days my embarrassment was lifted, I was able to talk to him without qualms, and above all listen and learn.

Don Florencio, my Floro from then on, was thirty-many years older than myself, so he was already well into his fifties, a few more years than I am now, although as he had the spirit and make-up of someone much younger, perhaps because he worked very hard and had not just sat around despite his position, he did not seem like it; he continued on living with his parents and his brother since the two sisters had gotten married, one well and the other badly.

The family had a lot of money, but the father and the two sons were hard workers. They had a lumberyard and a cabinetmaker's workshop where they made very fine furniture for rich people, and they also had many houses and various farms. Not like my family, who didn't have a dime or a place to drop dead, but were honorable.

Floro was so in love with me, and I with him to tell you the truth because a kinder, more affectionate person with more education and standing I had not seen in my life, that he wanted me to meet his family soon, and that we get married as soon as possible; he said that now that he had found me he didn't have to wait a minute longer than absolutely necessary, so I had to leave the tailor shop to dedicate myself to sewing my trousseau, helped by my mother and my workshop companions, since the two drones of my sisters did very little.

Although money was scarce in my house, mother used what little savings she had to buy a whole piece of fabric, and out of that we got many sheets and pillowcases, two tablecloths with their napkins and other necessary things, and father dedicated some money he had saved to buy a calf and some lambs, and between Mr. Macario, Mrs. Pepa and my friends they made me several dresses, a good coat and some shirts: all that was much more than I had ever had.

In order for me to meet his family, my Floro took me to his house, a large house that his father had built, with three floors, corrals and patios, with a lot of staff to take care of everything, and there his parents, his brother Nicasio (whom I already knew), were waiting for us and one of the sisters who was pregnant and was spending time with them.

His parents, who seemed older than my grandparents, who Rest In Peace, were also very affectionate with me. They had ordered preparation of an afternoon snack with more things than we ate on Christmas Eve, everything seemed very tasty but mother had warned me to eat little, so that I did not look like a starving woman, which I was not, and to sample only some of what they were going to offer me, so I followed her advice, and although everything looked scrumptious I held back, but they insisted so much that in the end I ate a bit of almost everything, which gave them good joy.

The sister, Celestina, was very weak because perhaps she was too old to have a pregnancy, but she immediately appreciated me and told me that she would always be like an older sister to me and that she would help me in whatever way I needed.

The meeting was very nice and when I got home and told my mother about it, she was very happy, and said that I deserved that and more.

We immediately set the date for the reading of the banns, and from that moment it was continuous running every day, I had so many tasks to juggle, so many things to finish that time passed in a breath and before I knew it the wedding day had arrived.

My future father-in-law had given us the house in the Plaza, because although in the one where they lived there was plenty of room for the two of us, Floro's mother, with very good sense, thought that it would be better and easier for me to be alone with my husband, something which I always thanked her for because the change would have been immense, too much for me, and furthermore my family would not have had the freedom or the confidence to come to see me, or they would not have liked being among such rich people, and with which they wouldn't know how to talk or what to talk about.

They brought us some furniture worthy of royalty from the Warehouse, and they set up a kitchen that had everything you can imagine, all good and upmarket.

I was even afraid to touch something in case it broke....

As in matters of cooking and preparing meals I have never been very good, because at home it was always my mother who was in charge of doing it and when I returned from the workshop everything was ready, my Floro told me not to worry about that because he had already hired a good cook, a maid to do the chores and another maid for me, that all I had to do was to be happy and love him a lot always, so look what a big change there would be in my life.

For the day of the wedding, his family gave me a beautiful black crepe dress, silk stockings, very fine leather ankle boots, a white linen shirt and some linen panties! I had never used panties before, because what we did was move the hem from behind the camisole to the front and fasten it well with some pins, and that was a new garment for me, although I knew about them and knew they were used by rich people. The ones they gave me were like breeches and on the bottom edges they had lace to match those of the shirt. The whole outfit was very beautiful and from that moment on I never stopped wearing them, because my sister-in-law Celestina had taken care of ordering two dozen from some nuns who made all the underwear for her and the women of the family and she wanted me to be one of them.

We got married in Santa Clara, a very cozy and charming convent and the church that morning was beautiful: adorned with many flowers and candles and with the smell of incense floating in the air.

My sisters behaved well, even Jacinta, who was already beginning to get up to her sad tricks, and when we were now husband and wife we all went to Floro's parents' house for breakfast. In addition to the chocolate with croutons that they served us and other sweets, my mother had made a very good cake that everyone liked very much, we finished very happy and I liked seeing the two families in such good harmony.

My husband wanted us to have a honeymoon, to rest from all the hustle and bustle we had had and above all to start getting to know each other without being surrounded by people, so we went on a honeymoon to Toledo.

I had never been out of Turgalium, and I was a little scared to be away from my family and the places and people I knew, but he had that caprice for me, and he said that I would always be happy remembering it, and for sure it has been truly like that.

As soon as breakfast was over, we went to what was already our house to change clothes and started the journey. It was many leagues, very far and it took us three days to get there, but at night we stopped at inns where we freshened up, we removed the dust that had stuck to our clothes, we could eat well and rest.

The first time we slept together I had a lot of qualms. I had never been with any man alone in a room before, and neither did I know what was expected of me, or what I had to do, but with his knowing how to act and his affection he explained everything to me so that I would not be afraid, and he said that what we were going to do was the greatest thing that could happen between a man and a woman, that at first it was going to hurt a little, but that later on, when I got used to it, I would like it a lot, as it was, and although I got all the bottom sheet of the bed full of blood, the truth is that it did not hurt, although it did scare me thinking it was a hemorrhage, as sometimes happened with my nose and I had to put my head back until the flow was cut. But thanks be to God it wasn't like the nose thing, and after the act I slept straight through the night like a dormouse.

I really liked Toledo. It was a very big city, with many people on the streets, there were shops where you could buy everything and many churches. We went into many of them that had very beautiful paintings of one they called El Greco, although if I do want to tell you the truth, all of those who were portrayed in the paintings seemed very sad and thin. My Floro explained to me that it was because that man had a defect in his eyesight and that he saw them that way, although in reality they were fat and happy, and since he was always right in what he said, I believed it because I knew it would be true.

After that first trip, I have done many: to take the waters at Mondariz or Alange, to Portugal (with the children, my Floro and Tomasa, and then she and I with Juan Carlos and Teresita when I became a widow), to El Escorial where Juan Carlos studied, to Madrid, first for my doctors and the dressmaker and later, when we set up house there to spend time with my daughter; in short, to many different places and cities, but I have never wanted to return to Toledo because the week we spent there was the most wonderful of all the ones that I had lived until then, and also of those that came later, even though there were many good ones.

My husband showed me the whole city, because he knew it very well from his business: we walked through very narrow streets where Muslims used to live, through others where the Jews had lived, the ones who had not left Spain when some old time kings threw them out of here, on another where the Christians were, all of them different, but living in harmony, as it should be. We went to the Alcazar, to the Cathedral, we even entered a Synagogue.... Everything was very nice and sometimes I would write something down on a piece of paper so that later I could tell my mother, she would surely like it a lot when I told her all the things that we had done.

At the inn where we stayed they gave us very good meals, but every time we were out on the street my Floro bought me everything we saw in the outdoor stalls: caramelized almonds, cream-filled buns, honey coated fritters... whatever he saw he wanted to buy for me, and he did not even taste it, but he had the whim of treating me like a queen, and since I was not used to anyone having ever treated me like that in my life, at first it gave me a bit of I don't know what, but one soon gets used to what's good, and after a few days I enjoyed receiving almost as much as he was happy giving.

We bought a very nice shawl for mother, as the one she had was very old and worn, and the poor thing never found money to buy another, with so many daughters who, as she said, needed more things and were of deserving age, a good walking stick for father and a jack-knife for my brother. For Jacinta and Eusebia he also bought some good scissors and two mirrors. The real truth is that this man of mine always went out of his way for everyone, always thinking of pleasing others.

For his family, since they already had everything, he bought some boxes of delicious sweets and some embroidered handkerchiefs for his mother and sister, and when the week passed, which went by in a flash, we returned to our city.

They all welcomed us with great pleasure and were very happy to see us, and after leaving the gifts we went to our house in the Plaza.

There the cook had prepared a good dinner for us, the maid had the house shining like a gold coin, and my maid came to help me when I was going to get ready for bed, but I told her "Beat it, beat it girl, I'm not so useless yet!" at which my Floro started to laugh and almost choked with laughter.

We started our married life.

He would go to the Warehouse in the morning and I, always used to not having free time, found myself with many hours to do whatever I wanted, so after visiting his parents and sister, I started going to some convents, to thank God for all the blessings He had given me, without doing anything to deserve it on my part, as they say.

At noon, the two of us would go to eat lunch at his parents' house, according to the custom, and when the men returned to work the three of us (his mother, his sister and I) stayed praying or sewing. I taught Celestina how to sew and between the two of us we made many things for the child she was going to have.

But since everything cannot be happiness, as a result of the upset she had had over her eloped sister, the poor thing had an abortion, and she almost died with that.

After that things went from bad to worse.

My Floro had told me everything that happened to the younger sister after she fell in love and ran away with a cattle trader, and it broke my soul every time I thought about her, what that creature would be going through with the rejection of her family, but even though the women of the house talked to each other about the affair, as soon as there was a man present, mostly my father-in-law, we shut up because the three of us knew that you couldn't speak out loud in that house on that subject.

Celestina, who was very touched after losing her son, flickered out like a candle and one evil day she passed away. It affected me a lot because it was one disaster on top of another: my father had caught pneumonia after getting wet one day when he was bustling around in the corral that we had next to the butcher shop, and he had died not a month before; my husband had even sent a doctor to auscultate and try to heal my father, but could not do anything and my poor mother was alone with three children still unmarried and with little to live on. Luckily my brother, who as I told you was good as gold, took over the butcher shop and little by little they were able to stay afloat, but at the cost of many sacrifices and many bad times and I, supported by my husband always, helped them in everything that was in my power.

But Celestina's death was a blow to her entire family; I had never seen grown men cry like that until that day came. If before we were in mourning, even if we weren't wearing black, for the Tomasa affair, when Celestina died, that was the straw that broke the camel's back. Their parents did not lift their heads, the brothers were always downcast and they had to go to work and deal with the carpenters and customers, even more than before, because the father had secluded himself at home and had no interest whatsoever in either warehouse or wood nor for furniture, with what that man had been, who before that misfortune happened was always the first to come and the last to leave the premises, and had built an empire at the cost of his work and effort.

The only good thing about that terrible time is that I got pregnant.

I was happy, but my husband was much more. As he was quite old, perhaps he thought that he would never have a child, but God rewarded him for being such a good, religious and honest man.

Although I was fine, since Celestina's pregnancy had gone wrong, everyone around me had me wrapped up in cotton, always watching me and treating me as if I were a porcelain doll. I kept telling them that I was fine, that all I had was a craving for lupins.

Me and my big mouth.... Every day, at noon and at night, my husband would show up with a big paper cone filled to the top and his greatest joy of the day was when he saw me eating them.

The news we had from Tomasa was getting worse and worse, so one fine day, commending myself to God and the devil because I didn't know how my Floro was going to react, I asked him to go to that town where she lived, Jaraichico, and assure her that although she could not return to her parents' house, in ours she would always have a bed and food and everything she needed; he listened to me, went and returned in great sorrow to see how his sister was, but even wishing to, he could not bring her by force. We had to wait until she took that step.

Our child was born well, thanks be to God, and thank goodness the two grandmothers were able to know him, although for a very short time because they left us right away, my mother-in-law for all the accumulated grief of losing her two daughters, and my mother, who was very much younger than my mother-in-law, started to get sick with an infection from some cavities in a molar, from there it spread to her whole body and in less than a week she was gone too. Deaths and more deaths haunted our families and we could do nothing but pray and cry for those who were leaving us.

My father-in-law and Nicasio were left alone in the big house, looked after by the maids and fed by the good dishes of the cook, who tried to make them appetizing dishes every day without success, because my brother-in-law since his mother died was acting in the same way as his father and he didn't even leave the house, so it was my poor Floro who had to take care of everything: accounts, carpenters, warehouses, collecting the rents of the houses, keeping up the farms, everything had to be controlled by him, the work of three people had fallen upon him suddenly. At seven in the morning he was already there working, I had to send him food with the maid because he couldn't even come home to rest for a while, and it was midnight when he came back at night. It was like that one day after another.

I used to go to my father-in-law's house in the morning and in the afternoon. I took Juan Carlos to be with them, who was the only thing that seemed to distract them, I made sure everything was fine and that they didn't lack anything. As soon as I left there I went to organize my late parents' house, because by then it was a total mess. Eusebia had gotten married and no longer lived there, only Jacinta and my brother remained, and she did not take care of anything, not the house or clothes or food, all the time hanging out in the street with others like her. So I would leave my child at home with the nanny, I would take the meals that I had told the cook to prepare, and I would clean and tidy up a bit. Imagine, I had nothing to do in my own house, but I worked more in theirs than I had ever done before, but my brother made me feel so sorry, working so hard from sunrise to sunset to get a few pesetas that I did it with pleasure, because I had more than them and I liked to share.

It was a difficult time.

And things got even worse when Nicasio died of a fever. The whole family was ruined in a very few years.

When Juan Carlos was two years old, I became pregnant again. At least some joys came to us in the midst of so much pain and suffering, and my Floro could not have been more content; with my pregnancies years peeled away from him and he did not care about all the work and responsibility he had, always thinking of providing well for myself and the children.

Carmencita was born, a beautiful, fat and good girl who never gave us a bad night. It was like a toy for Juan Carlos: he looked at her, kissed her and when the nanny or I let him take her, watching over her so that she did not slip from his hands, his joy was so great that everyone around felt all our sorrows and miseries falling away.

In this way, the months and years went by when my Floro received a notice from his sister to come and pick her up.

Tomasa came to live with us and we would never part again until her death a year ago. I miss her every day, and even more on dates like yesterday. How she would have enjoyed seeing our little girl getting married! Such a heartfelt ceremony, even if we weren't in church, and then everyone enjoying the snack we had prepared.... But life is like that, it gives you a little and it takes a lot from you and the sooner we know that, the better we will manage to carry on.

Since Tomasa came to live and with two children in it, our house was always full of activity, because, although at first my sister-in-law arrived very deteriorated, little by little and between all of us we managed to get her back to being like my husband told me she had been before the whole long episode. And since she had a kind of joking and cheerful nature, always thinking up something new, once she forgot all the bitter times she'd had to swallow, living with her became very easy.

For me she has been a mother, sister, friend and companion all in one package. She taught me many things, she comforted me when I needed it, she always helped me, no word ever came out of her mouth that could hurt or annoy me, and although sometimes I later realized that I had not done the right thing, she never criticized my decisions.

Taking into account all the bad things that we had been through and my brother and sister thrashing about, that was still an undoubtedly happy time. The children grew up healthy and happy, my Floro was still working many hours a day, but he was happy when he could spend even an hour with them, Tomasa had recovered, the house was running smoothly and my husband and I loved each other more and more every day.

We went to the vineyard and we all enjoyed the freshet, the hens, the burros that were there. Often we put Carmencita into a saddlebag and she loved telling the burro "giddup! giddup!" in her baby talk, and the two children laughed when they saw a lizard sunning, or anything. Yes it was a happy time.

And the first summer that we took them to Nazaret and Figueira, in Portugal? How those little creatures enjoyed it, seeing the sea and putting their little feet in the water.... Juan Carlos was very protective of his sister and would not let go of her hand, even if three adults were there to watch over them. The only pity is that my Floro could not be there all the time with us, only one week at the beginning when he took us because he wanted us to get well settled in, and another when he picked us up, but Tomasa and I would walk along the beach with our umbrellas while the children napped, or at night, when

Nanny had already put them to bed, we sat on a terrace that we had in the house we rented, we had a sarsaparilla and we spent the hours so comfortable, talking or quiet because we were both so happy to be together, that many times we didn't even have to talk.

When Juan Carlos was a little over four years old and Carmencita was two, the girl caught scarlet fever. She got very sick. Juan Carlos wanted to be with her, but the doctor told us it was very contagious, so even though he cried and pleaded we didn't let him come near her room.

Little by little, the girl was fading and two days after the first fevers, one morning she left us.

All the sorrow in the world is too little to explain how we felt. We couldn't believe what was happening to us, what had happened to us. It was as if my husband had been beaten and couldn't move. In one night his hair, which was very pretty, chestnut brown and all kinky and curly, turned white. Black coloring appeared under his eyes and only disappeared when Teresita was born. He couldn't speak, just cry and cry, hugging the girl with a soul-breaking sorrow.

Tomasa couldn't believe it either: just a few days before the girl was running around the house laughing behind her brother and she was trying to get her to stop because she was knitting a woolen jacket for her, and she wanted to measure to see how it fit her, and the two creatures, they did nothing but trick her and hide behind everything they got hold of.

And me? For those who have not gone through it, it is difficult to understand the pain of a mother, to see that something that has come out of you, the fruit of love, and that just by looking at it gave you all the happiness, is taken away from you in that way, there are no words that can express what you feel. What a shame and what a great pain! The only thing that came out of my mouth were bad words against God, I who have always been very religious and have never spoken badly to anyone, those days only toads and snakes came out of my mouth, and what I would have liked was to be dead myself.

Because, although I had lost my parents, my husband's mother and sister and I must have been used to death by now, nothing was comparable to being left without my daughter. Or so it seemed to me then. How little did I know about the blow that would fall years later ....

When they put Carmencita in her little white coffin to take her away forever, my screams and cries thundered through the house. My husband and everyone around believed that I had gone crazy and only with the love and patience of my Floro and Tomasa over time I was able to come back to life, although a part of me went that day when they took my little girl, and to this day, more than twenty-six years have passed, there is not a single day that I don't see her, playing and laughing, looking at everything with interest and making our life happy.

Last night, when I saw Teresita recently married, I imagined my other daughter next to me and tears came to my eyes. Everyone present believed that they were tears of joy and I did not want to say no, that who I was thinking about was my other girl that I could enjoy for so little time.

After that loss the house became sad. None of us had any desire for anything and I the least, even as I tried to pretend that I was all right for the sake of the boy, because all he did was ask about his sister.

He, who had cared for her, loved and protected her so much since she was born, could not understand why she was not at home, and when the nanny told him that she was in heaven playing with the angels, the only thing he said to all of us was that he wanted to go there too, so please would we take him away immediately, and that he was going to tell Carmencita to come home again, that our house was very good, even if it wasn't heaven.

It broke my soul just hearing him and when he thought we weren't listening to him he cried softly and said: "Carmencita, come down from heaven; I'm waiting for you to play" and then he stayed still, as if waiting, until between crying and hiccups, he fell asleep on the floor. Oh what hard times we had!

Months passed, we survived the tragedy, although we thought we would not, and I got pregnant again. I think it was the greatest joy for all of us in many, many years, although this time I had a very difficult pregnancy.

I was so tired and exhausted that I could do nothing at all the whole day, I was walking like a specter, roaming around the house when I was not vomiting, it must be that I was very afraid and that I remembered my girl.

But in November it was all over: Teresita was born, the most precious thing you can imagine, it seemed that she was already weeks old, as big and fat as she was and my Floro cried, but this time with joy. I had a fever and lost my milk, but we soon found a wet-nurse, Justa, who unfortunately had lost her son and had milk to give and spill, so she came to live with us and the girl suckled and drank her milk and got filled up with ease.

For Juan Carlos, who still missed his other sister, it was as if life suddenly came back to him and since he was older we could let him hold his little sister several times a day.

Happiness came home again.

We all spent hours looking at the girl, laughing along with whatever sweet gesture or babble or pout she made, and although we were spoiling her a bit and we knew it, we were so happy to hold her, hug her and cradle her that she was hardly in her cradle, for even asleep we fought over holding her in our arms.

My father-in-law died, of old age and of accumulated sorrows.

We were very sorry, but we were all so engrossed with Teresita that that death was not like the others, or maybe it is that we were already 'inured to pain,' as they say.

My Floro wisely decided that we should move to the big house. Because in the one in the main square we were already like lice between the seams, with the children, the two of us, Tomasa and the whole service we could hardly stir. But I think his main reason was to be not always reminded of Carmencita, he always thought of everything before it even occurred to us.

In the new house we had plenty of rooms and we settled down like royalty. My sisters were left with their mouths open seeing how all the rooms had turned out, because my Floro spared no expense and the apartment we dedicated to our home was more than beautiful, and every time I entered any room I was amazed how it was possible for me to live there, at all the good things that God blessed us with, despite how difficult I became with Him when the Carmencita affair, but at that terrible time all my nerves were upset, I say that would be why I was so impossible.

When Teresita's teeth began to poke out, how we laughed when we gave her a piece of bread crust to suck on...! It seems that I'm seeing it, everyone around looking and laughing with her, because it was such a good and funny sight we couldn't stand it! And the same day that she was nine months old, she began to say pa-pa, pa-pa, and Floro was drooling with joy, what a moment....

But a few days later tragedy hit us again. My husband did not wake up.

If when the girl left us I believed that there could be no greater pain in the world, I was not ready for that blow: all of a sudden everything fell on my shoulders, and at the age of twenty-six I found myself without the person I loved the most and had ever loved the most, the best and kindest man in the world and for whom I had been the first thing since he met me, with two children and a sister-in-law in my charge, because she had nothing to live on and depended on us for everything.

The patrimony that existed belonged to my children, since the portions of Nicasio and Celestina had passed to my husband, and also the same with Tomasa's part when my father-in-law disinherited her, but I had neither education nor studies to continue with the lumberyard nor with the cabinetmaking, and I was too sad and sorry to think about business, Juan Carlos was only seven years old, Tomasa did not know how to work or send others to work, so with the help of my departed husband's cousins we liquidated and sold all the material, we dismissed the carpenters and the outfit was closed. But we kept the building.

A real shame to do that because it was a very prosperous business and with which we lived very well; having more or less did not matter much to me, because I never forgot how my life had been until my Floro appeared in it, but the circumstances rule and one has to be content with what comes.

From those sales we got good money and along with what we already had at home, because my husband always liked to have a good deal of money for what might happen, we were able to live for several years, without wasting, but without missing anything.

The world was at war, but both of us and our children were not affected, if you want me to tell you the truth, because we had plenty of food and we both knew how to get by without much, in my case for my upbringing, the way I was born and raised with no luxuries, and in hers for the life she had in the bad marriage until she came back to us.

But money was beginning to be lacking everywhere, people needed loans to cope with necessary things, and since we had a lot of capital that did not give returns because they were houses and farms that we did not know how to manage, I came up with the idea of selling something and start lending to those who needed it and thus earn some pesetas. Tomasa, as always, agreed with my decision. Or she made me believe that she did.

I sold a house first and the money they gave me for it was now you see it now you don't, but soon the people I lent to began to return it to me and it was not a bad business altogether.

The children continued to grow and, despite all the worries we had, they were our joy, perhaps the only one in those difficult years.

When we were a little organized in our routines, she looking after the house and I with my loans, we had another misfortune: Teresita got wet one day going to school and as she was a little shy she did not say anything to the nun in her class. When she came home many hours later, with a shivering and a high fever, I didn't know what to do, I got nervous, but between Tomasa and Nurse Justa, who immediately understood the situation, we were able to move forward, although since then she has rheumatism and there are days that my poor dear cannot move for the pains she has, but thanks to the Virgin and all the novenas and promises that we all made at home, she survived. For many years I wore the habit of the Virgin of Perpetual Help because I promised it, and went to the Lord of Health hermitage every day to thank Him. Because I don't know if my heart could have endured another death....

We were living. I kept selling properties and sometimes the loans turned out well, sometimes so-so and sometimes bad, very bad, because the people to whom I gave money did not return it to me. As I almost never demanded guarantees and I only had some paper with the signature or, if they did not know how to sign, with a cross, I could not do anything either, the only thing was to trust my instinct and see if they were or had been good people before the need, but as I remembered the hardships that many times were gone through at my parents' house, before and after I got married, I was quite soft, as Tomasa told me, who always looked after me and gave me good advice without harassing me. We both did what we could.

My children grew up, they had many cousins and friends to play with, the Great War ended and we all noticed the effects and in case we didn't have enough the flu epidemic, which they called "the Spanish flu," wiped out more than fifty million people in the two years it lasted, but thanks be to God we didn't get the booby prize that time and the whole family escaped well.

Juan Carlos, when he finished his first studies in Turgalium, decided to become a lawyer and my husband's cousins recommended El Escorial to me and my sister-in-law as the best university in all Spain, because it was a place where they were given the best training and all those who attended were from very good families.

For me, the daughter of a butcher and of artisan origin, it was very important that my children got the education that I had not been able to get, because good learning always opens many doors, so before the course began in the fall of 1923, Tomasa and I went to see everything with our own eyes.

It is not that we did not trust what they told us, but both of us had already gone through enough calamities in our lives and furthermore separating from him was an idea very hard to swallow, because he was not even sixteen years old and it was going to be the first time he was away from home, and we had him very spoiled, if I tell the truth, especially his aunt, who stared at him with her mouth open at everything he had to say, so one day in July we made tracks, and accompanied by a priest and Cousin Santiago, we showed up there.

In our city at that time it was terribly hot, you could only be on the street in the early morning and at night, the stones and the granite boulders seemed to spit fire, so it was a pleasant surprise when we arrived at El Escorial and it was cool not only at night, but even during siesta time we had to wear a shawl around our shoulders so as not to get cold.

We stayed in a good inn, and the day after we arrived we went to the Monastery, which was the most beautiful thing I had ever seen in my life, and it seems to me that Tomasa also thought the same.

After seeing and going through everything, the four of us went to see the Prior, with whom we had previously made an appointment, so that he could tell us the plan and show us where our son was going to be. I did not want to talk much at first, for that was why I had learned people by my side, but after a while and seeing what that man was like, my shame was removed and I asked everything I wanted to know.

Father Prior explained to us that the Augustinians had been there since 1885, take note, that was before I was born, but that it was not until seven years later that the Queen gave them authorization to adapt an old warehouse and the Hospedería de los Agustinos to the one that everyone called "La Campaña," so that higher studies could be carried out there.

These studies, among which stood out those of the Law Faculty, were private university studies and the students who studied there later had to go to a State University to validate them, but the Augustinian Prior told us that with the prestige that the the teachers had, the good and complete training of the students and the Augustinian spirit, the fame of its center had spread at all levels: public, political and intellectual, and that although it was considered an elite center, not for that, or perhaps therefore, did they neglect other values.

I tried to find out about all this and the rest that he told us, although I knew that later my companions would explain it to me in simpler words, since that man was very cultured and knowledgeable, and sometimes I lost myself in what he said.

He showed us where the classes were given, where the students lived and all the other facilities, and although being in that place cost a lot of money, Tomasa and I decided that it was the best thing for Juan Carlos, that living with other students would be very good for him, instead of being in a house full of women.

In his class, which would be for the youngest of all, there would only be twenty-one if he stayed, which seemed like a good number for them to give him a lot of attention, so the next day before leaving back we had him enrolled.

And as soon as we rested a bit at home, we went back to packing our bags and the whole family plus the service went to Figueira da Foz for the summer, as in previous years. We especially wanted to enjoy our child, because we both knew that once we left him at the Monastery, we would not see him again until he had holidays at Christmas. And surely by then he would be quite changed. We had a very happy few weeks and we all enjoyed ourselves.

When we returned we had to get cracking, because in addition to buying all the clothes that Juan Carlos had to take for his wardrobe, we had to mark them with his name, the number they had assigned him, the class to which he belonged... he half jokingly, half serious, said: "looks like they're going to register me as a prisoner." But he was happy about where he was going.

Three days before he had to start his studies, my sister-in-law and I were already in El Escorial, this time accompanied by Teresita and Nurse Justa, because the girl wanted to be with her brother for as long as possible and we decided to take her, which was a very good idea because she liked everything a lot and so the parting with her brother went a little out of her head, since every time she started to say something about Juan Carlos, one of us asked her about something we had shown her, and she didn't focus on the separation.

We stayed at the inn (the same one where we had been in the summer and where they already treated us as if we were family) one more week, in case Juan Carlos had any problems, but from the beginning he was very content there and we returned to our city, happy with how things were going.

The house was a little sad again, because Juan Carlos was at an age when he went out and came in with his cousins or friends all the time, and there was always laughter or whispering among them, they devoured huge quantities of food from everything that was set before them, they talked about their plans, what they were going to do or not, and hearing them was a blessing, but Tomasa and I knew that, although it hurt to be without him, we had done the best for him and his future. Perhaps the one who had it worse than anyone else was Teresita: the two got along wonderfully and despite the difference of six years, as he liked children and she was very sensible for only ten, they were good companions and friends; but she was so sensitive she didn't even name him so that we would not grieve anymore, my poor dear, what a considerate girl she has always been.

The first time Juan Carlos returned from vacation we hardly recognized him: he had stretched out, he was thinner, very elegant, he talked more (he who was always so sparing in words...), and he even laughed more. He also had new glasses, very modern, and Tomasa said they were very chic, which is not that they were small, like we say *chicas* in Spanish, but something very good and elegant. They say it is a French word. It was a very happy Christmas and we all saw that he was very happy to have gone to study there, although he also missed us very much, just like we did, but all the sacrifices we had to make seemed little thinking about his future.

So we spent the eight years until he finished his degree that way. He was a brilliant student, he always passed all the subjects and made very good friends among his classmates, and although he was not given to revelry, as he liked to eat well they would go out for dinners or meals when they were free and without homework.

He came almost every vacation, because although some of his companions went on a trip during those days, my son knew the pleasure it gave us to have him at home, so many women alone, and what he did was to bring a friend with him, and so the house was filled with conversation and joy.

Between trimesters and trimesters we also went to see him and see if he needed anything, because although the Augustinians took care of their formation of the mind and spirit, and they told us that they fed them well, as he had always been very finicky, and at home we prepared everything to his liking, we were concerned that he might not be well fed, so when we visited him we loaded him up with loins, chorizos, hams, big balls of butter, very rich *perrunillas* pastries, and everything we could get our hands on, and during the school periods Tomasa also made herself responsible for sending packages by the regular bus as one of her obligations, and according to what he wrote and told us later, he and his friends gave a good account of everything and mounted huge snacks either in his room or in the gardens, the kind you don't just breeze through.

And as not everything was to study, study, study, he told us about the parties he went to with his friends, not only in El Escorial, where the cream of society there met for dances and musical or literary evenings, but also in Madrid, where they would go from time to time to spend two or three days to have a good time.

Tomasa was always on tenterhooks, fearful that some gold-digger would trick him, but Teresita and I quieted her fears, because we both knew that he was a sensible boy, too sensible for his years, but the circumstances of his life had led him to that.

When he finished his studies, with his law degree in hand, he returned home, and although we knew he was not going to practice, we prepared an office for him worthy of a marquis and in the next room he installed his library. I, who had never read anything other than the devotionals and the lives of saints, really liked entering that room — thinking that my son had many of those tomes in his head gave me so much joy that sometimes he said: "Mother, come and look at my books, they have sent me several new ones," and I always followed him like a lapdog.

Tomasa had taken up the habit of reading her serial novelettes again, and many afternoons her two friends, who were like two old and wrinkled raisins, came to our house and the three of them read aloud while we drank a cup of hot chocolate for our high tea. I didn't want to show disapproval, but life gives us enough problems without having to read and listen to ones in fascicles, so while they read and commented, I stayed with them, but I prayed and left them to their stories.

Juan Carlos began to take charge of administrating things, which was a great relief for me, because I had no education and I still don't even know how we managed all those years.

We all decided to rent a flat in Madrid, and so my children had another house available where they could spend time and we hit the nail on the head, because they went places that we did not have in Turgalium, visited museums, went to libraries and theaters, strolled through beautiful parks and gardens and could learn many things.

Teresita and her two close friends Julia and Carmen even took a cooking course and there they learned how to do everything, although neither of them had a need because the same in their family as in ours there were good cooks, but they enjoyed doing it and we, my sister-in-law and I, thought it was very good.

She also learned to play the piano and in order for her to be able to practice at home whenever she wanted to, I bought her a beautiful one, black, with ivory keys, mahogany wood and it even had golden holders to put candles or any type of lights. When she sat down to play and we listened to her that was a blessing.... She also took French classes and how a young lady should run her house, do needlework and behave in society, things that I had not been able to do when I was her age since my parents never had possibilities, but for my daughter everything was not enough.

As for Juan Carlos, who was still shy, his friend and partner at the Escorial during all the years he was there convinced him (with my help too) to take dance classes. Paco has always been very outgoing, and if you're by his side there are no sorrows, like last night at the wedding, one moment when he saw that I was quiet and a little sad, he came to give me a hug, he planted two kisses on my face and began to say so many silly things that I had no choice but to laugh. Well, as I was telling you, he and Paco went to an academy to learn to dance and when they came home it was a sight to see, one taking the girl's part and the other as a boy, even bowing and everything, it was hilarious, but what a joy to see them enjoying themselves...

Things around the world were not good and even those who had money in the banks could not get it; I had never liked having the pesetas in another place other than my safe, so in that particular it did not affect us, but it did in other things, because I sold some properties badly and if I had waited a little more it would have worked out, but now is not the time to regret.

And when we least expected it, at the beginning of the year thirty-five, Juan Carlos went and fell in love on us, like a schoolboy! It must be a family thing, because it happened just like his father, may God keep him in glory, from one day to the next he was declaring his love for me and the pain is the few years that we could be together, only seven, but if I tell the truth, there was not a single moment that we stopped loving each other and there was never a bad word or a disagreement between us, so as I was telling you, our boy fell in love with her and brought her home soon so that we could meet her.

We liked her very much because she is a woman with a personality that has no equal. Beautiful, educated, has traveled, studied, she belongs to a good family.... she has everything you could ask for and in the three years that they have now been married, they look just as in love as the first day. The only regret I have is that they still don't have any children, but that will come if God wishes.

Juan Carlos since he returned from his studies had to take care of the rental of the houses and the vineyards and the only farm that we have left (because I sold the Aldeanos) and sometimes he was very busy, but as Margarita's father has several farms and haciendas which are near Guadalupe, before the war and when he had free time they'd go for a stay in one of them, especially one they call "La Operetta," which is Margarita's favorite, and I am not surprised because it is a beautiful property. A few days before the war broke out, we went to spend a day there and we all liked it very much, Tomasa didn't even want to leave, the house doesn't lack the slightest convenience. And how much game there is! Everything from wild boars to partridges and rabbits, so with so many animals they have a well-stocked pantry.

Last year Tomasa caught a cold, then it worsened to pneumonia and in December she died. The poor thing was already very old and almost did not go out before she got the cold, but that was the drop that made the glass overflow, and what killed her.

After so many years without deaths in our house, it has been a very big blow for everyone, because the children have always seen her here with me, like another mother, and for me when I enter her room and I don't see her, I begin to tremble so, that Teresita has already decided that we are going to remove everything from there, because she cannot bear to see me with so much suffering.

If for them she had been like a mother, for me she was everything and I do not know what would have become of me if she had not been by my side. We always suffered and enjoyed together, and the great sorrow that I have because she is gone will never leave me. But you have to accept the Lord's designs and move on, even if you don't have the strength.

And the same year as Juan Carlos's wedding with Margarita, my Teresita met Jorge, that was a little more than two years ago, and her aunt and I saw right away that she was smitten by him, she who has never paid attention to all those who have approached her with serious pretensions, and look, she has had many, many suitors trailing her... I thought she was going to end up with Ricardo, because in Madrid they were always together, but in the end she could not decide... With this one it seems that it has been different from the beginning and my sister-in-law and I were very happy for her.

He seems a very good boy, he is from Madrid and he is alone here, the poor thing has been orphaned. His mother died about three years ago and his father at the beginning of the summer. The war caught them there in Madrid and the poor man and Jorge's brothers and sisters have suffered many calamities, and since the father had diabetes, and was without medicines and without the proper food, what happened to him happened; I felt very sad that his son was not able to bring him here, because between us and the Pacochinas (where they prepare meals for Jorge), we would have attended to and taken care of him; but as I always say in the end we should not complain because many are even worse off than us.... The only thing I ask now is that my daughter be as happy as she deserves and that the new life that began yesterday for her with so much love and hope never ends. For a mother to see her children healthy and happy is the greatest happiness there can be in the world and the two that I have are close by and concerned for me every moment, so all I want is for everything to continue like this until the Lord call me.

8. TERESA - DECEMBER 1938

—The third Christmas with war, it's not ending. And it seemed like it was going to be over quick, but no. On top of this, this morning I've had nausea again. I even vomited up the whole breakfast, and I ate it with such pleasure and hunger, but this has been happening to me these past few days and until eleven o'clock at least I don't feel right; I only straighten out after drinking a good-sized mug of the tea from the vineyards, and you know I don't like tea at all, but now it's the only thing that calms my stomach. And on top of that my period has been delayed, although it always comes right on time. From the first time, when I was eleven years old, something like that has never happened to me, not even when I had rheumatic fever; and look, I was really sick then, Margarita, you can't even imagine. Mother thought I wouldn't make it, but as I said, every twenty-eight days on the dot ....

Her sister-in-law interrupted her:

—My god! how can you be so silly? Don't you get it? What we have on the way here is a tiny tyke! You've pulled ahead of me, and look how much I like children, and your brother? I don't need tell you.... He really loves babies... My, my, a new baby in the family... You'll see when he finds out. Does Jorge know anything?

Teresa, whose face had suddenly flushed a glowing red as if she were a girl caught red-handed at mischief, sat up suddenly and slapping herself on the forehead began to laugh, a laugh modulated by a tinge of nervousness.

And I was worrying that maybe it was an outbreak of rheumatism! I Hope you're right and that's it, but don't say anything yet to Juan Carlos, or to mother or to anyone else. I'm also going to wait a little longer to tell Jorge, I don't want it to be a false alarm and then get everybody disappointed.... And don't even think about commenting to the Márquezes, they're both very handy and as soon as they find out, they'll begin making little doublets and weaving shawls and little outfits... And now we must continue with tonight's menu, with so much conversation time is running out on us and later on the cook will say she doesn't have time. I'll have to tell Juliana to come and help her a little, you know she's always willing and although she makes the other one dizzy with all her gossip, between the two of them they'll prepare a sumptuous dinner; our husbands are big eaters and we have to feed them. Teresa and Margarita were in the parlor of the mother of the first, and mother-in-law of the second, armed with pencil and paper and looking at Teresa's recipe books when Edelmira entered, who at fifty years old retained an agility that neither of the other two had. She came from her daily rounds of the convents, where she went not so much to pray as to see whether her goddaughters did, and despite it's being a very cold morning she wore only a small shawl that barely covered her, and was dressed in but a light skirt and blouse.

—But mother! How can you even think of going out like this? You're going to get pneumonia. Can you tell me why you aren't wearing the wool shawl that Juan Carlos bought you? With that you would be warm; and I do not want you to go out without stockings, those ankle boots are going to raise welts on your feet. It seems I have to be on top of you as if you were a little girl....

—Hush, hush, Edelmira answered without letting her daughter finish. —It's a wonderful day and the sun is out now. This morning at six o'clock when I went to San Pedro it was a bit chilly, but since I walk fast it hasn't bothered me too much, but since you don't like getting up early, by the time you set foot outside, half the day is gone, so you don't know if it's hot or cold; I'm going to see about Tomasa's room, because I haven't finished throwing away all the serials she had. Maybe I'll get them ready to give to her friends, who like that sort of stuff just like she did; and I need to see if my poor cats have eaten yet, because if I don't take care of them, they would starve to death, for all the attention you two pay them...

And she exited smiling, leaving the sisters-in-law to look at each other and burst out in loud laughter.

It was going to be the third Christmas of the war, the second without Aunt Tomasa and the first that Teresa would celebrate as a married lady, and perhaps expecting a child.

Her religious wedding, intimate and simple, with only a few friends accompanying them owing to the conflict that had divided the country, had been celebrated in the family home, since holding it in a church was all but impossible.

They had not even had their own wedding rings or the traditional ceremonial coins: they'd had to use the ones that Juan Carlos and Margarita lent them, since they could nowhere buy them, not for lack of money, but because gold and silver were scarce.

Everything had been far from the beautiful ceremony that her brother had had three years before, but Jorge and she did not want to wait any longer, because they did not know how long the war would continue, and the news that reached them from the rest of the world did not bode well either, so a priest friend agreed to celebrate the wedding, setting as the only condition that it be at home and without great ado.

Nor could she have the white wedding dress she had dreamed of; a simple blue dress, with white collar and cuffs, silk stockings, and shoes in the same two colors as the suit made up her entire outfit; and the few family members and friends invited were also dressed simply, as if their gathering were merely a usual one, not a wedding.

But they still had to be thankful that there was food, not as in other parts of the country where food had been in short supply for many months; so when the simple ceremony ended, everyone was able to enjoy a magnificent snack, with products they got from their farms and vineyard. Well prepared by the cook, who was helped by Teresa in order to lend an esthetic touch to the viands' presentation and decoration, they made a mouth-watering display.

The ladies had decided on a buffet, and the platters covered the entire surface of the large dining room table. Exquisite croquettes and pasties, shredded meat garnished with plums and raisins, deviled eggs, various kinds of cheeses, salad, tenderloin, chorizo and sliced ham cut in thin slices (the remains of the last slaughter, saved for the occasion), and an endless number of desserts made up the menu, of which all the attendees gave a good account, grateful for being able to taste delicacies that were not in their daily diet. They even served wine from their own vineyards, and Juan Carlos, no one knew how, had brought a few bottles of delicious liqueurs that, once opened, disappeared instantly.

The only sorrow overshadowing that day was the absences: neither her father nor her beloved Aunt Tomasa, a second mother to her, were there; Jorge's parents were also missing: his mother had passed away three years ago, his father had died on San Antonio's day this year. Those who remained, his two older sisters and two younger brothers, were in Madrid in a besieged area. Impossible to think about moving.

There was no honeymoon either, not even a little getaway, because many of the big cities were still under the control of Republican troops, and leaving their little city, so far a quiet redoubt, would have been asking for unnecessary trouble. In addition, the groom, in charge of telegraphic communications, could not leave his post, not even for the weekend. They would do so later, when the storm had subsided and conditions were more favorable.

Teresa had met her now husband at the New Year's Eve ball, just as predicted half-jokingly by her sister-in-law. The comment had been prophetic, and when the bells that introduced 1936 had just chimed, a friend introduced those two. He was dark, tall, thin and very handsome, with very pretty eyes behind round glasses to correct his myopia, a small mustache that was barely a line, black hair combed back, and thin hands with long and narrow fingers; he was dressed very elegantly in a dark three-piece suit; when he smiled he revealed very white teeth that contrasted with his bronzed complexion. He also had one of his upper front teeth split in half, which did not detract from any charm, but rather gave a mischievous note to his face.

After the introductions and the first pleasantries, what most caught Teresa's attention, apart from his physique and fine appearance, was how correctly he spoke, without swallowing any letters at the end (as everyone in the city did, even those with a fine education), and accompanied by an impeccable accent.

Together with her maid and companion, Juana la Bizca (Cross-eyed Juana), she had spent long periods in Madrid at the flat there, but she had never lost that characteristic Extremaduran touch: her diminutives continued to end in -ino, she used typical phrases of the region, and she vividly recalled that when she was a child, she and her friends had often made fun of someone they'd met who spoke with the palatal s: "*oh sho veddy, veddy fine sh*," giggling and saying that they would never fall in love with someone like that, what a riot and what a bore and what a situation having to be all the time with someone talking like that, with that hoity-toity stuck-up Castilian s-sh! Irony of fate that she was attracted to one who spoke just like that.

~. ~. ~. ~.

When her close friends, the Márquez girls, set up a flat in Madrid (something that was the fashion among the wealthy from the provinces), Edelmira, Tomasa and Juan Carlos opined, quite judiciously, that it would be a wonderful idea to do the same. The man of the house had already finished his studies, Teresita was eighteen years old, Edelmira's specialist doctor, whom she visited twice a year, also resided there, as well as her dressmaker, and the possibility that the daughter could spend time in the Capital in their own flat seemed ideal to everyone. For this purpose they rented a beautiful flat on Blasco de Garay street, in the Argüelles neighborhood, very central, spacious and bright, and close to the home of their friends.

At first, Nurse Justa, who had raised Teresa and considered herself more of her mother than her biological one, screamed to high heaven, warning of all the dangers and evils that could befall "my baby," but after inspecting and investigating everything, cunningly checking on the building's residents in seemingly causal conversations, patrolling the neighborhood to see with her own eyes "what was cooking" there, visiting the grocery stores where they would make the necessary purchases, and even attending a nearby cinema (where she almost crossed herself, amazed by the invention), she returned calmly to Turgalium with the two elderly ladies, and agreed to leave Teresita in the hands of "Cross-eyed Juana," who more than a maid acted as a señorita's companion, because she was naturally fine and lady-like, and above all clever, since she instantly captured any suggestion made to her, all which made her company very pleasant. Another maid, who served as cook and did other chores would also go.

Juana la Bizca was nice-looking, except for the defect in her eye resulting from a bad knock when she was still a child; her face was very harmonious: oval, fairly pronounced high cheekbones, a straight nose, a medium-sized mouth and a clear general complexion. Perhaps her loveliest feature was a rather long but prettily shaped neck, which she tried to show off by not adorning it with necklaces or other accessories such as kerchiefs or scarves, and by always wearing her hair to just below her ears. As she normally wore no uniform but a simple black dress, she could easily have passed for one of those salaried English confidantes who accompany their patroness on all outings.

This cross-eyed Juana was a faithful companion for many years and when Teresa married it had been only a year since she was no longer on the staff: she herself had gotten married, but she continued to frequent the family home and it was a rare day that she did not appear there. Her husband, a wealthy older man from Turgalium who fell in love with her like many others had before, but who was the only one who managed to end her single state, was a good man, and not only did he not want her to break off relations with her former employers (owing to her new, higher status), but if for some reason she had not been able to go see them one day, he worried and insisted on accompanying her, so that her ladies would not feel restless.

So Teresa's life was divided between Madrid and her city, taking the best of both places and enjoying when she lived alone with Juana and also when she returned to Turgalium, always being the focus of attention of all those who made up the family clan.

As Teresa was tall and pretty, with the careful upbringing of most of the well-off women of her time, very talkative without the need to gossip, very nice not only with her peers but with people of any rank, she was always surrounded by friends, and suitors constantly besieged her, but she didn't feel anything special for any of them; she had fun, laughed, danced, and talked to everyone but didn't want any formal commitment. That is why she had reached twenty-two years of age still single, and even though there were many good boys who would have counted it their greatest happiness if she had accepted them, she never wanted to. She wasn't sure of her feelings and she could wait; better said, she simply had no amorous feelings towards them. Her life was very full, and she did not have to depend on a husband to provide for her. When she got married, if she ever did, it would be for love and for love alone. The rest did not matter to her. Until that day came, she enjoyed what life offered her, which was a lot.

There was, during one of her long stays in Madrid, a suitor with whom she frequently went out. Ricardo was the son of one of her mother's longtime doctors, and she thought that maybe she could fall in love, but after thinking it over well and in spite of his insistence that they formalize their relationship, she resisted taking the step. And that despite the fact that Ricardo was what was considered a very good catch: he was handsome, with abundant blond curly hair, tall, a doctor like his father with whom he shared a clinic, very outgoing and friendly, a connoisseur of all fashionable places, a great dancer and with ready money. All the girls hoped to win him, but when he met Teresita, as he always affectionately called her, he put aside all his commitments in order to dedicate all the free time he had to be with her: to theater premieres, strolling through Parque del Oeste or Casa de Campo, going to the cinema, or having dinner at the best restaurants, and entertaining her in the thousand ways that only he knew.

For Teresa that friendship, which was really all it was for her, was something very pleasant and she fully enjoyed his company, but despite the beautiful picture of a future together that Ricardo painted her, and despite everything he offered her, every day she found new excuses to put him off. They were fine like this, two good friends with many things in common, but for her that was the limit of the relationship.

The preparations for the wedding of Juan Carlos, had Teresa spending many weeks in a row in the capital with Margarita, helping the latter to buy her complete trousseau. She had seen Ricardo there very often, and the women, including her mother, felt somewhat obliged to invite him to the wedding, which he was delighted to attend and where he greatly enjoyed himself. Ricardo was fully integrated with all the other guests, displaying an unrivaled *savoir faire* and elegance, and even Juan Carlos, despite floating on his private cloud that day, called his sister's attention to the suitor's total interest in her. But Teresa was not sure.

She decided to wait until after Christmas season to make a decision. In January she would return to Madrid and see what would happen. She was in no rush. Everything could wait. And on the last day of the year, or the first of the new, at that moment of transition, everything took an unexpected turn. She met the one who would be her husband.

With Jorge, from the moment they were introduced, everything was different. The truth was that from that first moment he captivated her, she, who was not dreamy, not prone to infatuations nor to let herself be carried away. She was calm and sensible. But he was different from everyone she had known until then. And despite being two years younger, he breathed a maturity and a knowledge of life and things that she had not found in others.

Jorge had arrived at the small town only three days before, and in such a short space of time he had already accomplished many things. The first thing was to settle in. As Chief of Tele-Communications, he had the right to a home located behind the offices, which were in the city's Plaza Mayor; it was a very spacious apartment whose only drawback was the absence of balconies on the Plaza, but it had a beautiful roof terrace from which you could see all the palaces, towers and churches that surrounded the square, and in this flat he arranged his belongings, consisting mainly of books, his clothing (his great vice always), and an ocarina that his father had given him when he was an adolescent, which always accompanied him wherever he lived, and which he played for relaxation in the few moments that work, outings or study spared to him. Also, as soon as he arrived in the city, he looked for a good place to eat. There was unanimous agreement: they all recommended a certain inn, also located in the Plaza, which from that first day became his second home. There he had breakfast, lunch, high-tea, and dinner. Barely a week had passed since his arrival when a new custom began: the inn owner's daughters crossed the short space between the two buildings four times a day, carrying all the meals to his home. Thus the all-important victuals question was resolved.

An older man who worked with him recommended a good woman to do the housework and take care of his clothes, so at the age of nineteen in 1935 he found himself in a new city where indeed he knew no one, but with his life organized, secure pay and a job that, although it occupied him many hours, he really liked and which did leave him the occasional free hour to continue his studies. For his idea at the time was to spend but little time in Turgalium, the shortest possible, and return to live in his beloved Madrid and there continue his career as an engineer, combining it with work. His dear mother had died six months earlier, his sister Carolina had married a few days before, as had his younger brother, forced to, actually, but there were still enough people in the house on Espiritu Santo, and although things were not as they had been, to return home was his greatest yearning and hope.

Love and war changed his plans. He met Teresa. He fell in love and never thought about leaving the small town again. They started going out together and the two realized right away that they were made for each other, and a few days before the war broke out they became engaged. As the conflict never reached their city, despite the difficulties and shortcomings that surrounded them, the increase in work that Jorge had, the lack of mobility that prevented their going to other places and the inconveniences typical of a state in war, and although many on the two sides died every day, the courtship proceeded without incident, with great anticipation and love, and, not knowing how long the conflict might last, they decided not to wait for its conclusion, but to get married. Jorge was now twenty-two years old, he had no family of his own in the locality and the one he had in Madrid had dwindled even more when his father died months before, so he was eager to form a new one with his beloved Teresa. She had also found in her ardent fiancé the ideal complement and partner to her calm character, and at twenty-four she felt sure and confident in taking the definitive step. And although it was true that Jorge, unlike her other suitors, did not have much on the material side, he had a steady job, he was very intelligent, and she knew they would succeed. In addition, she had her own capital and products from the farms shared with her mother and brother, and despite the prospect that in the future she might not have the economic freedom that she had enjoyed all her life, she felt so sure of her love that she trusted those practical aspects of life would work themselves out.

Edelmira, her mother, would have liked them once married to live in the family home, even offering to leave the apartment where she lived, and proposing a tidying up of some rooms on the ground floor and her moving into them. She would say again and again: —Well, for the kind of life that I lead I don't need such a large apartment, with fewer rooms I can live very content, and so we would all be in the same house, together but not on top of each other, which is what the married household wants, and I also want my freedom and my independence.

But Teresa and Jorge decided to settle in the apartment that corresponded to him as part of his emoluments, a stipend that also included other expenses such as water, electricity and telephone, and that for him had the great advantage of being on the same floor as his workplace, just a few meters away. They therefore furnished and prepared the flat, making it a charming residence, with a glazed entrance, a beautiful parlor, a nice dining room, a sunny and cheerful living room, three bedrooms, a good bathroom and a pretty and spacious kitchen, plus a beautiful terrace on the top floor that was accessed from the house by going up a simple flight of stairs; here there were also additional rooms and a toilet, and after a few small arrangements and some coats of whitewash they made suitable quarters for the servants.

Teresa brought one of the daughters of the guardian family from Las Viñas, a smart girl named Juliana, and taught her to cook, patiently showing her many of the techniques and tricks that she herself had learned when she took a couple of cooking courses in Madrid, in a prestigious school whence proceeded the most famous chefs of the moment, and who, once they had mastered the trade, were distributed among the best establishments and restaurants throughout Spain. She and her Márquez friends had learned by chance of the existence of said School and did not let up until they were admitted there. The Haute Cuisine classes that were taught in that place were very gratifying: each day at three o'clock at the end of the practical lessons, they had the added extra incentive of tasting the menus that all the students prepared, which ranged from a simple vichyssoise or an Andalusian gazpacho, to the most elaborate desserts, going through learning how to prepare all kinds of soups, meats, eggs, game, fish and shellfish, as well as the ideal way to present them according to whatever the occasion was.

Thanks to the knowledge imparted by her señorita, Juliana had become a perfect cook, since to the techniques she learned she added a sense of saving and making use of remains, which economy later, with the wartime scarcities, proved to be very useful. With a simple partridge and a few potatoes she was able to prepare a delicious and comforting stew, some egg-battered breasts and a large plate of croquettes capable of feeding all the members of the house, and to that skill she added a fun character capable of dispelling the doldrums even in the darkest days. Her gratitude to her mistress, who had brought her out of the boring and hopeless existence that she led in the country, was so deep and sincere that she looked after her well-being and comfort as if instead of being a paid servant, she were a busy-body mother hen, and before Teresa even began to say that she wanted something, Juliana had placed it before her! Faithful, a storyteller, funny and always very affectionate, she was for Teresa a great joy to have around and also, in addition to her chores Juliana freed her from cumbersome situations, because her role did not end in the kitchen: she also saw to it that the rest of the service strictly fulfilled their obligations, and although little in size and years, she possessed such authority that no one dared confront her.

So Teresa and Jorge settled into their new home with everything organized, and despite its being war time, their life was happy. Only those morning annoyances overshadowed her existence a bit.... But, as her wise sister-in-law had told her, how foolish she had been for not having thought of the most obvious thing: a boy, or a girl, who would make her life even more perfect, if that was possible. She closed her eyes and gave thanks to God.

9. JUAN CARLOS - LAST DAY OF 1939

This morning Don Rosendo, Margarita's father, came to see us and to wish us a good start into the new year and above all to consult with me about his plans, because although I am not practicing as a lawyer, nor have I ever done so, he trusts my judgment a lot and also wanted me to explain to him the steps to follow when transferring most of his possessions in life.

With everything that has happened in the country in recent years, not to say the last decade, he is tired, he feels his aging, and what he most wants is to get rid of problems and spend his time as he pleases.

We talked about the subject for several hours and it seems to me that he already has everything very clear, and that as soon as the holidays are over, everything will begin to move, because he told me that after turning the matter over in his mind many times, now that he has made the decision he does not want to drag out the process.

His intention in principle is to give La Operetta hacienda to Margarita, and if he does so I would be very happy for her, because I know how much she likes it and the good memories she has of all the stays there when she was little, added to the ones that continued to accumulate as an adult. The hacienda is beautiful, or it was before the war, and the last time we were in it, a couple of months before the war broke out, it was in full operation, with all kinds of well cared for and fattened animals, trees full of fruit, gardens overflowing with vegetables and the fields with wheat and barley crops that were a delight to see, but after the punishment suffered in that part of our region, and with the skirmishes fought there, I do not know the state of things now. The house is still standing and well, the administrator has told him, although my father-in-law assumes that this is an euphemism and that inside it will be chaotic and a real disaster; but as he told me, it is already something that those vandals have not destroyed it and burned it down as they have done with many. And as I replied, even if it is a cliché and a common place, everything can be fixed except death, and with time, health, and a good will, the damage can be repaired if there is any.

In sum, we spent some very good hours together, for my father-in-law is a gentleman from head to toe, very sensible and reasonable, and in the four years that I have been part of that family at no time have we had the slightest touch of disagreement, because for me (who was raised among women), his company is highly esteemed, and the times we can be together, the conversations we have, everything we share, makes me feel like he is the father that I don't have, whom I hardly remember, and yet whom I have missed so much. My father-in-law is a cultivated man with whom you can talk about everything, he is well read, and added to his education is an innate knowledge of the common man; I consider it a deference on his part to come and consult with me. We will see how everything develops in the coming months.

This year that ends today has brought us some great joys, such as the end of the damnable war and the birth of my niece Manuela. The two things have been very important in our life, each in a different style.

I really like children and so far we have not had any, despite trying every day, but if they do not come, I am not worried either because the One who governs all our designs will know why they are not sent to us, so I lived minute by minute the pregnancy of my sister Teresa, looking forward to the birth. The girl is beautiful and I am her proud godfather. I even think she already recognizes me, but when I say it Jorge laughs and give me all kinds of technicalities about babies that I don't want to hear. I'll stick with my idea, it doesn't hurt anyone and it makes me happy.

We celebrated her baptism in a big way, as the occasion especially demanded, after the wedding that her parents had, so austere and simple due to the circumstances in which we found ourselves because of the war, and that day we ate, drank —even me!— we sang and we danced like we hadn't had the chance for years. The girl was so good and nice, so clean and funny that she even sucked on the water the priest poured on her head, and it seemed that she was laughing doing it, but maybe at thirty-one years I am becoming as goofy as they say that grandparents are....

Because speaking of ages, the truth is that I, by character and life circumstances, have always seemed much older than the years on my identity card. It is possible that the first years of my existence marked me, with the deaths of my sister Carmencita first and later on of my father, who curiously died on the same day Manuela was born years later, turning that date that has always been sad in our family into one of happiness. Maybe my father's spirit has settled in the girl and she will turn out just as good, judicious and hard-working as he was.

Time will tell us.

And what I was commenting on about the years is not an exaggeration, to which I am not given, but a verification of reality. When Carmencita disappeared, without even saying goodbye, something changed in me, for I had many cousins, but none of them felt like they were mine, like that girl. She was my little playmate in the house and at four years of age, I did not really take in that hackneyed phrase "she has gone to heaven." It didn't make much sense, or none, and I didn't understand it, so when Teresa came I was already prepared not to let anyone take her too, not to heaven or anywhere else; this time I would watch over her and take care of her.

But watching over her, my father escaped me...

So since then I had a double function because I had to act as brother and father. I got older suddenly because mother and Aunt Tomasa were also there, and only I could take care of all of them.

And so it has always been like that. My friends, and even Margarita, sometimes tell me that I am too protective of my sister, that I have not let her breathe or have a normal life, which is not true, so one day when Teresa and I were talking about it, in confidence and with sincerity on both sides, I asked her bluntly and she said no, that I was and had always been the best brother and father that anyone could dream of, so I decided to turn a deaf ear to future comments from others about the matter.

Despite the dramas of my early years, my childhood and pre-adolescence were very happy, surrounded by a lot of love, always supported by my mother and my aunt. It is possible that they spoiled me more than other parents do their kids, but I did not abuse, I was a good student because it seemed to me that it was my obligation, I came and went as I pleased (living in a small city where we all knew each other helped a lot), and I don't have what they now call traumas from that period. As I have always liked reading a lot, from a very young age I could spend hours doing it, and I did not have the same need as many others to be in noisy and boisterous environments all the time.

I'm shy, or maybe that's not the right word to define myself. It may be that before speaking I prefer to listen and when I meet someone, once the introductions are over, I like to observe and know how they think and where they are coming from before delivering a speech or letting loose with a lecture. But when I am with friends or with someone who is no longer alien to me, my shyness evaporates and I talk as much as anyone.

Some time ago, when I was still in school, I started to write a kind of diary and after my father-in-law left today I have been reading it because it seemed to me that today, finishing not only a year but also a decade, was the right time to do so, and it would be like a reminder of things I have lived. It had been a long time since I reviewed those papers, and although I have spent several hours with that task, I think it has been worth it. In addition, it has been a way of getting out of the way and leaving Margarita alone, who is with my sister organizing tonight's dinner that we will all share; then we will go to wait for the New Year celebrations and swallow the grapes at the Casino that reopens after the forced closing of the last three years.

After that "stroll down memory lane" I have been re-reading my dear Proust because, although I try to keep up to date with new literature, I still love and remain faithful to my favorite authors and he is one of them. He seems so extraordinary to me, with that exquisite choice of words to relate the smallest detail, that I greatly enjoy it when I decide to spend time in his company.

Margarita, who cannot stand those she disparagingly calls inverted fags (without realizing that by joining the two terms she is making them "normal"), when she sees me engrossed in one of his volumes makes jokes about it because, although she doesn't knows his work in its entirety, I managed to get her to read some of it, but without much success since my wife, although she is reading a little more every day, is more given to light things, such as do not make her think much, and I love her so much that whatever she decides to do, to read or not to read, to choose simple novels or treatises on philosophy, is of no importance to me. We are so opposite in our tastes and hobbies that every day I marvel more and more at how well we get along, and how easy it is to live together.

But speaking of common literary tastes (of which we do not have many, if I stick to reality), there is an author we agree on: Jorge Manrique and his beautiful *Coplas on the death of his father*, although each one of us for different reasons. As we both know the poem by heart, it is enough for one to start with "Remember the sleeping soul..." for the other to continue with the next line and sometimes, when we wake up, it is a game we play. For her, I think it is simply something that she likes, without further connotations; for me, since I have not had the opportunity to live with my father as an adult, it is something else, but the important thing is that we both enjoy reciting it, and it takes me back to my student years with my classmates.

Because those years impregnated my mind with many wonderful times and many and such good memories... But each era has its compensations, complaining about my life now would be like a slap at everything that heaven gives me, which I often wonder whether it isn't too much.

Although... one of the things that I have missed, since I left school several years ago, is being able to play tennis and whenever circumstances have allowed, I have always taken up my racket to smack the ball a few times. Perhaps now that this terrible conflict is over I will have more opportunities to return to practice, or even to promote the creation of some courts here in Turgalium. That would benefit many of us, because after what we've been through, leisure time would be good for all of us. We will see.

As I tend to be of constant affections, I continue to surround myself here with my usual friends, my cousins and also Margarita's brothers and sisters, although I do not forget the many companions I had during those eight years at El Escorial, and especially my group of "the four drudges," as the older ones jokingly called us. I only see my friend Paco, almost daily, since I had the great luck that when he finished his studies and started working, his first assignment was Turgalium, but I have not lost contact with the other two either, although this was in epistolary form. We exchanged long letters weekly, where we continued to debate everything from the political situation that we had to live through, to other more ordinary things such as jobs, love affairs and family. And of course, when there was an important event like a wedding, we always tried to get together, as happened when Margarita and I got married: everyone came to the festivities; they enjoyed themselves, and we enjoyed their company.

Unfortunately, during these past three years, with the war, things could not continue that way, communications were increasingly difficult, though I had Jorge to hook me into the frequent use of telegrams, so I have been able to continue giving them news occasionally. The four of us have escaped alive, our wounds are not physical, but not for this less painful, because many of those we knew have left us forever, and although their memory will be alive in our hearts, the idea of their non-existence hurts.

Speaking of friends, my last thought, now that the afternoon is over, goes to my brother-in-law and the great luck I have had when a year ago he became part of our family.

The end-of-the-year festivals and parties were never things that attracted me much. Not even as a young man. It seemed to me that people felt an obligation to have fun and so I always tried to evade such activities, staying home with a good book and listening to music. But then I had to change my mind when I met Margarita at the passing of 1934 to 1935. And when the year was about to change again as we just got back from our honeymoon, although I would have preferred to stay quietly at home, I could not refuse my wife's wishes. She loves to dance, wear her outfits and have a great time making jokes with everyone and about everything, and I enjoy seeing her happy so much that there is nothing that compensates me more in life. On that occasion Teresa preferred to come with us instead of going with her friends, she told us that she would meet them there, and that she really wanted to be with Margarita that night.

At that party we met Jorge. He was introduced to us on a day like today three years ago and from the first moment I saw that my sister liked him. I did too. He was a boy of only nineteen, very young but very mature for his age, with very clear ideas; and although due to circumstances he had had to abandon his engineering career for the time being (which was and I think continues to be his true vocation), and go to work when he passed the telegrapher tests, his idea was to continue studying as soon as the occasion was propitious.

He came from a bohemian family, but he was very conservative, very focused, and we fit in from the beginning, and seeing that both Teresa and he felt an undoubted attraction to each other, I played match-maker for the first time in my life, and invited him to have a drink at my house the next day.

He was in awe of my library, of which I am so proud, and there, without the noise inherent in parties where there are many people, we were able to talk calmly about many things. His opinions confirmed everything I had intuited the night before and a bond was forged between us that has only strengthened and become closer every day.

In these years, in addition to occupying a front row seat and witnessing the progress of his love, engagement, marriage and the birth of his daughter, I have tried to teach him and guide him in aspects in which he, due to his young age and the medium in which he grew up, was not very knowledgeable. Eight years is not a big difference when people are old, but at our age they do represent a lot, so I have been able to reprise my father-like role and guide him in some things.

Although at the beginning of our acquaintance and friendship he insisted that his stay in Turgalium was provisional, and that what he really wanted was to live in Madrid again above all things, with the passage of the months his mind changed, perhaps seeing that we all are very happy here, although we could have lived anywhere else; then came the war and all plans were altered, he was left without a father, his family dispersed and Madrid went from being a city of childhood, adolescence and good memories, to an unknown place; where things were never going to be the way they had been, or how he remembered them. He was acclimatizing to our city and our habits, he saw the advantages of residing in a small place, enjoying nature and the countryside that he loves so much, always having a plate of food (even in the most difficult days of the war, we never noticed that anything was missing), and I believe from my heart that Jorge is happy where he is now and it would be strange if one day he decided to leave our small city. He has already put down roots, which makes me happy, and I think how pleasant it will be when we are very old to sit before a decanter of good wine from Las Viñas and speak of things divine and human...

10. JUAN CARLOS - 1941

Reunion with friends

Monologue

My old classmates have just left. Now they have a lot of hours ahead of them until they reach their destination, Adrià and Josetxu especially, because Paco, living in Turgalium, has it much easier, but the reunion has been worth the effort for all of us, and we needed to be together again after such a long time apart.

We debated where, how and when, and after great deliberations as always happens with us, they came to the conclusion that the perfect place would be La Operetta in spring, although I let them know that the farm is still not as I want it to be in the near future, and that maybe meeting in a city and staying in a hotel would be more comfortable for them, but they said no way and everything turned out well, perfect I could say; We settled in without problems, the weather was good and we had two and a half days, the four alone as in those years that now seem so far away even though only ten have passed, without interference and with hours and hours of pleasant conversations, good meals that the cook prepared for us, Cañamero wines, and those who wished to, sampling other stupendous liqueurs.

Arranging the get together was not easy because the three of them work (I do too, and a lot, but not for a salary like they, and I have total freedom of movement), two live in remote cities, Paco and I are married... well, many variants to juggle, but we have succeeded.

Margarita is in Madrid with her sisters, entrusting the dressmaker with summer clothes; she decided to "get out of the way" according to her expression, so that I could be alone and in peace and fully enjoy myself with my friends. She is a person with such tact and sensitivity that she anticipates my needs before they even arise. How lucky I was the day I met her! It has only given me joy and love, and my existence cannot be better or more complete... I cannot ask for more in life, well maybe yes, maybe I wish everything would continue like this forever, until God calls me to his side.

The four of us talked about everything, the divine and the human until our jaws hurt. We reviewed what our life has been like in recent years since the last time we were together at my wedding, six years ago, and we have agreed to have at least one annual meeting, now that it seems that everything has stabilized, and that life goes on. We are no longer who we were, not so much because of the years that have passed, but because of the war we have lived through, but the affection and the union remain unchanged and that is so difficult... It often happens that people with whom you have been united in a time of your life then disappear forever, and only vague memories remain, if any. Not in our case. The ties that we forged for eight years, when we were still so young and innocent (even though we thought we knew everything), are stronger than those of blood and can only be broken when the day comes that we are not alive, when we disappear, and I hope that won't come to pass for a long time.

Adrià has taken over the family textile business, he is doing well, although with a lot of work, fighting with workers and trying to understand their positions, although he does not leave his more intellectual side and continues to read voraciously as he did, and since the war ended he continues attending concerts and becoming fully involved in all of Barcelona's cultural life.... He has a full life and a girlfriend whom he will marry soon. From what he has told us about her, she seems the perfect complement to his personality, and we all have wished him the best of luck. He's a great guy and he deserves the best.

Josetxu also continues in his family's shipping company. With the World War that we have upon us, although we Spaniards have gotten out of this one, his business is booming, and he told us that his normal working hours are a minimum of fifteen or sixteen hours, so he does not have much time left, none at all, and when he falls into bed he is so exhausted that even though he tries to read something "useful for the spirit," at the first line he feels the book slipping from his hands, he stops resisting and falls asleep without further ado.

Paco, whom I am lucky enough to see almost every day, has it easier than the other two, because as he is simply a bank director, he has many afternoons left for his own recreation. Living in a small city also helps the quality of life, less haste, less pressure, less stress... but as a counterpart also less cultural life, fewer possibilities in many fields, although in our case, having each other and sharing so much, it is different. And there's always Madrid. He longs for his Andalusia, his cortijo and his fields, but he knows that now he has La Operetta at his disposal, with me or on his own, and that helps him dissipate the longing for his land.

Among all that we talked about these days, one topic could not be missing: our initiation to sex, and that is where the laughter of the four could be heard for kilometers. Now that with great sorrow I am alone, with my glass of good wine and a plate of ham and chorizo to accompany it, I relate it:

The first time I had a pollution was the first year I was in the School. I was sixteen years old and one morning when I woke up my pajamas were stained with a viscous and whitish liquid. I was very scared thinking if I must have peed during the night, which had not happened to me even as a child, not even when

Carmencita or my father died, and after examining the pajama bottoms as quietly as possible, I came to the conclusion that it was something else. My sex education was nil. I had grown up in a house full of women, including family and service, and the house always seemed to be full of women: cousins, my sister's friends, my mother's sisters, my aunt's friends... Men came to discuss matters with my mother, cousins to pick me up, other friends with whom I exchanged games or trading cards, but they never spent hours like women did. I can say that, unlike fellow students, as I found out later, I was quite childish and dumb for my age, and since I did not have a father to explain things about my body to me, I had not the slightest idea of anything. Once I was convinced that it was not a leak of pee and after I had badly washed my pants, as soon as I had the slightest opportunity, that is, at the first recess, I asked Paco.

Instead of being scared, as I had been, he laughed and told me that from now on I was a man. I have to clarify that Paco, in addition to having a living father, had and still has two older brothers, and they apparently had instructed him well on the matter and he, always with all his good heart, transferred his knowledge to me. Everything was normal, according to him, and he could already say that the event had "made me a man," with which my fears disappeared, but since we did not have time to continue talking, he summoned me for the afternoon, to give me some very useful lessons for life according to him. I spent the whole day distracted, I had no interest in any of the classes even my favorite ones, I ate reluctantly... all I wanted was for time to pass fast till the hour when Paco would explain everything to me and, finally, when my nerves were about to finish me off (Me! So calm by nature. Almost nothing alters me.), Paco appeared as if he were the great guru and told me that in a moment he was going to clarify all my concerns .

He told me everything was natural, it was the body's response to the beginning of sexuality and although on that occasion it had been spontaneous, the liquid could be caused to spurt out by acting with the hand or by inserting the penis into a suitable hole, such as a woman's pussy, which caused a pleasure like no other, but if you didn't have a woman near, the hand could do the job. I was a little uneasy with those explanations, but he told me not to worry, that he would teach me how to do it; although he also insisted that it was not good to abuse, that those acts were considered sins and therefore you had to confess if you wanted to receive communion and that they even had a name, onanism.

The next four nights passed uneventfully, although when I woke every morning I thoroughly checked my pajamas to see if there had been any involuntary escape, but the fifth while I was having a very unusual dream with a beautiful stranger who approached me and touched me where no one had ever done it before, I woke up with my member three times its normal size, and merely touching it with my fingertips made a hot liquid flow out. Everything was dark, the rest of my companions slept while an indescribable pleasure took over my entire being, leaving me both full and empty. That's where my sex life began.

Half an hour before the daily mass there were always one or two confessing fathers waiting for sinners (but usually with few clients). For another of the rules of the boarding school is that, unless for some extraordinary circumstance you had broken the fast, we had to receive communion every morning, or in the expression of the friars *"Receive Jesus Christ,"* since that would help us during the day and free us of the possible problems that could arise. We arrived at the Chapel a little after seven o'clock, with plenty of time to go to confession if necessary, since Mass did not begin until seven thirty, and we all had to be present, unless we were sick. There was no escape there.

After my discovery and awakening to what one could do with one's body, and the pleasure that derived from it, I observed that the queues in front of the two confessionals got longer and longer every day and Paco, who was such a smart and witty guy and nothing escaped his eyesight, immediately commented to me about the fact; between laughs and a bit daring comments, the two of us agreed that they must be doing something "rather handy."

Despite the secret of confession, something must have leaked, or the Friars observed the same as we did, because one morning, the professor of Ethics and Religion, instead of the usual program, gave us a talk about the sins that haunted us, and the divine punishment that awaited us if we dared to use our hands to give ourselves pleasure, as well as countless physical problems that would surely overtake us, and these ranged from going blind, to contracting horrible diseases, to going mad... in short, a terrible and creepy panorama. At that point, he must have assumed that we would all have experienced something by now, but if any of the students were still a virgin in that regard, the picture he painted for us was chilling, although in practice it only served to increase the intrigue and in many cases incite masturbating, to see to what extent the friar's claims were true.

I still didn't do anything to myself, but the nocturnal pollution continued, so I became expert at washing my pants before putting them in the laundry basket, which, as with the confessionals, filled up every day, although nobody commented openly about this. The kids only talked in their private cliques.

Apparently I was the most naive of our group, since the other three narrated without pause their experiences; so not to be less I decided to do an experiment, or in the words of my friends "jerk off," but the whole thing was not as easy as it was painted since there was not much privacy: in the dormitory, as I said, there were twenty-one of us, and when the father in charge turned off the light at eight in the evening there had to be the most absolute silence, so some involuntary sigh or moan would give you away instantly; the showers were common and we all used them at the same time, there was no separation, so those two places were "out of order." The toilets were left, the only place where we could be alone, but this so-called privacy was also relative because there were always queues waiting to use them in the morning, and in the ones we used when we were in class we weren't supposed to be in them for long either, since they only allowed us to be absent for a few minutes if the need was pressing. Our departures from the precinct were in groups and always under surveillance. The affair was complicated!

So when I decided that I was going to do it, after weighing all the pros and cons that the event would entail, and assuming that with just one time I would not go blind or go crazy, I asked Paco where he did it, and in the afternoon, after gym class while the rest of the students and friars were occupied in the Lonja, he took me to an area full of trees away from that recreation area, he sat under one which had a lot of vegetation around it, and with the greatest tranquility in the world he opened his pants, put his right hand inside the boxer shorts, and right there, gave me a practical demonstration.

The most curious thing of all was that I was the one who was ashamed, my face burned, I was overwhelmed and I kept looking around in case someone from school or outside appeared, as if I were the culprit - if we are talking about guilt - while my friend finished with his business, cleaned himself with a handkerchief, got up and said: "Let's go back to the group before they miss us," and that's what we did, without further comment; but despite how easy it all seemed, I continued with my doubts and imaginings that they would catch me the first time I did it, so I decided to have a series of excuses at hand so that, when the big day arrived, if a friar caught me *in fraganti delicti* my explanation would sound plausible, and I'd not end up in the Director's office.

In the meantime, our school life continued with the established routines, we learned without rest, every month that passed our intellect expanded, we did many activities of all kinds, we were immersed in a privileged world (and almost all of us knew it), where the political ups and downs and the changes in the different laws and education plans practically did not affect us, because ours was a Renaissance formation and it covered, or intended to cover, all knowledge; but although the months passed, I still did not decide to act and do something to myself and I did nothing, waiting for the right moment and thinking that, in the worst case scenario, when the Easter holidays arrived, once at home I would have a chance, so I relaxed, stopped looking for a suitable occasion and waited.

Finally we got vacation holidays, and although my friend Josetxu wanted the four of us to spend them together in San Sebastián, I did not have the strength not to go home, knowing what it meant for my mother, Teresa and Aunt Tomasa to have me some days with them. Their last letters were full of plans of what we would do, what we would eat, what places we would visit.... Even my little sister, who was almost ten years old, had written me a delicious letter telling me about her cousins and her friends. I couldn't fail them and I declined the invitation, although I really wanted to join them.

I arrived at my house, and just as during the Christmas holidays, everything returned to exclamations of joy and happiness on the part of the family as a whole, plus the service, and since we had not seen each other since the beginning of January, I also observed changes, although minimal. My mother was still as pretty as ever, but certain wrinkles had appeared at the corners of her lips and her eyes, Teresa was very tall and Aunt Tomasa, as ugly as usual, was duller, although as soon as a few days passed and she had me home again, she went back to her old self.

I returned to my lifelong friends: my cousin Sebastián and his two brothers and my friend Emilio Márquez. With them it was as if the months I'd been absent from there had not passed, and we resumed our conversations and entertainment immediately.

We had certain routines, simple but effective: in the morning we would go for a walk, ride our bikes or take a stroll, talking and trying to "fix the world." Then, generally, each of us would eat at home, rest for a while, and in the afternoon we would meet again.

In Holy Week we went to religious services, we dressed for processions in *capirucha*, and when no one could recognize us (or so we thought), we played little jokes; it was an uncomplicated teenage existence.

After Holy Thursday and Friday had passed, sometimes someone held a little party and we tried to sneak in, but almost never had success, so we simply watched from a window, wishing that time would pass and we'd soon be "grown up."

The first two days of my return home I did not have the opportunity to do "the thing," but since I did not want to delay it too much because I knew that the holidays would end soon, the third night, with the house in silence and while everyone was sleeping, I did. And my feelings were the most mixed, since, although I had pleasure, at the same time a sensation of emptiness and a terrible feeling of guilt invaded me, and with those sentiments I could no longer sleep for the rest of the night. I did not want to fall asleep in case I died that night being in mortal sin, as one of the friars had explained to us, and besides, I thought of what had happened to my father who went to bed and never got up again, so my restlessness was terrible, wishing the morning would finally come so I could go to confession, because although in those days I was reading a passionate theological treatise on the pain of Attrition and that of Contrition, in my state of mind I could not read a single line.

As soon as dawn came, before anyone else in the house even got up, I ran off to a church. After the confession I told myself that it was not worth it, going through the ordeal of such a terrible night, and that I would avoid such experiments and practices in the days to come. I would let nature take its course. So I continued washing my pajama pants and listening to what my three friends told me, but without doing the same.

The year we started our law studies, Paco's father thought it was the right time, as he had done with his two older children, for my friend to come face to face with a woman, or in other words, lose his virginity, and as he knew that my father could not introduce me to that world, or underworld, he decided to include me in the initiation excursion.

Madrid that year was already a large city, since it had more than 800,000 inhabitants, about 8,000 cars circulated through its streets and avenues, and the trams also filled them. Little by little it had become a modern and cosmopolitan capital; the city was full of hotels, cafes, theaters, restaurants and banks and for the two of us, although we had visited it many times before, this time it was something different, first of all because we went hand in hand with a great connoisseur of the Villa y Corte who had a mission, and secondly (and almost more importantly), because we came from an environment very closed to what real life was; we had access to great pictorial and literary works, the conversations were of the highest level, we could debate everything that was passing through our heads... but there were no women on the horizon....

Don Curro first took us to have a good meal at the Casino de Madrid on Calle Alcalá, an institution of which he was a member despite not residing in Madrid, and before going to the dining room he gave us a tour so that we could see all dependencies first hand. The Casino was located in a beautiful building in which French and Baroque trends were mixed, and the best artists and craftsmen of the time intervened in the decoration of the interiors, as Don Curro explained to us. It had its origin back in 1836 when a group gathering at the Café del Príncipe decided to call it that, and in 1903 they acquired some land between Alcalá and Aduana streets to build their new headquarters there. Just seeing the imposing façade and entering the Patio de Honor with its glazed vault, where natural light filters in, was great, and the two of us climbed up the main staircase happily — we lived in a magnificent and beautiful place and therefore we were not impressed easily by anything, but we realized that it was an extraordinary building and that all the interior details were exquisite. My friend's father showed us the beautiful rooms where big parties were held and also the exclusive rooms of the members, including the Library, which we now as law students were keenly interested in, because its collection was mainly on these themes, and although when we entered there it seemed that everything was wood, with a more detailed look we realized that all the shelves and the stairs to reach the highest ones were made of iron to prevent fires.

We also visited the Terrace, located on the top floor of the building, where at that time they were preparing for the celebration of a party that would take place that night. We saw the nightclub and imagined what it would be like to be there, accompanied by beautiful partenaires, dancing and enjoying ourselves one day.

When we finally went to the dining room reserved for the members, the food they served us was quite distant from the menus that we tasted at school even on Saturday or Sunday (which was when the daily routine of peas and stew was broken), and the three of us chose the excellent menu of the day: a minced meat soup, over-roasted split sea bream, and a veal ragout of which the accompanying vegetables melted in the mouth; and he insisted that we accompany the delicious delicacies we were eating with a glass of wine, something that we were not used to but that we welcomed happily, it released our tongues and relaxed us, and when after a delicious caramel souffle for dessert and coffee we got up, the three of us were in an excellent mood, and in the words of Paco "ready to devour the world."

Don Curro then took us to a beautiful bar, in which there was a magnificent collection of bottles strategically placed all over its walls, and with that we entertained ourselves for more than an hour, trying to decipher its content while we had another drink, this time of a rich liqueur. Each moment we were more loquacious and happy.

And finally, the three of us walking, on that beautiful spring afternoon, we arrived at the place where our initiation to women would take place. We entered a building on Calle Montera that was no different from those next to it, and, after going up two floors in an elevator that made a hellish noise and seemed about to collapse at any moment, we reached our destination: a flat that, from the outside and judging by the large mahogany wood entrance door, was stately and similar to others behind which the activities or families that occupied them we supposed were more respectable.

There we were received by a lady who must have been French, named Madame Petite Fleur, not very tall, middle-aged, but still attractive, quite painted and well-groomed, with a huge chignon on top of her head, and perched on very high heels, but despite that she did not reach our shoulders.

She knew my friend's father well and greeted him very effusively, and after the introductions and mention of the motive for our visit, she took both of us to a fairly spacious room, decorated in red and a bit too ornate, in which armchairs and sofas were scattered along the walls. No one was there. As we sat down, a waiter appeared, a Philippine boy who must have been our age, smiling and showing his white teeth, and perfectly uniformed, carrying a huge tray with glasses and bottles of various drinks.

The two of us had already drunk two, one at lunch and the next on our way up after, and having a third seemed to us that it would go beyond our little resistance to alcohol, but nevertheless we accepted the offer, expectant of what would come next. And it came.

In a few minutes, five very pretty girls appeared, quite scantily clad, who walked in front of us calling us "darling" and "handsome" and also saying some slightly risqué phrases, between laughter and smiles, and caressing our faces. It was the first time the two of us had been so close to scantily clad women, because the ones we knew from our family or circle of friends, didn't have the habit of parading like that or talking so fresh! ...and something started to grow. They didn't give us the option of choosing, and two of them (a brunette and a redhead whose hair reached almost to her waist) took us by the hand and led us down a long corridor with many closed doors to two rooms and where Paco and I parted company.

I had been taken in hand by the brunette, a very pretty girl, tall, with a very good figure and a big smile that filled her face.

The only thing that spoiled her looks was a missing tooth, but otherwise you couldn't fault her. As soon as we entered the bedroom, which is what it was, she walked over to a gramophone on a low table and put on a sensuous song. She sat on the edge of the bed and with graceful movements began to remove my jacket, undo the knot in my tie and unbutton my shirt, and once I was a little lighter, she proceeded to do the same with her clothes, as she danced and wiggled to the music. In a short time her upper part was completely naked: two large breasts, white and firm, immediately appeared and I, who was looking at her absorbed, felt a humid rush between my legs, an ineffable pleasure but also overwhelmingly embarrassing for not having been able hold back. She, though, redoubled her movements to the rhythm of the music, delicately approached me, took off my pants and underpants (which were soaked by then), proceeded to shed what little clothes she had left and lay down beside me, caressing my whole body until in a very short time my member was hard and wanting more.

With great care, she guided me until she had me totally inside her, and from that moment on, our bodies matched each other, and a few minutes later I felt the wonderful joy of exploding inside her. I would have liked that moment never to end, such was the pleasure I felt, but it ended and although we continued lying down for a long time, we were two separate entities again. But I wanted more still and she, after carefully washing me and speaking to me in a low whispering tone, began to run her tongue over my flaccid member while I touched her breasts and carefully took her nipples with the tips of my fingers, afraid of hurting her and again the great miracle occurred: in a very short time I was ready for a second attack and this time it was even better than the previous one.

Finally, exhausted but happy, we ended the session. I didn't even get to know her name or any personal information, but I enjoyed her body for a long time. We got dressed and returned to the living room where we had met, she gave me a chaste kiss on the cheek and disappeared, leaving me wondering whether it had all been a dream or reality. At once Paco appeared with the redhead, who did the same thing with him that the brunette had done with me, and the two of us stayed there alone until Don Curro came back for us and settled accounts.

On the street he asked us if we had liked the experience. What could we say? Like was too short a word to express how my friend and I felt, so we spoke little and went to dinner at the hotel where we would spend the night.

While they served us dinner, Don Curro told us that he had preferred to take us to that house, as he had previously done with his older sons, because he knew that the girls who worked there were clean and experienced, although very expensive, and that that was important for a first time when nerves sometimes betray even the most macho, but he said we should refrain as much as possible from frequenting these types of establishments, and limit their use for when the urge to be with a woman was unbearable. We both told him that we were in agreement, although my friend and I would have returned there that same night, despite the physical exhaustion that we both felt.

After a great dinner, that night we slept like angels, and when I woke up my member was harder and more anxious than ever, so, since I already had to go to confession anyway, I relieved myself twice until my desires became bearable and afterwards Paco told me that the same thing had happened to him. Youth was bursting within us and we would have to hold things at bay.

We didn't have to go back to El Escorial until the afternoon, so we spent that morning walking through the Botanical Garden, showing off our immense knowledge of the plants and trees there, and leaving my friend's father with his mouth open, and after a long walk around the premises we went to see some paintings in the Prado museum. It was curious because suddenly in many of the paintings that we looked at, breasts appeared, and women with insinuating gestures and scantily dressed; and that happened with paintings that we knew very well but in which we had not before noticed such details.

Remnants of the previous afternoon were still thrashing about in our minds...

And from there, on a faster visit than I would have liked, we went to Cuesta de Moyano, to buy some books at the stalls.

It was night when he dropped us off at school again. The past hours could not have been better, but we were back to normal, although carrying within us an indelible experience. We had made good use of the time.

In the next few days, as soon as we had the chance, we told Josetxu and Adrià what we had done over the weekend. We were now among the "grown-ups." We four university students had luckily all decided to pursue a law degree, with which our union was further strengthened if such was possible. Our schedule, although intense, was different from the four previous years: we dedicated the mornings to classes and the afternoons to study, but we had much more freedom and the friar Fathers were not on top of us at all times, they already knew us well, and they knew what each one was capable of, so one of the afternoons in which we had free time and had decided to leave the premises and go to have our high tea in the town, was the ideal occasion to tell them our story play by play and without sparing any detail.

They continued in their virginity, so Paco and I decided to act as sponsors and introduce them to the same bordello in which we had been initiated. As there was little time left until the end of the course, the four of us deemed excellent the suggestion of Paco (who was always the most daring and determined of the group), to spend a few days together in Madrid before separating for the summer. Each of us would go to spend the long lazy summer vacation with his family and, except for some short encounters, we would not meet again until September.

We passed the course not only without difficulty but with very high marks, and the summer break beckoned as a long period with no obligations other than what we wished to impose upon ourselves, so it seemed more than fair to award ourselves the Grand Prize for all our effort. As we wanted to stretch and use our money on something that was really worthwhile, that is to say women, we decided not to go to one of the big hotels but to spend the nights of our stay in a pension on Espoz y Mina street, of which we had good references in terms of cleanliness and friendliness. This way we ensured that the bases were covered if money started to run low.

The morning we arrived, after settling into our rooms, we decided to go visit an inn located in the Cava Baja called Mesón del Segoviano, a spot of good report, and there have Josetxu and Adrià imbibe wines to accompany the delicious tapas that were served there, so that, as happened with our initiation a few months earlier, they would sally forth uninhibited and relaxed when their moment of truth arrived.

This inn was very popular not only for the quality of its culinary offerings, but also as a meeting place for people of the most varied nature, who also found a special attraction every Friday: the arrival of the "Ordinario de Illescas," a wagon drawn by mules owned by a long dynasty of carters, who carried their wares to the adjacent markets; writers, painters and poets often met in the entrance hall of said inn, and there, between glasses of wine and stronger liquors, expounded their theories and made known, to those who wanted to hear, the latest about their work. Only a few years before they had offered a great tribute to the writer from Burgos, Francisco Grandmontagne, in which up to a hundred personalities of Spanish literature, such as Azorín and Antonio Machado, had participated, and to us, bookworms who knew the their writings almost by heart, the possibility of crossing paths, even very briefly, with authors we read offered us a plus, but on that occasion, whether it was because of the early hour or for any other reason, we did not meet any.

However, it was very pleasant there and we spent more time than initially planned, although it was not in vain: when we left we were all relaxed and the two neophytes were ready for whatever lay ahead of them.

We arrived at the women's house without an appointment, since we did not know that was required, even though Paco and I posed as cognoscenti, but there were no problems: the French madam received us as smiling and friendly as the previous time, still on her high heels and with her big chignon, and as soon as we explained the reason for our visit, she took Josetxu and Adrià with her to the same room where she had taken us, and very kindly asked us to wait a few moments.

Our idea was not to lose the occasion either, and as long as we were there to have a good time with some of the girls, but apparently we were wrong, or at least in part, since when the madam returned she began to talk to us about the matter as a mere commercial exchange: *Do ut facias*, I give so you do, in the purest example of Roman Law that we had learned in the course, and when she told us the price for the "service" to our friends we almost fell backwards. We had no idea (and logically we had not asked Don Curro either) that it was so expensive, but all of a sudden we remembered that my friend's father has commented on it in passing, so we paid and went for a walk while they finished. The Frenchwoman told us not to be in a hurry to return; that sometimes the initiation rites took a bit of time and that we needn't worry, that our friends were in good hands and when they had finished, if we hadn't returned, they would be waiting for us in the hall.

As we knew it would be at least three hours, we decided to walk back to the pension, rest there for a while, replenish our meager wallets and be ready to return to collect our friends. Time flew by and before we realized it, not three but four hours had passed, so we had to take a cab to get our friends, who were just leaving their respective bedrooms at the time of our arrival.

Neither Paco nor I, knowing the fees, wanted to do anything. There would be times in the future. We knew how to get there, we were old clients and we also knew that we would have to make an appointment and bring money, loads of money... We both felt so experienced, sophisticated and grown that, despite the initial frustration at not having also participated in the spree, we accepted the fact like sportsmen and received our friends as they deserved.

Although on the way to the whorehouse we had instructed them not to behave as we had done when we were confronted for the first time with a naked or semi-naked woman, all the warnings seem to have fallen on deaf ears and, according to what they told us, the same thing had happened to them: they could not contain themselves, and their following performance was a carbon copy of ours.

So, with the primary mission that had brought us to Madrid accomplished, we were able to dedicate ourselves to enjoying everything the capital had to offer. The following year everything would change with the collapse of the American stock markets, but we were in 1928, we were so young (the four of us were twenty years old at the time), and despite the uncertainty in which the country lived, with constant crises and under the threats of fascism and communism, for us life was wonderful. The first night, assuming that Josetxu and Adrià would not be up to many adventures, we decided to go to the Calderon theater, which until the previous year had been known as the Odeon Theater, and was located in a beautiful building on Atocha street. We all knew the exterior from the many times we had all passed by, but none of us had seen the interior, which pleasantly surprised us with its exquisite stained glass windows in the lobby, the paintings that decorated the vault, and the great capacity.

That night the program was the zarzuela "Doña Francisquita," which had premiered at the Apolo theater a few years before, and which we did not know, so to the pleasure of the place was added the possible enjoyment of the operetta. We knew it was based on the comedy of Lope de Vega (an author that the four of us liked a lot) "*La discreta enamorada*," the music had been set by Amadeo Vives to a libretto by Federico Romero and Fernández-Shaw.

It was a lyrical comedy in three acts, set in the romantic Madrid of the mid 19th century during carnival season, with music that stuck right away and we all enjoyed the choice we had made. When we left there, the four of us hummed the song "You know where the fire is from the smoke" as if we had heard it many times.

We finished late, but the night was young for us so we went to recharge our batteries at a bar called Alegría, which was in the Cuatro Calles, crossroads between the Carrera de San Jerónimo and the streets of Seville, Principe and de la Cruz, a site that students from courses higher than ours had spoken wonders about, and that did not disappoint us. What we ate and drank there, in addition to being of more than reasonable prices, not to say cheap, was of unsurpassed quality and the murals that adorned its walls, with caricatures of politicians and famous people of the time did not leave us indifferent, for we laughingly commented on them. The modernist-style restaurant had the latest advances in terms of coffee makers, lighting and seats, and the waiters were true professionals, dressed in black and wearing a kind of white apron that was nothing more than a large napkin knotted at the waist, and with a bow tie around the neck that gave them a very French look.

It was a full day and although neither Paco nor I had "performed," the summation of all our activities was highly positive; when we finally arrived at our pension late at night and the watchman opened the door for us, we were tired but exultant and we could have continued much longer, but Adrià thought that we still had many days ahead and urged us to reserve our strength, with which we all agreed.

The next day, after the owner of the pension regaled us with a sumptuous breakfast (she had amiably protested that we had skipped all meals the previous day and said she wanted to make up for it in a big way), we decided to spend part of the day in the Jardines del Buen Retiro and leave the night for something more exciting, and as the temperature was very fine, thither we went, walking and recalling everything we had done the day before. Adrià and Josetxu were relaxed, but just as what had happened to us, they wanted more, they had the bug of wanting to be with women again, even if they were for pay, but we convinced them, as the "initiating fathers" Paco and I had become, that it was better not to abuse nature, that we would return another time, and finally we arrived at the park.

Although the four of us had been there previously, knowing that it was a must on our vacation trip, Adrià, who was very meticulous and overly punctilious about those sorts of things, had prepared some sheets where he explained many details that we did not know, and they did come in handy and allowed us to know a little more deeply what we were going to visit. According to his research (although in order not to exhaust ourselves since we were no longer in school time, he had summarized the information and ignored many data and dates), the origin of the park and its installations dated from the time of Felipe IV and were built in the first half of the seventeenth century for the king's enjoyment at the request of Gaspar de Guzmán y Pimentel, who encouraged the monarch to expand the Royal Room that was next to the Jerónimo's Monastery, and build a palatial residence there. It took ten years to build it and at that time it was located on the outskirts of Madrid; one hundred and fifty years passed, until Carlos III allowed the public to enter for recreational purposes, although it was not until the second half of the 19th century, when it was under the ownership of the Madrid City Council, that its use became fully popular.

The initial palace had an exterior of a plain and austere style, which contrasted with the lavish interior ornamentation where the spacious rooms were adorned with beautiful paintings and the coffered ceilings displayed bright colors. The initial gardens, which were projected at the same time as the palace and like it did not have an integral plan, was determinative for the layout of asymmetric and interlocking compositions, without a determined axial order.

The park Los Jardines del Buen Retiro was later accessed by a series of ten gates, the most famous of them being that of Felipe IV (also called Mariana de Neoburgo), which was the one through which we entered. Initially, according to what Adrià told us, an iron fence had been put up to delimit the enclosure and separate the gardens from the streets that surround them and little by little, especially after its use passed to the town, more gates had been added, some for the public and others simply for service, to facilitate access for citizens. Making an exhaustive list of what the park contains would take me too long, so I am going to limit myself to note here the most interesting things that were in my friend's work, which I still have and has served me more than once over the years to refresh my memory when accompanying family or friends to visit the venue.

Once inside, the first thing that catches the visitor's attention is the immense number of trees, more than nineteen thousand, of one hundred and sixty-seven different species, and for us who came from families with farms and lands, and lovers of vegetation, such variety attracted us greatly. Especially, and as a concrete example, we stopped for a long time before what is called "Bald Cypress," a magnificent specimen, with a difficult botanical name (Ahuehuete) that is more than 200 years old, but which experts say is in the flower of life, and it is by far the oldest tree in the capital. This tree is of a very rare botanical species and has a few relatives in Aranjuez. All of them arrived on the peninsula around the year 1783, after having spent a period of adaptation in Tenerife. Around this precious and long-lived specimen, many and varied legends have been hatched, the first being that it is coeval with the park, but that is practically impossible since that species was not yet known in the middle of the 17th century; it is true, however, that according to experts such trees can live up to two thousand years.

Although we would have liked to spend more time contemplating the bald cypress and recounting our experiences with our own trees, such as Paco's, who at his Andalusian hacienda also had several old olive trees over two hundred years old, time was pressing if we wanted to do the route that

Adrià had prepared for us, so we went to see some of the more than fifty monuments that had been distributed throughout the Buen Retiro during its more than three hundred and fifty years of existence, and that's how we arrived at the Casa de Vacas, which in its beginnings and for a long time was an authentic dairy and milk distributer when it was inaugurated and for a long time after. From there we went to visit briefly the Casita del Pescador and immediately after to see the magnificent sculpture of the Fallen Angel, which is the only known public statue dedicated to the Devil. Its sculptor, Ricardo Bellver, was inspired by Milton's work "Paradise Lost," and because we had studied and analyzed this work in depth, when we contemplated the statue we all began to recite passages as if we were cockatoos, so that those who were close did not know whether to clap or laugh, but they opted for the former, which led us to get Josetxu to give them a small lecture on the divine and the human. It was fun.

We went to see several fountains: the one with the seagulls, which, even though they were not real ones, were fluttering through the Madrid skies far from their seas, the Fountain of the Galapagos, which from its construction until the reign of Isabel II supplied water to the Villa and Corte, that of General Martínez Campos and several others until we finally reached the Rosería rose gardens, which, given the date of our visit, was fantastic, an explosion of colors and fragrances. The Master Gardener, Cecilio Rodríguez, had arranged all the flowers and plants with such taste that Adrià took out his notebook and began to take notes and draw diagrams of how everything was arranged in order to try to reproduce it in the garden of his house in Barcelona, although we told him that the climate there was different and that he would have to change some of the species so as not to be disappointed.

We went to the Crystal Palace, which had initially been built as a greenhouse for exotic plants that were to be displayed at the Philippine General Exposition; to Velázquez's palace (which we mistakenly believed was named after the painter, but which was actually named after the architect who built it); we visited the Central Observatory, which was born in 1856 as a telegraph station but which in 1887 became the headquarters of the Meteorological Institute; we approached the Music Temple and from our colleague's notes we learned that only three years before, in 1925, the City Council had decided to put up a Music kiosk, adding it to the recreation area that had been installed in 1868, which consisted of the Zoo, the Exhibitions, and the Gardens, thus increasing the possibilities of fun for locals. And finally we came to the pond. Our feet were tired, but our minds were alert despite our full bellies (because we had stopped to eat a couple of times).

The Buen Retiro pond was created at the same time as the park and its initial function was to supply water to the Palace, the Gardens and the Fountains. Its creator, Cristóbal de Aguirre, had to construct several successive works until he managed to bring the water necessary for this purpose. In 1868 its management passed to the Madrid City Council, which dedicated it mainly to recreational purposes and as a visual haven for visitors; at its pier we took two boats which the four of us enjoyed rowing, but it was Josetxu, since he practiced rowing as a sport during his summers in his native San Sebastián, who gave us a demonstration of how to row without becoming exhausted. On the banks of the pond, we stopped to admire the magnificent sculptural group dedicated to Alfonso XII, along with the Egyptian Fountain, and the four ferris wheels still in use.

The hours had flown by, and it was getting dark when we went back to the pension to change and go to another show, but the visit had been fruitful and we were all glad we did it. We decided without any discussion that that night we would go to a variety theater that our older colleagues had also told us about, the Eslava, located on Arenal street, between Puerta del Sol and Opera, where Celia Gámez performed as the first star in a show called "*Las Castigadoras*," and with this decision we aced out!

As with the Calderon, we hadn't know about this theater either, which according to the program had been born in 1871 as a warehouse for musical instruments and a concert hall, promoted by a nephew of Hilarión Eslava, and which later would become a theater and a café; it was very popular among its Madrid patrons for the erotic daring of the works that were performed there. The interior of the theater, in the Mudejar style with its tall and fragile columns that formed the arches, did not leave us indifferent and we spent a long time admiring the elegance of the hall. The theater was dedicated to popular genres and reviews, and had gone through several difficult times, with many ups and downs and even bloody episodes — in 1922 a crime was said to have been committed there, owing to literary rivalries, to which were added jealously because apparently the murderer's wife had slept with the other and he therefore felt the "moral obligation" to terminate his life. Be that as it may, they said the ghost of the dead man used to walk among the actors when they were on stage, and sometimes his audacity went so far as to rise to the stalls. The night we went he didn't show up, or if he did we were so engrossed in the comedy that we didn't notice.

When Celia Gámez premiered Las Castigadoras, the theater returned to its plentitude, and despite the fact that more than a year had passed since that opening night, the place was completely packed when we entered.

Las Castigadoras, the work of Joaquín Mariño and Francisco Lozano Bolea was a picaresque story in seven acts, a vaudeville of musical works, a colorful and quite spicy review that we, little used to that genre and coming from where we came, loved, and we joined in the songs as if we were regulars. We thoroughly enjoyed ourselves and the best was yet to come.

At the end of the vaudeville, and while we were still lingering around the exit, we saw the cast of the play come out through a semi-hidden door. We got closer to see better, and what was our surprise when four beautiful girls, smiling and animated, said good night to us. Emboldened, we went to them, or rather, Paco approached them with a firm step and a resolute manner, and suggested an invitation to go for a drink with us, and to our astonishment they said yes. We couldn't believe our luck so before they repented, the eight of us went out to a nearby cafe that was still open.

We spent hours with them and from the beginning we realized that with the four of them we would have many opportunities, and that it was not a thing to despise, so we went on to the direct attack. And when after seeing the sunrise we invited them to breakfast on hot chocolate with churros and left them at the pension they lived in, having made dates for the next night after leaving the show, we already knew without having to speak that the tourism visit was over and that we were going to focus on those girls who had fallen to us from heaven.

We slept most of the day and when it was time for the performance we returned to the theater laden with flowers and boxes of chocolates to please them.

As we already knew the work, we sang full out and we paid special attention to the long legs and the sculptural bodies that our stars had, who winked at us from the stage, seeing that we had returned as promised. From the moment we picked them up and after again spending some very fun hours with them, we were certain we could take them to bed, and as in our pension that was unthinkable, Paco, taking the initiative again, hired a room in a good hotel where we would take turns. Josetxu was in charge of setting the hours that would correspond to each one of us, and everything was ready for the adventure the following night.

At that point we already knew the work by heart and we could have jumped on stage to sing and dance, but we didn't care, what interested was what interested, everything else was accessory. Everything went according to our plans and, to make the story a bit shorter, I got the second turn, so I didn't have to wait too long. When my time came, pretending a sophisticated ease that I did not have, I went to the hotel with the lady on my arm; she was called Carmina (later I would find out that that was her *nom de guerre* and that in fact her name was Petra, and also that she was from a small town in Extremadura not far from my city, coincidences of life), a beautiful girl and with a really spectacular figure, and once in the room, she was the one who directed the whole thing from beginning to end. She undressed herself, she undressed me, and during the three hours of shift that corresponded to me the only task was to enjoy and enjoy. I would have liked to have more hours, all she had free, and I was about to take another room for myself, as I imagine the rest also felt, but we were a group, the four drudges, and I did not.

We spent the rest of our vacation in total madness: we slept late, went to the theater, then had something to eat while we waited for our turn, we enjoyed ourselves like sybarites with our companions, we accompanied our "assigned" girl to her pension, we ate and rested a bit and went to it again. We all lost a lot of weight and had silly faces, but the experience was sublime and the four of us were delighted.

But the vacation was ending. We would have to say goodbye to our starlets, whom during our stay we had showered with gifts and even promises that could never be fulfilled, but the ardor and desire of youth is like that, and if we had to make promises in exchange for good and rich carnal favors, we didn't care. I said goodbye to Petra with great sorrow, but not before assuring her that I would see her again soon, as soon as my family obligations allowed it, and the other three did the same. The four of us spent those last hours together, sharing experiences of the last few days and even recounting intimate and somewhat rough details, and each one returned to our place of origin.

But Petra had gotten under my skin, and two weeks later I returned to Madrid to enjoy her body. And I kept doing it as soon as the slightest opportunity presented itself, sometimes making excuses so strange that even I laughed at them. By the time I returned to El Escorial for the new year, our relationship was well established and consolidated, there was no commitment by either party, but we were both devoted to each other, we enjoyed each other's company, we ate and drank and, mainly, we spent hours naked, enjoying sex.

As time, months and years went by, little by little she began with small demands. Petra was still in the review, but she knew that age is a handicap in that profession, and she wanted to stabilize her life and formalize our relationship in some way, if not with a wedding (totally unthinkable on my part), with some kind of alliance. And I was not up for that job. Gifts, many. Money, too, but that's where my commitment ended.

I finished my studies, got my degree, more years passed and little by little the relationship faded. It had served a long period of my life, but it was time to turn the page; it wasn't fair to make Petra miss opportunities by waiting for me, when deep down she knew she had no future with me. We saw each other for the last time at the beginning of the winter of the year thirty-four, we said goodbye with love and without any misunderstanding between us, we enjoyed each other enormously, so much that I wondered if I had made the right decision, we wished each other the best in life. I have not seen her again, nor have I missed her: a few weeks later I met my great love, Margarita, the woman of my life, who is so smart and so skillful that being naked with her and getting into her body brings me to a state of total glory. I do not need more. I already have everything any human being could want.

During my lucubrations about those experiences, those ancient stories, total night has fallen, my bottle is almost empty and the snacks have disappeared. I'm going to bed now. I hope my friends will arrive soon and well at their destinations, and above all my main desire is that it not take so long to meet again. I need them and they need me and so it will always be.

A small snake, Margarita calls them serpents, even if they are eight inches long, has curled itself around the leg of the chair. It seems asleep, I'll leave it alone, it doesn't hurt anyone. If my wife were here now she would be screaming and urging me to kill it.... She doesn't want us to have any serpents in the house.

11. FUNERAL - END OF MAY 1942

TERESA, sister

The priest, wearing a black chasuble and all the attributes due to the occasion, said at that time:

Pulvis es et in pulverem reverteris. Oremus.

But Teresa, despite knowing the meaning of those words, did not hear them. Her gaze was fixed on the place where there should have been the coffin containing the remains of what until just a few days ago had been her brother, her only and most beloved brother, and although the tears welled up in her eyes, through them she tried to see beyond, trying in vain to imagine her brother asleep there, resting like any other day and ready to wake up and tell her what he had done the day before.

The child she carried in her womb stirred restlessly, bringing her to the present, announcing a life that began while another had ended, and perhaps that is why, when the priest came down from the altar to offer his condolences, her legs failed her and she nearly fell to the floor, her pain was such that unconsciousness at that moment would almost have been a blessing. Her mind wandered.

When she returned to reality, she realized that she would never see her brother again. In her mind she said goodbye, and suddenly so many memories came back to her...

—Look what I have brought you, Teresita, a little white kitten to play with you! Her brother spoke to her.

Little Teresa looked at her cousin Piluca, and the two of them got up running from the big round table where they were having a snack and rushed towards the kitten who stared at them, and immediately turned around, having lost all interest in his new owner and her friend.

This was one of her oldest and fondest memories of her brother Juan Carlos, six years older than she and, since the death of her father (whom she had never known), the "man of the house." For the father of the two had died when she was only nine months old, leaving a heartbroken widow, a young and beautiful woman, alone and with two children who would grow up cared for and always enfolded in the immense love not only of their mother, but also of Aunt Tomasa, the deceased's sister, who lived with her sister-in-law and nephews.

Teresa never missed her father, never had the feeling of being an orphan, something that did not happen with her brother, who every night, when he was alone in his room, looked at the crucifix that was above his bed and asked God why he had taken their father, why they were left alone, without a man to guide them, without a guide to direct them, without a direction to follow. And for years, every night, he asked himself the same questions.

But he never got answers. Or at least satisfactory answers for a child, which is what he was.

As the men began to pay their condolences by passing before them and bowing their heads, she looked at her mother, leaning on Jorge and dissolving in tears, without either of them yet able to understand the scope of what they were experiencing at that moment. A great veil, thick and black, covered not only her face but also her understanding of what was occurring. It might be said she was in a trance, but that would have been oversimplifying her state, because what she really was, what she felt, was dead herself.

She took Edelmira, her mother, by the arm, leaned on her, they supported each other, while one of her cousins, Piluca, held her, and surrounded by relatives and friends, the three of them left their private Golgotha on their way home.

MARGARITA, wife

Pulvis es et in pulverem reverteris. Oremus.

Finally, in a short time, everything would end.

The minutes had seemed like hours since she entered the church, contrary to the previous days, in which each hour had passed with the speed of a minute.

But soon she would be totally free. Free to do whatever she wished. Free to love. Free to dream. Free!

Although she recognized that Juan Carlos had been a beautiful person, so fine and educated, so cultured and enlightened, always such a gentleman, and putting the love he felt for her above all other considerations, she had never been in love with him, that was for sure.

She looked at her sister-in-law, pregnant and about to faint, at her mother-in-law, at the friends and the rest of the relatives who accompanied them, and for a moment something similar to grief crossed her mind. But it was only a moment and she brushed it away right away, as you do with an annoying fly. A few more hours and she would leave behind what, for the past few years, had been her family; her body was still there, but her mind had flown elsewhere even before she entered the gloomy church for the grim ceremony. She was definitely bored, but very soon she would be free. The very idea made her smile.

Thank goodness the thick veil that covered her face would prevent prying eyes from seeing it. She continued with the ritual, getting up and kneeling, and when at last the priest approached with the hyssop, to sprinkle the place where the coffin should have been, she faked a swoon and sat down.

JORGE, brother-in-law

Pulvis es et in pulverem reverteris. Oremus.

A few days earlier, while he was at work, a pair of civil guards had given him the news. Not in his worst nightmares could he have imagined anything worse. His brother-in-law, the only brother of his beloved wife, had been murdered. Everything was confusing, although it seemed that members of the maquis had perpetrated the crime. But Jorge's analytical mind knew something didn't fit.

And now, after many hours of hectic activity, they were finally all gathered, celebrating the funeral of the victim in the church, although the remains of his body were not there. They had been interred in an unfamiliar cemetery, something very different from what Juan Carlos, between joking and earnestness, had always asked, almost since they had met: to rest with his father and be near him once he was dead, since he had not been able to enjoy his company while he was alive. Jorge would see to it that he fulfilled what he had promised, even if he had to wait a long time to do so.

It had been a few years of friendship and brotherhood; exactly from the first day they met they had found that they had many points in common: their love of music, of good literature and, above all, of Teresa. The age difference was never an obstacle between them; on the contrary: Juan Carlos saw in Jorge the little brother he never had, while the latter relied on the wisdom and knowledge that his brother-in-law had, and together they formed a good team. There was never the slightest disagreement between them and now he was gone. Why? What a senseless murder, and of such an excellent person. He had been thinking about the subject for days and every time he understood it less and less.... He looked at his wife and feared not only for her but also for the child they were expecting.

He looked at his mother-in-law, whose vacant gaze made him wonder why he hadn't been more assertive and prevented her from going to church. Too late now.

And finally, his gaze tracing the rest of the pew they were on, his eyes fell on Margarita, the widow. Through the veils that covered her face, he thought he detected a smile. That increased the uneasy feeling that had been haunting him since he and Manolo had seen Juan Carlos with his head shattered. He looked at her again, this time openly, and only found someone with closed eyes, a tightly puckered mouth, and a generally dejected appearance, so he told himself that he must have interpreted as a smile what was rather a grimace.

He could not continue thinking because he had to stand in front of the altar, leading the direct relatives so that the friends and neighbors who filled the temple could file by offering their condolences. He rose together with the other family members and for the moment put aside his impressions.

EDELMIRA, mother

Pulvis es et in pulverem reverteris. Oremus.

My God, my God, how many deaths do I have to go through until mine comes? Why haven't you taken me, I'm useless anyway....

When we buried Tomasa I thought I would be the next one, because of my age and because of everything, there have already been too many deaths that I have had to live in these fifty-four years, and every time one falls on me I feel like I'm not going to be able to keep on living. If when you took my parents, my in-laws, Carmencita and my Floro, it took me so long to move forward, what will become of us now, without my son who was the center of my existence? How can I get up every day and know that I will never see him again? Why do you put me through all these ordeals? Why you test me so much?

You know, God, I miss Tomasa a lot, but I thank you my God, because she doesn't have to drink this bitter drink. This tragedy would have carried her off; my son, her beloved child, whom she loved like nothing or no one in the world, has left us in the prime of life, he is no longer and will never be with us again, he who was incapable of killing even a fly and... even the field snakes he let live...

How could something like this have happened? What have we done to make you vent your anger? I believed that just being good and following your commands was enough, forgive me my God, I no longer know what I'm saying or what my head suspects, and please give us strength, we're going to need a lot of that to move on.

My only possible consolation now is that I still have Teresita, Margarita, and my precious Manuela, but this blow is going to be too much for us. Goodbye, my son. Wait for me. Hopefully we'll see each other soon.

SEBASTIÁN, cousin and friend

Pulvis es et in pulverem reverteris. Oremus.

Even seeing it with my own eyes, I am still unable to believe what is happening, where we are and why. My cousin, my friend, my brother has died and we don't even have the consolation of having his remains present, even that has been stolen from us.

What can I say about my cousin? Everything and nothing. He was my brother by choice, which is more than some brothers are by blood ties, and since we were children we have been together. His house was my house, mine was his, and all my memories of childhood, adolescence, youth and now maturity are and will always be linked to him. As Juan Carlos has no father or brothers, I think mine were a good substitute for him, and we all love him, we have loved him, so deeply that I cannot find the words to say it. This murder doesn't make any sense. He is, was, now, a peaceful man, always so polite and correct with everyone. Something does not fit here, but it's not the time to digress, the time will come, but the only reality is that he has left us and he will never come again.

And not a week ago we were together in a bar in the plaza, commenting on the next harvest, talking about the fields, we both protesting a little about how the day laborers are a pain in the ass... in short, the usual, while we had a coffee. Right then I saw, I noted, felt, that you were more alive than ever, more animated and with more projects. You, who were naturally very calm and who always weighed any decision, no matter how minimal, that day you were very talkative and you told me about your plans to continue modernizing the hacienda and make the house you have there even better, since each time you spend more seasons in it... the enormous support in all your decisions that you have always found in Margarita, your wife, who is always so beautiful and funny, and the great luck that you both had, having found a good steward just a few months before, Antonio, that he was giving you good ideas and unburdening you from a lot of work. Now all that should have been put in the past....

My cousin seemed different and I was happy for him and for everyone. When I later told that conversation to Teresa, my cousin and especially my close friend since childhood, whom I saw every day, even if it was only for an hour, she also saw it as a good sign. Perhaps, we both commented that day, finally at thirty-four years of age Juan Carlos was going to give himself free rein, he was going to forget his shyness and develop all the great potential that he had always had.

My gaze went to my cousin, but before reaching her it settled for a moment on Margarita, the widow, and through the veil I saw her smiling. Perhaps the emotion of the moment was playing tricks on me, so I lowered my eyes and when I looked back, her eyes were closed and she was clasping her hands in what seemed like great pain. But I couldn't keep looking. The priest called us up to the altar to receive the condolences.

AMA JUSTA, Teresa's nurse

Pulvis es et in pulverem reverteris. Oremus.

Mother of Perpetual Help, Virgins of Heavun and All Saints of the heav'ly court! How has happened this tragedy? What will happens with my child now? Because the old lady already has many deaths on her and knows what that is, but my girl? My girl only had that about Doña Tomasa, and the pour soul died of pure old in her bed while she was sleeping, which is not a bad way to go, if we look right, but this, this doesn't make any sense to me. Jeez, and I say, even if no one asks me, Jeez, why did Juan Carlos have to go to that farm? Because what he really, really liked was hang out all day with those fat books in his lieberry... That whole farm thing was from her, the Margalita that has evybody drooling not me I don't swallow it, she's some happy sinner, jeez what a diff'ence with my girl, someone like her had to look for Juan Carlos, the one he married a lot of big shot and a lot of stories but not what he needed, look at her there she is laughing, she oughta be ashamed, his body still warm. But I don't care about that, lightning can split her, my girl is the one that worries me, my Teresita, she sucked on my breasts and I know her more than if I borned her, and with another pregnancy on top, that Jorge seems not to stop at night... Oh my girl of my soul! Oh my Teresa of my heart! My poor little dear, so stuck together with Juan Carlos, two kids who got along better and loved each other has not been seen in the world... How will you stand it, what a blow, my child... Oh dear mother of heavun! May God take us confessed!

PILUCA, cousin

Pulvis es et in pulverem reverteris. Oremus.

This is not the time to think about it and even less to say it aloud, not even to myself, but deep down I never liked Margarita, with so much ease and freshness and with those international airs that she used to put on, but I do have to admit that she is pretty and she is really nice, and when you are by her side you laugh and laugh, she will put you in her pocket, even if you don't want to.

When Teresa and I met her, she had just arrived from Argentina, and the truth is, although neither my cousin nor I were what they call "yokels," or small-town women, and we had traveled and lived in different cities, the truth is that Teresa, as well as I, were the typical ladies from the provinces, and Margarita was different, she had a totally different way of seeing things from us and from the rest of our friends, and she acted with a naturalness that always made us think she was not natural. We have always been judgmental.

And when she married my cousin, I still didn't like her, and I don't think Teresa did either, but she adores her brother and it would seem to her that if he had chosen her, he would have good reasons, and my cousin is so polite and discreet that she would never make a negative comment about her sister-in-law, even though she thought it. Not even to me, and look, there are no secrets between us, but I suppose it is a matter of tact and delicacy and she has plenty of that, so even though we both have seen life in a different way, we have tried, in a tacit agreement, to ignore things about her that did not seem very appropriate, and I also have to admit that Margarita with her glibness, her impudence and her funny jokes, has always continued to wrap us in her web.

And now we are here, praying for the soul of her husband, my dear cousin, who has been another brother to me. What I don't know is how my relationship with Margarita is going to be from today on, since we will no longer have the link that we have had until today and without Juan Carlos in between, I don't know, I don't know. She is not the kind of friend I would ever choose.

I look at the pew where she is, and through the veil it seems to me that I see her smile.

It's not possible. Perhaps she has taken a pill so that her nerves do not play tricks on her, because what we have experienced in recent days has been a nightmare.

I look again.

She is sitting with her head down and I don't see her features.

And I have to go over to comfort my cousin and my aunt and walk them home. Today another torture begins for them. All of us who loved you, and there are many of us, will miss you, Juan Carlos. Rest in peace.

MANOLO, friend and dentist
Pulvis es et in pulverem reverteris. Oremus.

I have no words to express the horror that Jorge and I encountered that black day, Juan Carlos. How did it happen? You, always so rational, with your immense knowledge of everything, maybe you could explain it to me, because I don't see any meaning in your death, with all the meaning that your life had. Those who were there that awful day pointed us towards the Maquis. But against you? All of us who knew you knew that you were incapable of hurting anyone, not even those who had hurt you... You didn't even have disgruntled laborers, you were not a prey for the Maquis, yet it seems they were the ones who destroyed you. And I say it seems because neither Jorge nor I, the last of us to see you, believe it. In your murder a lot is obscure... In the terror of the act, whoever pulled the trigger, at least they have not taken your wife, your passion and your life, but is she smiling now? I think I'd better continue praying because with what has happened my mind seems to be raving...

JULIANA, Teresa's cook
Pulvis es et in pulverem reverteris. Oremus.
The radiu say there's lots, but lots of those manquis runnin round, that there are many, but many of those manquis loose in the fields, let's see if nothin happens to my parents and my sisters in the Vin'ards. And my lady, who don't raise her head since it happened. The Don Jorge also's like a dyin coal that don't eat, and what that man enjoys eatin ... and Doña Edelmira what'll it end up, oh Jeez what she's gone through.... But the one who really matters to me is my señorita, who with the preg'ancy and the roomtisum was not well, and now this great tradjdy.... And look you, there is the Marg'rita as if she ain't in this dance, dint I seen her laughinA behind the veil she put on... any day she's givin us a surprise, and if not, sometime...

ANTONIO, administrator
Pulvis es et in pulverem reverteris. Oremus.

Some days! And now this endless funeral. The priest has spent hours praising the excellences of the deceased. What does he know? I say... as if so much prayer and so much crying could serve to bring him to life, what a bore... and the body's not even here. This all really bugs me but I had no choice... come and endure and here I am, I am the hacienda's steward and if I had not come they would have all jumped on me and criticized me and looked askance at me. I don't care about that, but Margarita always says that you have to keep up appearances... Anyway, I hope this ends soon and every gopher goes back to his hole and the storm dies down.

EMILIO MARQUEZ, friend

Pulvis es et in pulverem reverteris. Oremus.

Despite the fact that every day, from the moment I learned of the terrible misfortune, I try to remind myself that Juan Carlos is dead and that nothing and no one is going to give him back to us, I can't get used to the idea. It is something so terrible that I have not slept or even closed my eyes all these nights. How could something like this have happened? I don't understand it and I don't think I'll ever understand it. And all the years that we have shared crowd around me as if they were one day. Because we were friends since childhood, forever, and I don't have many memories in which Juan Carlos doesn't appear. At four years, at seven, at eleven, at eighteen... always friends, truly and from the heart. So many memories, so much affection... Even in his years at Escorial we did not separate, because during the course we exchanged long letters and as soon as we had holidays we enjoyed the free time in Turgalium or on the beaches of Portugal, where our families used to spend the summer together. Not even when he got married was our union undone, because a person who is closer to his friends like he was cannot be found. How can I believe that I will never see you again, my dear companion of games and of so many adventures? Do you remember the day we bet on a dinner at La Cumbre to see who would kill the most doves? We were tied and then you purposely missed a shot to let me win... always so considerate in all your acts... And the filthy coots, which you thought were ducks and I believed they were fish until the old guy who looked after the garden of the Marquesa undeceived us and told us they were some kind of hens? Do you remember that day in La Albuera, when we decided to hunt a few coots and not only did we not kill any, but those that were there showered us with bird shit? And how we laughed and laughed while returning home, stinking, our clothes soaked with their excrement, and our heads too. Do you remember the first time I got drunk and how you kept my parents from knowing? And that time in Figueira when we were going after some girls and we got lost? I could remind you of more than a thousand episodes and that would not cover all of them. Juan Carlos, what happened makes no sense, and you are not here to explain it to me as you always did when I did not understand something. Who am I going to consult now? We all loved you and we shall always love you. How could you have gone like this, in this hard way? What will become of your dear Margarita now? Haven't you thought about that? There she is now, listening to the prayers of the priest, but look! It seems to me that she is smiling... I must be hallucinating, may God forgive me for believing such a thing.... Friend, we still have many things pending to do together, and the first of them we do will be to hunt down those nasty coots ... Go prepare your shotgun while I go meet you. And rest always in peace.

DON ROSENDO, father-in-law

Pulvis es et in pulverem reverteris. Oremus.

What a nightmare! It's hard to believe what is happening. How this has happened? Is it fair that now that the damn war is over, we have to keep protecting ourselves so that these vermin don't kill us? It seems that yes, there is no escape from their hatred and their evil, but Juan Carlos? This has neither head nor tail, because this boy not only has never hurt anyone, never, and when I say never I can say it very loudly so that everyone can hear me, and although by family and training his tendencies were conservative, due to his great intellectual training he has listened, if necessary and the occasion presented itself, to the opinions and point of view of those of the opposite side. If I have to define him with a single word, I would say of him that he is fair. When he fell in love with Margarita, from the first time she brought him home, for me that was a holiday, because she is my daughter, I love her very much, but I admit that perhaps we have all spoiled her too much and she has come out a little frivolous. Of course not succumbing to her graces was difficult, but perhaps I should have been a more severe father, I don't know and today it's difficult to think, my head is spinning, that's why I think it was a blessing from heaven that Juan Carlos fell so madly in love with her; because a better person, better suitor was hard to find. He has (or had, and it is very hard for me to have to speak already in the past tense of my beloved son-in-law) everything that any woman could wish for: tall and good-looking, elegant, exquisite education and manners, great knowledge and intellectual training, money, gentle and sensible, much loved by all those around him, you couldn't fault him. Perhaps only one: he was too much in love with his wife, my daughter, with whom I don't know what will happen now, because as I said, she has very frivolous and crazy tendencies and has little brain. Her husband was the perfect counterpoint, and although I myself have witnessed how he always gave in and bowed to the nonsense and absurdities that Margarita sometimes proposed, I also knew that when it came to something serious, or a great crisis, she would accept his criteria, because she is not stupid; crazy, empty-headed and irresponsible yes, and it is difficult for me to recognize these traits because she is my most beloved daughter, but her head is full of insubstantial things and she hasn't changed over the years... Oh my God, what will become of her now without that retaining wall that was her husband? It scares me to think about it, there she is and it seems that she is smiling. Is it possible? I do not think that her stupidity goes that far, my eyesight is deceiving me... I have to go up front now in order to receive all those who are accompanying us today and offering their condolences. Goodbye, dear Juan Carlos, I have loved you like my own children. Rest in peace.

LOLA, Margarita's sister
Pulvis es et in pulverem reverteris. Oremus.

Oh! Poor guy, what bad luck, what happened to him... What a horrible and foolish thing, to die now, as young as he was. Anyway, this life is very strange and you never know what will come the next moment. We'll see how Margarita accepts the whole thing, now that it seemed that she had focused a little and that she was more sensible, because my sister is a charm, but totally spoiled and capricious... We are the ones to blame, what can I say? But it was very difficult to deny her anything, with that likability that she has and that good humor that removes all sorrows. Thinking of sorrows, poor Juan Carlos, such a wonderful, polite and charming guy. Since we met him the whole family were delighted with him and he was the perfect counterpoint for her, although later we saw that he also spoiled her in everything and more. What a shame, poor guy.... There she is now, surrounded by all of us, look, she seems to be smiling.... Is it possible she could be so crazy? I must be dreaming, let's see I'll look back again... she's definitely smiling.... For God's sake, what is going through that head so that she can't behave even at a time like this? I'm ashamed. I'm going to look again: now she's serious, her lips pursed. I was wrong. This affair is not for laughter or smiles. Poor guy.

The MARQUEZES, friends of the family
Pulvis es et in pulverem reverteris. Oremus.

Julia: Even though we are in church, I can't stop talking, Carmen. I cannot. This is beyond me, and if I'm like this, can you imagine for a moment how it must be for Teresa and Edelmira and the rest of the family? I don't want to comment on Margarita, because a while ago I saw her smiling, well, each one reacts to death in a different way and we already know that she is very particular, not like us... and Juan Carlos always so in love and crazy about her, I have not seen more different characters in my life, no one can deny that, nor that she is very animated, but what I do know is that she is too much of a shock, very different from the rest of her family, very different, Carmen, when we were with them we saw that, but she, you know, always with her dances, with her costumes and with her jokes. A stupid head, if you want my opinion, let's see now how she deals with this drama, if she will stop her nonsense and settle down a bit, because Carmen, as far as economics goes, there are no problems, Juan Carlos had everything well arranged and she, on her own, has the Operetta, but I don't trust her at all and maybe any one of these days she will get involved with someone, and if something like that happens it would be a kick in the ass for this family, Carmen, that you know the same as I how they are, better and finer people are difficult to find in the whole world, and we both know very well, although we have never commented on it, that the same on the part of Edelmira as for our parents, if Juan Carlos had decided for one of us the two families would have welcomed his decision with great pleasure, but that is beside the point and getting into another topic, since he fell in love with her from the first moment he saw her, I am talking for the sake of talking, Carmen, but now he's gone; we just must think of the many and such good memories and all the time we spent together. And our brothers I don't know how they are going to handle it, with how close the three have always been, because Juan Carlos, despite having his three intimate friends from El Escorial, has never, but never ever, neglected them, Carmen, and you know it, and he was really close to his lifelong friends, I mean his cousins and our brothers. It will be very difficult to be without him; such a great loss, a man in the prime of life as they always say, but which in this case is true, Carmen, my head is like a drum, it is too much pain and too much pain that I feel and we do not even have his body ....

Carmen: Shut up, don't talk anymore and pray.

PACO, his close friend
Pulvis es et in pulverem reverteris. Oremus.
A little over a month ago, when Miguel Hernandez died of tuberculosis in the Alicante jail, you came to see me at work, and although neither of us shared his political ideas, we did admire his poetry a lot, and right there, in unison, we recited his Elegy to Ramón Sijé, alternating our voices each triplet and both almost ending in tears, for different reasons; it seemed such a beautiful poem, so beautiful... but now I will not be able to read it again or recite it without associating it with you, without your beloved image juxtaposed, soul mate, my companion... my friend and faithful companion for eight years, sharing so many happy hours spent together every day, when we were interns in Escorial, so many experiences, so much complicity.

We studied and lived, and not even the political maelstrom of those years prevented our accumulating knowledge that would help us navigate through life, which we had expected to be long, but now "A hard slap, an icy blow, an unseen killer's ax, a brutal push has struck you low." Do you remember when I recited those words? We both got a lump in our throats, although as we didn't want to look soft and tried to hide it. But now I don't have to hide anything. You have left and your murderer has killed not only you, he has also taken a part of my life, perhaps the most human, and nothing will ever be as it was, but I am asking you for an appointment, do not fail me, we still have many things to talk about, soul mate, buddy.

JOSETXU, friend and fellow student
Pulvis es et in pulverem reverteris. Oremus.
This is not like you, Juan Carlos. Hadn't we arranged for the four of us to meet next week? You have always been formal with your commitments and now you can no longer keep that last appointment. What happened? How did you, always so

careful, allow this to happen? I do not understand, I do not understand anything, but a phrase is trying to break through my sleepy mind: you are gone forever, you are gone and we can never experience things together, or relive our adventures, which have been many. Do you remember when you and Paco took us on that "initiation" trip? Can you still remember the long hours we spent talking about our favorite painters? The intellectual discussions we had? We were the "drudges quartet" and we did not care if they called us that, on the contrary, it seemed almost an honor to us, and when in the first years some of the older guys asked us for help because they could not solve something, you and we were all there to give it to them, but you were always the first, without hesitation or doubts... I do not understand your death, this death so early. Why have you left like this, without even warning? The year you got married, and you, as the oldest of the four, did it the first, when we met for the ceremony we agreed that the change of status was not going to undermine our union, and the pact was to meet several times a year to be able to continue talking about everything, continue to fix the world with our salon philosophies... then the war came for three long years and we could not do as planned, but the lack of physical presence did not lessen our relationship, did not dilute it, on the contrary, it was strengthened by the distance, and when at last we could see each other again, all alive, the four of us together, we quite believed that things would continue like that until the grim reaper claimed us in old age. For this we have overcome the horrors of war? Have all the miseries and deprivations, all the pain and loss been for nothing? You are gone, and even today you have not come here to say goodbye to us. Where are you, my friend? My heart cries so much for you, for your absence. Do you remember when we talked about how subjective pain is? How, even though you empathize with the pain of others, it is yours that really matters? I think of your poor mother, your sister, Margarita, the rest of the people who loved you, and I know that now their pain is great, but mine is immense, precisely because it is mine, and you are not here, as on other occasions when I was afflicted with grief, to help me with your words, to relieve me of so much suffering, my friend, my brother. None were like you and none will ever be... and I am so selfish that I don't even want you to rest in peace; what I want, what I wish with all my soul is that you were here, undead, not with a shattered head, that head that held so much wisdom and so much love towards your fellow men... I would like us to be at the funeral of another, of someone known but not such a dear person, I do not resign myself to saying goodbye, I want you to continue alive, and so you will be in my heart until we can meet again, and for the next appointment do not fail me, that will be the final one, where the four drudges will be reunited for ever to talk and laugh and share and we'll have all eternity to do it. *Agur, ¡Hurrengo arte!*

ADRIÀ, another intimate

Pulvis es et in pulverem reverteris. Oremus.

Dies Irae. The day of anger. Such a beautiful poem, with repetitive music that gets inside your skin, and reaches the most recondite place of the soul, that you taught us to appreciate. Now it sounds for you and I cannot stand it. I'm bleeding, although I have no injuries. I bleed for you, friend, partner, brother, the best of the best.... The Angel, with his trumpet, is calling the souls of those who have died. You did not have to be there yet, you did not have to be even close to the right hand of the Father, you had to be with me, with us... many more years, many, for we need you. Don't listen to the trumpet that calls you, turn around and come back. It is not an appointment that you have to keep yet. Let a few years go by. When your hair becomes gray, when your body is overcome by age, when your sight and hearing fail you, when you are old, very old, follow the Angel, then it will be a joy to finally meet your parents, the heavenly and the earthly, whom you always adored despite the little time you had together. Do not do like your father, do not listen to the trumpet, disobey for once in your life, listen to me in that, do not listen to him. Return. Do you remember when you explained to us the panel of your favorite painting with the representation of Hell and the pain of the souls that were there? You would never fall there, that does not worry me, you have to be somewhere else, but not yet, wait. I keep hearing the music, but your body is not here. What if they have deceived us? Could it be that everything is a joke and that in a while you will appear smiling at us? It would not be your style, but I like the idea and I think I will tell Paco and Josetxu... but no, although my heart denies it, my reason forces me to accept the terrible reality.... *Recordare Iesu pie, ne me perdas ille die.*

Adéu amic, germà, if you finally decide to stay in heaven, find me a place by your side, *saps que molt t'estimo, adéu germà.*

12. JORGE - AUGUST 1942

Letter from Jorge to Marisa.

Turgalium, August 27, 1942

Dear sister and dear all,

Although I have already communicated to you by telegram the birth of our new son, in this letter I will give you more details.

Teresa is doing quite well, under the circumstances. She is still very sad about the death of Juan Carlos, but this month it seems that a respite has come, first with the birth of our child and a few days later with the news about all the maquis that were killed in Alía.

The boy, whom we have baptized with the name of his uncle, has some health problems; his little heart is not very strong and the doctor insists that we need to be very careful with all the ailments typical of babies, because a simple cold could degenerate into something serious. All of Teresa's suffering in these last three months may have been passed on to him, and this is a double cause of grief for her, although I insist that she must try to have positive thoughts always, and that now she needs to concentrate on raising Juan Carlos the best we possibly can.

But we both realize that this child is not like our precious Manuela: every day she is more and more beautiful and yesterday she was three years old. This little girl makes us happy every minute we spend with her; of course the circumstances now are not the same as when she was born, but we will have to be up to whatever comes next.

The boy is very weak, so much so that it seems that he does not even have the strength to cry, and he stays in his crib between feedings without moving. The little angel has not given us a bad night yet, although this, instead of giving us rest, worries us even more, in fact, we both spend the nights awake looking at him and checking that he is well; we will have to pray that little by little he gather strength.

Now I am taking advantage of these waking hours to write to you since during the day it is impossible for me to do so.

Marisa, when you came here with Carolina and your two children, Luisito and Demetrín, you met Juan Carlos and were able to see first-hand what an extraordinary person he was, the great culture he possessed, how fine and exquisitely he always behaved and already then we commented on how much you liked him. You did not have the same opinion of Margarita, although we tried to explain to you that despite being so open and outgoing, she is not a bad person, but that her character is, or I would say better was, very different. Now I am remembering the word you used all the time to refer to her, "party girl"... Carolina is not as clever as you are (as you have always caught on the fly the real essence of the people you met), and she found her funny, charming and very generous, things that are true, although it is also true that the one who was really generous was Juan Carlos. They always say that when someone leaves for eternity, all that is said about such a person is nothing but praise, but in this specific case his praise is the truth, I can attest to that.

From the day I met him, and later when I got into a relationship with Teresa, he "adopted" me, and everything his became mine too: his extensive knowledge, his humanity, his home, his immense library, everything.... Even his wine cellar, and note that he had it well stocked even though he was not a drinker; Juan Carlos was a fabulous being, one of those who are not easily found, with clear ideas, great intelligence, magnificent training and, above all, a good man who added to all his virtues the great simplicity with which he acted at all times of his life. If I tell you that I miss him very much, you, the person who knows me like no one else, you will know to what extent I am suffering. He has been family, but the most important thing is that he has been a friend, a great friend who has guided me on many occasions with wise advice and there we see the difference in age, and how different our training was, because he had the enormous luck of studying for eight years in one of the best centers in Spain, if not the best, and had lived in a refined and very privileged environment and I, on the contrary, had to leave my degree, and start working very young in order to have a secure post (as mother wanted for all of us), and then the war came and altered all the initial plans. I know that you will not read these last comments as a complaint, because they are not; at twenty-six years old I am very content and happy with the family that I have formed, and given how the outlook is, having a secure job is a bargain, a Godsend, and also now I supplement my salary by giving classes in mathematics, physics and chemistry, and I have more students than I can accept; I simply confirm the fact of how fortunate I have been to have had the privilege of meeting him and enjoying these years of his friendship and affection.

A while ago, looking at the calendar, I saw that in a few weeks we must begin the harvest in the Vineyards and will you believe, dear sister, that I have started to tremble? The idea that he won't be with me this year was a thought that has struck me, and I suddenly felt his absence as happens to me so many times when I go to do something which I used to do with him, as in this particular case that I am telling you about, because even with the war already started in the fall of '36, I had my first experience as a "landed squire" so to speak. I had never seen a grape harvest. To my understanding there were grapes that were eaten, fresh or as raisins, and there was wine that was drunk. That is as far as my knowledge went. When I accompanied him that first time he patiently and carefully explained the whole harvest ritual to me, and I saw the whole process that begins with a lively team of women, the grape harvesters, who go vine by vine cutting the bunches of grapes until their baskets are full, taking good care to do it in specific areas and not to mix the white grapes with the black ones, since the former will give white wine and the black ones red wine. With the baskets brimming full, they return to the winepress and empty them into a large basket that hangs from a Roman balance and record the weight; from there to the granite basin, the Lagareta, where a couple of peasants tread the grapes and squeeze them until all the juice is extracted, and later it is emptied into large clay urns, the *tinajonas*, and then begins the production of the wine itself. He even made me step on grapes! I thought I was going to be disgusted or repelled, but it was a very pleasant feeling, and for someone raised in an urban environment as I was, a unique experience, which has already become an annual appointment; and even the guardian, "uncle Joaquín," as soon as he saw us appear, said: "Don Jorge, shake a leg, the grapes are waiting for you." I don't think I can go this year, everything is too recent....

And what I'm telling you is just one example of the thousands that I could quote you. It has been a terrible and tragic loss and it is hard not to think about his absence.

What can I tell you about Margarita? She is taking the whole thing quite calmly in my opinion, and the last thing she told us is that she wants to go live on her hacienda, that she feels suffocating and drowning down here. Teresa gets chills when we talk about it. She cannot understand, and neither can I, if you ask me, how she can even think of being there again, the scene of such a terrible tragedy and a place where Juan Carlos was so happy; but that is one of the many strange things that I cannot get out of my mind.

I don't know if you have read about the maquis in the newspapers. Here it has been all the talk, and in our family in particular a reason for rest, since according to all indications one of them would be the one who murdered Juan Carlos.

As we already told you when you came, many of them are entrenched in Extremadura, a poor land of rich landowners, latifundistas par excellence, and in the Sierra de Guadalupe there are many little chiefs, who with the aid and help of the neighbors of the towns in the area continue to commit crimes, shielding behind the theory that the government we now have is illegitimate. When the war broke out, many of those towns were ruled by the Republicans and the repression has been strong, very strong. In the case of Alía, the civil guard shot twenty-four members of the maquis in front of the entire town in a rapid and extrajudicial execution, since those of the *Benemérita* feared that if they were imprisoned and all the legal machinery had to start up there would be more problems. As a corporal put it to me: "When the dog is dead, so is it's madness...."

You know me almost better than anyone, and you know that I have always been a peaceful person who does not like violence, and that when I met my brother-in-law I adopted his theory of "live and let live," but in this specific case it is possible that justice has been done, although not in the right way, and that some have paid for terrible actions that others have committed, because I'm not sure that certain episodes that have been attributed to them have been carried out by them, but if you can find one or some guilty of something, it is simple and even human to add charges that others have done. The sad thing, in our particular case, is that killing a few, or all of them, is not going to give Juan Carlos back to us, and that is a fact. If any of those undesirables committed the vileness of murdering him in cold blood, when he was sleeping and without any possibility of defense, it would be a comfort to know that his murderer has paid in the same coin, but I have my doubts, which every day increase more and more, whether it was really the maquis who did it. It is not a topic to discuss in a letter, it is something so macabre that just the idea makes me nauseous, but it has been on my mind for months. There are many things that do not fit, and although you know that I am very rational and generally do not get carried away by hunches, in this matter if I follow my instinct something tells me that we do not know, and perhaps we will never know, what happened that fateful day, nor what is still happening, because there are so many loose pieces in this puzzle that I have not yet been able to unravel its meaning. As you can understand, I cannot comment on any of those thoughts with Teresa, or with her mother, they have enough to cope with, but I have spoken about my theories with cousin Sebastián as well as with our good friend Manolo, the dentist, and with Emilio Márquez, whom you met on your trip, sensible and discreet people who will not gossip, and the three of them (especially Manolo who was with me in the removal of the corpse), agree with what I think, but as I was saying, it is not a topic for a letter or for the phone, although I would like to talk about it in depth with Demetrio and with you. I hope you can repeat the visit soon. It would be a good idea for you to be here with us in these difficult times, and having you nearby would lift Teresa's spirits a lot. Let's see if Demetrio can fix his affairs in the ministry and get a free fortnight. Being with the family is very important and here you know that food you will not lack, although we are also a bit at the mercy of rationing and black-marketeers, but nothing compared to Madrid.

I'll keep you up to date with what's happening in our little world. Let's hope that Margarita gives up her plan, which I insist seems crazy to us, although she affirms that there is no longer any danger as they've killed the criminals in the area, but I imagine that there will still be many on the loose. Her father, a very sensible gentleman, I suppose will go with her and will not leave her alone if she continues with the stubborn plan of moving, or if not, her sisters, with whom she has always been very close. Time will tell us.

Now I have to leave you, the little one has woken up. Do not stop sending us news, give the children a kiss from their uncles, aunts, and cousins, and you receive all our love.

Your brother,

Jorge

13. TERESA - DECEMBER 1942

Letter from Teresa to the Márquez sisters.

Turgalium, December 23, 1942

Dear Julia and Carmen,

I have just seen your brother Emilio and he has told me that you will not return for Christmas because you continue to be engaged with your mother's doctors' appointments and traveling with her now is not the most advisable thing to do. Not having you around is another sorrow for me to add to this year, which as you well know has been appalling.

It started so well that I thought it would be perfect, enjoying the girl, carrying the pregnancy with enthusiasm, although with my own discomfort, but you already know how much Jorge and I like children, and being able to start forming a large family has been from the beginning our fond hope and intention.

But then in May came the blow. I still can't believe that my dear Juan Carlos has left us forever, and many times when I'm doing something I say to myself: "I have to tell him this afternoon," "Let's see what my brother thinks about this, it's so funny he will laugh for hours" and so on with whatever is happening. Because the reality is so overwhelming that I imagine it will be a long time before I accept it, if that moment ever comes.

My mother, as you know, is crazy with pain. There have been too many deaths that she has had to go through in her life, and thank goodness I have managed to get her to talk about it, because some days I have feared that she also would leave us. She refused to go out, and you know very well how much she likes her morning excursions to convents and churches; she refused to eat, and although she has always been very spartan, the way she was this season was already reaching tremendous limits, she did not even take care of her beloved cats, to the point that I had to take care of the poor animals, with the little that I like them, but necessity forces. Gradually it seems that we were pulling her out of the hole and when my child was born she suggested naming him after my brother, something to which we delightedly agreed.

But the baby came with many problems and Jorge has already told you the outcome. With only four months the little angel has also left us. It has been a terrible blow for everyone; even the girl keeps asking me where he is and already it's been almost a week. I don't know how I am, if I tell you the truth. I wake up like an automaton, because I have no choice, and I am sleepwalking all day. My child has also left, as did my brother, and the pain we have is so immense, the pain so great that I don't know what will happen to us. Jorge is feeling the same way, but since he has to work and see people, he bites the bullet when he is at the office, although when he gets home he collapses, and even as he tries not to mention anything so as not to burden me even more, as soon as he thinks I am not looking at him, I see him cleaning his glasses that have been misted by tears. I do not want to repeat, but we are broken.

In addition, the last month of our little one's life has been exhausting: we did not sleep, we did not eat, we could do nothing but be with him every minute of the day, vainly waiting for the miracle to occur and he would carry on. I have spent hours on my knees, asking God to let us have him, imploring for his life, but you can see that this year the Lord has decided to leave us on our own, and you can see how we are doing... without having been able to recover from Juan Carlos's death this has been the last straw. You know how Jorge and my brother fit in from the beginning. The two, rather bland in character, as soon as they were together, it seemed somebody had wound them up and they came to life.... More than one night I have gone to bed at two o'clock, tired of waiting for them to finish talking and talking about the divine and the human. The two shared many hobbies, and things that my husband had not had the opportunity to do, such as hunting, my brother taught him as if he were a teacher guiding his disciple. Do you remember the joy Jorge got when Juan Carlos gave him his first shotgun? He looked like a child on Three Kings Day.... And when that day in Las Viñas he killed his first partridge? I don't think he wanted us to eat it, maybe we should have let them desiccate it, but then Juan Carlos and he gave a good account when we served it with some potatoes.... So many memories and so many happy moments and now you see everything is all in the past. We can never make more shared stories to tell when we grow old. What a blow and what anguish, my God, there are times when it seems to me that even my faith fails, I try to be strong because my mother needs me, Manuela needs me, Jorge needs me, and I need them and I need my two, my two Juan Carloses, but I can't even say it out loud so as not to burden them more.

And just in case we didn't have enough, Margarita finally went to live on the hacienda, as she had been saying for a long time that she was going to do. I don't even know how she can be there, and sleep in the same room after what happened in that room. Look, I loved La Operetta and the good times we had there, but after the tragedy, not even a million dollars would drag me there. Just thinking about whether my brother woke up and found himself face to face with his murderer I tremble, although Jorge has told us in every imaginable way that when he was killed he was asleep. What vileness and what terror.

We tried to convince Margarita in every possible way not to go, but once they caught that gang of soulless people from the maquis and executed them, she said that she felt safe, that the environment here gave her a lot of stress, that each person and each object makes her remember her husband and that she couldn't take it anymore.

I miss her a lot because, even with all the suffering and pain she has, sometimes she returns to her old self and distracts me for a moment, but I also understand that she wants to be closer to her blood family, although you already know that I have always considered her as the sister I did not have. Another loss, and they add up to three in this difficult year.

Jorge is not convinced that it was someone from the Maquis who killed Juan Carlos. Not many things fit for him, but with me he does not want to talk about the matter. Just yesterday he was whispering in a low voice with my cousin Sebastián, and as soon as he saw that I entered the room, he changed the subject. It is not the first time that has happened and when I have asked my cousin about it before, the only thing he answers is: "your husband is very intelligent," which I already know, but that does not clarify anything about the secrets that are going on, in short, each one of us has a way of bearing pain and dragging along our miseries.

My dear friends, this holiday will not be like others. Nothing will ever be the same after this year. Our double mourning does not allow us even to think about the birth of the Christ-child, but we have to move on for Manuela. The girl cannot grow up in such a sad environment, or see me cry every moment because, even though we think they don't know, children are very insightful and understand everything.

We can only pray and ask the Most High in heaven that His will be done always. Jorge is, I wouldn't say fine, but given the circumstances he is holding up, and he sends you many greetings. Give my regards to your whole family, a big hug to your mother, and you two receive my sincere love as always, while I hope we can see each other again soon.

Your longtime friend who misses you so much:

Teresa

EPILOGUE
14. MARGARITA - AUTUMN 1967

Who could have told me that suddenly, at my age, I was going to fall in love for the first time in my life like a fifteen-year-old? No one, not even myself, would have believed it if someone had told me.

But that's the way it was and now I'm not going to deny it, because the most certain thing is that soon I will have to give an account and it is better not to contradict the evidence.

Because men fell in love with me, but I didn't.

I have always had a way of being liked, not only by men, but also by women, and by that I do not mean that I was a target for dykes, no, what I mean is that as soon as I spent a while talking to some woman, even one of those serious, pious ones, I immediately noticed that I put them in my pocket, that they were going to accept my opinions, sometimes so different from theirs, and that they went from not knowing me at all to wanting to be my friends for whatever.

With men it was even easier, perhaps because what they like is to have a good looker next to them, attractive, friendly, who can distract them from whatever they have on their mind and, at the same time, does not bother them. That is why the one with the most and the one with the least, as soon as he can, takes a mistress with whom the only obligation he has is to pay, take care of her expenses and she will be always there, at his disposal for whatever he pleases, without obligations nor ties as happens with the legitimate ones, which generally involves much more onerous disbursements, and from which on many occasions they get nothing more than complaints, regrets and negatives.

I have always been very likable, very out-going, pretty and to top it off smart and sharp; perhaps I could not be classified as very intelligent for serious studies, but I have caught onto what was around me instantly and I have overcome obstacles without problems, and look, I have had to live in difficult times, in which there have been wars, epidemics and misery, because as I always say when I get serious, in each generation there is always at least one catastrophe of the great ones. If you live long, you will have several, and that has been the case and will always continue to be whether we like it or not, and if not, look a bit to history and do numbers.

But to tell the truth, none of those calamities have touched me seriously. In the Great War I was too young to even know that there was one, and even if I had been older, everything that was happening was very far away and had nothing to do with my life. With what they called the Spanish flu that devastated the whole world, ditto of the same — it did not touch anyone in my family. When the civil war came, we spent it in a city that was not occupied, we had enough food and our life, although it changed a little because we did not have parties or entertainment and we sometimes thought of those who did not have what we did, we went on. Our war ended, although I never thought of it as mine, and another World War came, but our country was left out because the one we had experienced was very recent, and it did not affect me at all.

Well, I keep confessing, although without a priest by my side, I have never liked prayers and religions, even if for many years I have had to put on an act, do theater, especially in front of Juan Carlos's family, who are all very self-righteous. Jorge is the only one who seems to me to deviate a bit from that line, but he was so involved with all of them that it looks to me that he did a bit as I did, and he followed the flow so as not to have questions or problems, but the thing is as I say, you never know what is inside a person, you do not even know who you have next to you day by day, and then surprises come to you.

About my childhood and adolescence I can only sing and tell wonders. We lived in a small city, with everything at hand and without missing anything. My parents were always in a very good financial position and they gave us everything we needed and more.

Being the youngest of the siblings and with years of difference with all of them, I was always the doll and the object of all the pampering and cuddling, not only when I was a child but all my life. I was pardoned for everything from babyish antics to rudeness when I was no longer so youthful, and there was nothing I craved that I didn't get right away.

And that's what I said before: everyone loved my charm and my agreeability. Even my father, a quite serious man of few words, made exceptions for me and liked me to tell him what I was doing and what I was not doing, and although sometimes I knew that he did not agree with my ideas, more liberal and modern than his, he allowed me things that my brothers and sisters were forbidden.

And with my mother it was the same. If someone tried to say something against me, and I say tried, she would jump like a tiger defending its cub. That has been my pain, when she left us forever, because I could still have had her with me for many years, but they say that the good ones leave first, and I cried for my mother as I had never done before, and it is possible never after. There were many occasions when I needed her and I would have wanted with all my soul to have her close. I had genuine sorrow for her and it was a long time until I got over her loss.

Despite being born and growing up in a small town, I knew many large cities in Spain and spent long periods of time in Madrid, summers in San Sebastián, or on the beaches of

Portugal. I made many excursions around the region with my sisters or my friends, we moved a lot and everywhere I went I always knew how to get friends right away.

And suitors.

Because that was another thing, I had them like blowflies since I was fourteen years old, and since then I had to put up with the eternal promises of love, the compliments, the letters and poems that the most enlightened people wrote me, and the gifts of flowers, chocolates and trinkets that all of them gave to me, while I tried to be friends with everyone but without committing myself to anyone, because I liked to have fun — but from there to a serious commitment there were miles, leagues and furlongs, and I wanted to continue having my freedom, which is worth more than all the millions in the world.

I debuted in a beautiful party in Madrid. There were six of us who did it at the same time and, although all of them were beautiful, that day I stood out as the best of the group. My white silk suit, simple but very elegant, clung to my body like a second skin, because my dressmaker knew every curve of my body and in her creations she always highlighted what suited me the most. As I knew that I am not nor have I ever been given to unnecessary adornments, that I have always liked pure and simple lines better, what she sewed that day she made absolutely perfect... We got a beautiful silk, with an incredible drape and as soon as the dressmaker saw it, she imagined the model she would make: something very simple, with long sleeves to the wrists, tight at the waist, bust and hips, and from there some almost hidden folds that would allow me to move and dance without problems. Between the two of us we decided that the front would not have a plunging neckline, reserving this for the back, with an opening on the back down to my waist, that did not show anything but hinted at everything, and the hem instead of reaching the floor and covering the shoes, ended a little below the half leg, something daring but that allowed me to show off my ankles and the beautiful sandals my uncle and aunt had sent me from Argentina, medium-heeled, silver and with buckles in which small crystals adorned the closure, and matching with a small bag that they had also given me.

To complete the outfit, she made me a small lace toreador jacket, purely decorative since if it had been cold it would not have kept me from freezing, which afterward I have used on countless occasions and have always been very fond of.

My usual hairdresser made me a low bun, without combs or other ornaments, because, although my hair has always been very abundant, and at that time it reached my waist, it was not suitable to wear it loose on that occasion, and despite the fact that the bun was very austere, or perhaps because of that, the face and eyes stood out more.

My eyes, just like my mother's, are the best thing I have: they are of a changing green depending on the time of day or mood, bright and expressive and I don't even need to paint them because my eyelashes are very black and thick and they are the perfect setting to highlight them.

My sisters inherit the noses of my mother's side: thin but aquiline that make their profile ugly, but mine resembles my father's and is straight and small, well formed and without lumps or protrusions anywhere, so I was lucky and didn't have to be one of those big snouts.

My mouth is normal, neither big nor small, with thin lips, but with very good shape. Sometimes I would have liked to have them a little fuller, but with a brush and a lipstick I make them fat when the occasion calls for it and for better luck I have very white, healthy and well aligned teeth, smiling or laughing has always been a good weapon with which to attack any situation.

I don't complain about my figure either, not even now that the years are leaving their mark, because since I have liked to walk all my life, no fat has been deposited in undesirable places, and although sometimes I was a little too thin for the prevailing tastes, I have always preferred it to looking like a balloon or feel swollen, like others.

That is to say, summarizing the particulars of the physical: I am and have always been one of those few lucky people who have felt happy with myself, and I have not pestered others or complained about whether I would like to be taller, or more blonde, or less this or more that. Living and living happily is what has always moved me, the physical aspect has been given to me and as such I accept it.

The coming-out was a complete success. That night, in addition to opening the doors to future dances and parties, I met many important and interesting people.

The father of one of the *debutantes* had a great position in the Government of the nation, the father of another was a General, one of those all loaded with medals, the third, was the owner of an important bank, the next would be the future Duchess of Bujio Blanco del Este, and the parents of the latter were the owners of half of Spain. The farms that they had in Extremadura and Andalusia could have supplied animals and cereals to the whole of Europe for many months, and then there was me, from a very good family, but in terms of possessions, titles, power or money they were not enough for the standards of my companions, and never will be.

My inclusion in that soirée was fortuitous, like most things that have happened to me all my life, because in a hunt that my older brothers had organized I met the one who later became the Duchess, a very fine and charming girl, who had been accompanying her father, sick with gout and who took advantage of the slightest excuse to skip the iron diet that he had to follow, and with whom I fit in from the first moment. We spent three days together, laughing at everything and everyone, talking about trifles and sometimes even serious things, and in one of those conversations it came out that she would be a *debutante* in a couple of months and she asked me if I had already done it, or when I would.

As I do not like to pretend what I am not (although some people have criticized me as false and accommodating), I told her the truth: I had not been introduced in society and I doubted that that would happen to me, because my mother, who was the one who came from a more illustrious family and therefore more given to social relations and the initiation rites proper to girls, was no longer among us, and I assumed my father did not have the slightest interest, and my sisters, since they had not had that ceremony, the most logical thing would be, they wouldn't promote any initiative in that regard, which had not crossed my mind either.

Lolin, which was my new friend's name, told me that it couldn't be, that she would fix everything from that moment, because I was definitely going to debut the same day as her and her friends, to leave everything in her hands. And I did.

The result was that when the hunt was over, everything was agreed: I would debut in society at the end of October at a party in the Ritz salons.

Lolin had convinced my father, sweet-talked my sisters, and they were all excited and delighted with the project. The only thing I had to do was agree, all that first phase was given to me.

But then came the madness. My sisters and I, along with the service, moved to Madrid, to an apartment that my father rented near the Museo Del Prado, and the three of us set out so that when the day came, everything would be perfect. I was only seventeen years old, but they were already reaching an age in which if they did not find a husband soon they would join the ranks of the dreaded spinsters, so the possibility of meeting many potential ones had them excited and they consented to everything, even to what I asked and asked them incessantly ... without problems.

I met the rest of the *debutantes*, we formed a wonderful crew and the experience would have been wonderful even without the debut, but with it was much more. The day was getting closer, but the six of us didn't even have time to get nervous. We went out in the morning, we walked in the afternoon and there was always a show to fill the nights. It was a great few weeks.

The scheduled date arrived. My father and my brothers had come from our town for that special occasion since it was the first time such a thing would happen in our family and we all, in our best regalia, headed to the Ritz.

My father, a tall and thin man, was very elegant in his tailcoat, patent leather shoes and a top hat that he had bought for the occasion. My brothers, acting as my sisters' escorts, not only did not detract from the group, but they elevated it and both my sisters, in flowing gauze dresses, one turquoise blue and the other green with small silver flowers embroidered on the skirt, were gorgeous. Our entire group was imposing in its beauty and elegance and the entrance into the little room, from which we would later enter the great ballroom, was triumphant.

The week before the event, my friends and I stopped our adventures a bit and focused on perfecting our waltzes, we got used to walking with little steps, smiling and behaving like real ladies, which we already knew but the reminder didn't hurt, so we were all prepared. And our parents and companions too.

But each one kept secret what her outfit was like, our confidences did not go that far, perhaps because deep down we were just a handful of big girls, who on the one hand were a little scared and on the other, even if it was unconsciously, wanted to outshine the rest.

My outfit was the simplest of all. Also the most beautiful and elegant.

When the six of us entered the room where the dance was to take place our mouths formed as if we were going to pronounce -Oh! The large and beautiful chandeliers in the ceiling illuminated everything, the French-style chairs upholstered in gold brocade were lined up around the huge room, and waiters in spotless uniforms passed through it, offering guests glasses of French champagne, small sandwiches, and endless appetizers. All very fine.

They introduced us, we attacked the initial waltz with our partners who, except in the case of Lolin, were our fathers, and from then on the night was a whirlwind of fun and pleasure.

And my two sisters met and found their future husbands. All perfect.

We stayed in Madrid for a few months that were perhaps the best of my life, my sisters consolidated their courtships, little by little they began to prepare their trousseaus and when spring came we returned to our town, each of us with thousands of projects in mind, and all happy with how things had developed.

Time passed and the moment of truth arrived: they were ending their maidenhood and leaving our family to start new ones.

My sisters decided to get married on the same day, and it seemed like a good idea to all of us because we had a lot of relatives abroad and that way made it easier for them.

It was a beautiful double ceremony with so many guests. There wasn't room for a pin in the Monastery and everything turned out perfect: the outfits, the food, the guests... My father, although he was sorry that his two older daughters wouldn't be with him anymore, was happy because the new members who had entered our family were impeccable, very fine boys, with good professions and a better future.

As the indirect cause of these marriages, I loved the idea of having two houses permanently open in Madrid, where I could go whenever I wanted and for no special reason, and so it was. I was also entering an age when I was no longer so young, so in the capital I would always find better game than in the town.

For the weddings, my aunt and uncle who lived in Argentina came and convinced my father to let me go with them to spend a long time there. At first he did not like to be suddenly without his three daughters, but together we convinced him and the matter was sealed: I would travel to Buenos Aires.

I didn't know much about geography, but I knew we did have to cross the Atlantic Ocean to get there, and since I wasn't going to go alone, I didn't worry about anything but my suitcases and having everything I needed for the trip and the stay.

The only condition set by my father was that my maid accompany me: despite the fact that the ticket price was very high, he preferred to make that disbursement than to let me be alone in an unknown country, although in reality, as I insisted, I wasn't going to be alone there since in addition to my uncle and aunt, all my cousins would be in the house, but in that particular he did not give in and later I was glad.

The three months that my uncle and aunt spent with us flew by, between hunts, excursions and various parties that everyone made in their honor, some welcoming and the most farewell parties, since they were very dear people and had not been among us for many years, and after Christmas and New Year's Eve celebrations and Reyes, almost without realizing it, the day of departure arrived.

We left on a steamboat from Lisbon. Up to there my father and my brothers had accompanied us and the three of them acted like it was the last time they would see me: they gave me more hugs than before in my whole life, but I was happy and calm because I knew it would be a marvelous adventure, as it indeed turned out.

The trip lasted nearly two months, although we did not have a single minute of boredom. The days flew by, every night there were parties, shows, music... the cabins were impeccable, the food better than I had ever eaten, we played tennis, long games of cards and although we did not make many ports until we reached the American continent, the sea did not play a trick on us and we could enjoy beautiful days, bathed in the sun, and spectacular nights in the double light of the moon, the one that was above and the one that was reflected in the water, with star-studded skies and balsamic air.

I met many people: Spaniards who returned to their adopted country, as happened in the case of my aunt and uncle, where they had made their fortune but longed for their homeland and had come to visit their relatives, Argentines who had taken the leap to meet the mother country, English, French, Germans... all very educated and very fine people, with whom spending so many hours was a real pleasure.

But after such a long journey, we also all waited impatiently for our arrival, and to be able to step on solid ground. Because that time on board, in a sense it was a bit unreal, it seemed like being in a bubble. The days of the week did not count, neither week-days nor week-ends, there everything was a party, a permanent vacation, and in the end many of the passengers yearned to return to their normality.

The night before disembarking, the party that the captain gave us was memorable and we danced, ate, drank and had fun until well into the wee hours and, accompanied by the swarm of suitors that followed me daily, I even shed a tear thinking I would not see them again, but they had obtained all the details and information about my uncle and aunt beforehand so that this eventuality did not occur.

We finally disembarked at the port of Buenos Aires, better equipped than the one we left in Lisbon and there, after all the boring customs procedures, the chauffeur of my relatives was waiting for us, and although we were loaded with trunks, suitcases and packages we settled in perfectly and we got home.

Their apartment (because that's what they call what we call a flat here) was beautiful, very spacious, bright and with many exterior windows, as well as a couple of large terraces, and it was located on Avenida Alvear, the most important street of the city, a street with a lot of life at all hours and with a lot of traffic. Although I had spent time in Madrid and other cities, I came from a town, where the number of vehicles was very small and the number of people as well, so I loved all that incessant traffic. Leaning out of a window or sitting on the terrace and watching the constant flow of people entering and leaving the stores was already entertainment. Not to speak of the cows! Because a typical custom of the city of Buenos Aires was that the cows were milked in the middle of the street, especially in the most important avenues, and people left the flats with their milk carafes to buy freshly milked milk. That was something that I really liked because I was used to seeing cows passing through the streets of my town too, although on the less traveled ones, and they didn't think of milking them there, they were just passing through, but still, it reminded me.

Buenos Aires had everything a big city could wish for: pretty squares, well-kept streets and avenues, a multitude of shops of all kinds, museums, nightclubs, and many bookstores. I had never been very given to reading, but on that trip I became fond of reading and that has given me many hours of pleasure later.

The country, according to what I was told, had gone through difficult times after the American crash of '29, the coup d'état of '30, the frauds of all kinds that they had to endure and many more things in which I do not want to extend myself now, but an unforeseen circumstance (the great drought that the United States began to suffer in 1932), was the spark for things to improve and for cereal exports to skyrocket, also opening new markets for Argentine meats, allowing the economy to take off, and during that period many public works could be carried out for the benefit of all. Money was moving, people were happy and it showed.

I'm sure my uncle and aunt would have really liked for me to fall in love with one of the wonderful guys that they presented to me, because that way they would have assured that I would stay and live there, but I just kept wanting to have fun and not have serious commitments, so although some of the boys were very handsome and fun to be with, and I could have had a very good life if I had agreed to their proposals, I managed not to do it since I knew that in that case I would have had to give up living in Spain, and that I didn't feel like doing.

I spent many months in Argentina, I learned to dance the tango well, I got to know many beautiful cities, I visited huge white sand beaches, I had a great time and finally it was time to return.

With sorrow and tears I said goodbye to everyone, because they had behaved fantastically well, not only with me but also with my maid, whom during those months they showered with gifts and attentions, and by a heartbeat I was almost left without her because the chauffeur had his eye on her since the first day, and he kept courting her all the long months we were there, but luckily she did not let herself be won over and came back with me.

If on the way out I had trunks, suitcases and bags, when I returned it was crazy: in addition to everything I had bought for myself, and the gifts for family and friends, everyone seemed to have agreed to entertain me and to want me to have a memory of them or of the country; the truth is that more generous people I have never met again in my life... I had to fill a trunk and three extra suitcases with everything I received, pearls, bracelets, Manila shawls, precious fabrics to make me suits, a list now would be endless.... Everything seemed excessive and although at first I was reluctant to accept some of the most valuable gifts, I immediately realized that they did it from the heart, with a lot of affection and to refuse and not to accept them could be taken as a very ugly thing and even bad manners, so I took them delighted.

The ship that took us to Spain happened to be the same one on which we had gone to Argentina, and therefore the Captain and the Officers were in a sense almost like family. Even the chamber maid who was in charge of cleaning the cabin was the same, so, although this time I did not have my uncle and aunt for support, from the first moment I felt at home and ready to enjoy again.

The journey was a little longer than the previous one, something about the currents the Captain explained to us, but I didn't care about a couple of weeks or so more, what I wanted was to have a good time and in that particular it was marvelous.

The same thing that happened on the way out, happened again: my father and my brothers were waiting for us. Meeting them again was wonderful and then I realized how much I had missed them.... My brothers were as handsome and as nice as ever, but I noticed my father was very sad and old, he must have been feeling very lonely during the long time that I was away, because as soon as a few days passed, he returned to his old self, and he told me every moment: "You make my life happy, my daughter, with you around all sorrows flee," and it must be true.

The funniest thing was that when we arrived everyone noticed immediately that my maid and I had lost the Extremaduran accent, and had picked up the porteño accent. We hadn't even realized it, while in the other environment, but that sweet touch has never left me, and to tell the truth over the years I have accentuated it because I like it a lot.

Going home had its advantages but also some disadvantages, because with my uncle and aunt I had enjoyed much more freedom, and in the months of the return trip I did not have to give an account to anyone of what I did or did not, and for me, who have always been very free —having tics and concerns about what people may think of me have never agreed with my nature — from the beginning of my arriving I rebelled because it seemed unfair that what men have always been allowed to do or say has been forbidden to us women, although little by little, with a lot of sleight of hand I managed to do what I wanted without major problems.

When the end of the year came, my brothers had been invited by some friends to a soirée that was held at the Casino de Turgalium, and although at first they were not willing for me to go along with them, I managed to convince them.

My existence changed there, who would imagine it?

The party was fantastic, with a good orchestra that played all the fashionable rhythms and we were having a great time when they introduced me to Juan Carlos.

He was a tall boy, impeccably dressed, very polite and since he seemed very shy I took him out to dance.

What came after that dance was a whirlwind because he fell madly in love with me, something that I was already used to, which happened with many, and somehow I got involved in everything that happened later.

To tell the truth, I was not in love and I never was afterwards, but it is true that he was a very fine boy, very cultured and once I got to know him and he put aside his shyness, I liked being with him. He did not have that possessive eagerness that I had found in others, perhaps because he was widely read or because he had suffered a lot, although he apparently led a privileged life.

His family had money and that had allowed them to give him an exquisite education, and the years he spent in El Escorial studying law had completed the good foundation he already had, because that place was very elitist and restricted, and they did not admit just anyone.

Shortly after meeting we became engaged.

My father and my brothers inquired to see if it would be a good match for me, and not only did they find no problems, but the more they knew, the more they liked it. Especially my father, who from the beginning liked him and always loved him very much, so things went on maybe a little faster than I would have liked, but he didn't give me much time to think about what I was getting into.

Juan Carlos soon insisted on introducing me to his mother and aunt, with whom he had lived again since he finished his studies. I had already met his only sister, Teresa, almost at the same time when I had met him.

Teresa and he got along perfectly. I have always had a very good relationship with all my siblings, especially with the boys, but those two were like peas in a pod, and from the beginning I realized how close they were, with what genuine love they loved each other, and how they respected even the smallest opinions of the other; then, once married, I have never heard a bad word between them or critical comment to third parties, not even to me. They treated each other with affection and respect that made me a little envious, because the joys of one of them were always a source of joy for the other, and when they were together, talking or silent, they had a harmony and a sympathy that many would like to have, in short, they got along wonderfully, so, instinctively seeing that if in the future there was a point of friction with him it would be because of the little sister, I always tried to get along very well with her, which was very easy because she was also very nice, fine and polite, very talkative but not critical, and although our customs were opposite, we always respected and loved each other.

Meeting his mother and aunt was a horse of another color, and the truth is that I was a bit hesitant to do so, although I knew that both my boyfriend and his sister would be there to smooth out any possible motive for friction, there wouldn't be any, and all would go well, but going to his house was like making everything official, without being able to turn back later without damaging my reputation, and for a moment I was thinking about not going, leaving the introductions for later and for everything to slow down a bit, but Juan Carlos was so impatient to get me closer to his people that I gave up.

When they were introduced to me, I was already aware of the aunt's story. Juan Carlos had given me a let's say soft version, but my brothers told me what was circulating in the region, so I knew the matter from different sources. A case of very bad luck and a lot of recklessness, which was the spark that ignited the decline of her family, and the worst part was undoubtedly taken by her, because when she managed to get out of that situation she was left, as vulgarly said, without a pot to piss in, upon the charity of her brother and her sister-in-law, who were very good and took her under their wings.

The mother came from a family of little means, had married very young the father of Juan Carlos and the misfortunes and deaths did not stop chasing her for years. She became a widow very soon and had to raise not only her two children but also take care of her sister-in-law, and all this without having any training or support, because her immediate family had neither the means nor the education to do so, and the few relatives who were left by her husband were not very helpful, so the poor woman, not very well advised in my opinion, became a moneylender and as a result of that the family lost a good part of the great capital they had at the time of Juan Carlos's father's death; although to tell the truth they still had enough left.

The house where they lived was wonderful, a magnificent three-story house with many balconies, and as for me, who likes the air, the sun, and rooms that are not gloomy or dark, I loved it.

And the two ladies couldn't be nicer. The mother, seeing how crazy Juan Carlos was for me, immediately treated me like a beloved daughter and with Aunt Tomasa, who was very hearty and funny although ugly as a demon, I laughed a lot, so I passed her exam without problems and with honors, come on, I put them in my pocket, as I always did with older people, and although that family was very sanctimonious and I was very open and liberal, I think they accepted me as I was.... Maybe Teresa had already told them a bit and that is why everything was easier, but these are speculations that occur to me.

As I said, the whole matter of courtship, engagement and request for my hand was very fast and in a few months I found myself at the gates of the wedding. At that point in the events I had to carry on, although more than one night I would wake up thinking if I had made the right decision, but those doubts and fears would vanish when the day came; to everyone around me my marriage and the person with whom I was going to contract it seemed the best of the best: a good match, a very educated and cultivated person, a family lover, serious, and above all crazy about me, willing to kiss the ground that I stepped on and able to give me everything I wanted.... I couldn't raise any objection but my nocturnal doubts persisted.

I ordered my trousseau, the wedding invitations were sent, everything related to the ceremony, the banquet, the honeymoon was arranged.... Everything was ready. Everything but me. My doubts grew and grew as the days passed and what was clear to me was that I appreciated my boyfriend, I could even say that I loved him, but I did not feel passion or desire for him. Nor is it that I had had those feelings for others before, but I saw my friends as they looked spellbound at their future husbands, even my sisters who were already married, and what was evident is that I was not in love.

I consulted my doubts with a priest I knew who seemed to me more open than the rest of his colleagues in office, and the only thing he told me and made clear is that marriage was not a game, that the main mission was to procreate and live in holiness, that love and respect were more important than love affairs and passion, because the latter are soon exhausted, and without the former, the marriage ends in disaster, and many more stories; but the truth is that it went in one ear and out the other, because what I wanted to hear from him was to tell me loud and clear that if I was not in love I should not marry, and that he did not tell me.

And since everything comes in this life, even the things we love the most sometimes, the wedding day also arrived.

The two families, relatives, friends and acquaintances were happy, I imagine for us; and the day ended well: everyone had fun, perhaps I was the only one who was not as elated, but if someone noticed it, I would attribute it to emotion of the moment, to the fatigue of the preparations, or simply to nerves. My father, who knew me well and who did not miss a detail, thought that I had finally matured, and that idea, apart from filling him with joy, gave him the option of believing that his work with me was over: I was now married and from that moment on it would be my husband who would have to take responsibility for my behavior.

Juan Carlos was ecstatic. He was the happiest guy in the whole world and every time he looked at me I felt all his love and also a bit of pity for not feeling the same, but that's the way it was. My hope was that one fine day I would wake up and stare at him rapt and mad with love for him.

But no. It was not to happen so.

We went on a honeymoon, a honeymoon that was not bitter, but not so sweet either. Maybe I should have suggested going to Paris or Mallorca, but with all the mixed feelings, I didn't even think about it at the time, and since Juan Carlos had already reserved everything for Galicia and it was an area that I did not know, there we planted ourselves .

My sisters, with experience of marriage, had enlightened me about what the first night would be like because I, despite having always been outgoing in all aspects, had no experience at the level of sex. My knowledge was limited to kisses and hugs with some guys before the engagement, and during the courtship with my boyfriend the caresses, although they were a bit more intense, did not reach anything serious. In addition, in the year thirty-five, despite the fact that divorce had already been established in Spain and what they called free love was practiced, still in certain conservative sectors, as the ones in which I moved and let alone in the family of my boyfriend, what was expected is that the brides would arrive chaste and pure to marriage, and that is how I arrived: a virgin and in the same way my mother brought me into the world, although some people had their doubts about it, seeing how I behaved and how it I always had done: with much more freedom than most, if not all, of my acquaintances.

I was warned, as I say, that that night would not be pleasant, but the truth is that it was not unpleasant either. Juan Carlos was a very sensitive boy, and although later by other experiences that life has given me I have realized that he did not have that much experience either, he behaved with great delicacy and we spent the first days dodging the sexual obstacles that were presenting themselves.

But I didn't feel anything, or anything special to be more exact. When we had finished the act, relaxed and satisfied, he fell asleep with a big smile that filled his face, while I watched the hours go by without being able to fall asleep and tossing and turning not only in bed, but also turning over many thoughts in my head.

The trip was beautiful, I could not say that it was fun like others I had done before, but maybe the days of fun and laughter for any little nonsense had passed for me. I do not know.

We visited beautiful beaches, but we couldn't even think of bathing in them because the weather was cold and there was that fine Galician rain most days, although that did not deter us from going on excursions. My mother-in-law and Aunt Tomasa had given me a fantastic fur coat, and with that and an umbrella I was ready for whatever they threw at me, and Juan Carlos had a good coat that reached almost to his feet, so neither the drip nor the chill mattered to us. We ate more seafood than I had in all the previous years. We went to shows when we stopped in big cities. We bought gifts for the family and many things for me. My husband was a very generous man and it was enough for me to look at something in any shop window and say how beautiful it was and a few hours later a boy would come to where we were staying with a package for me. And as I have always liked receiving gifts since I was a child, opening them made me very excited and I noticed how happy he was when he saw my surprised face.

After visiting the Apostle Santiago (whom I fervently asked to grant me to feel in love with my husband one day), we returned to Turgalium. Married life began for us.

They had our house ready, above where Juan Carlos's family lived, a spacious and beautiful apartment, with all the comforts and well furnished; a good service staff at our command, money to spend and fulfill our whims; the close relatives, that is to say Edelmira, Teresa and Aunt Tomasa, thought everything we did was perfect; my husband adored me more and more every day that passed. However, I already knew, or sensed, that I had been wrong about that wedding.

When the war broke out we did not notice great changes. Although in some parts of the country they had a very bad time, in our small city we were safe, and in the town where my father and my brothers were living too. Since we had farms, we didn't spend a single day without food, but there was fear, a lot of fear, because we could not know the outcome and every time we heard of the bestialities that were happening in other places, the burning of convents, rapes of the nuns, destruction and death everywhere, you actually felt ill. Both sides carried out atrocities and one day they will have to be held accountable, because they say that if you don't pay it in this world, you will pay it in another, but in our case, even with the inconvenience of not being able to travel, or have parties or do many things that we would have done in times of peace, we could not complain.

My sisters (who normally lived in Madrid), thanks to God the war didn't catch them there either, because when everything exploded they had the good fortune to be spending a few days at my father's house on their way to Portugal for the summer; the two couples with their children and the service, and the two of us had rented a house in Figueira da Foz and over there we thought we would all be together, enjoying the sea and the cool nights, with outings, excursions, parties and dances.... I was very excited to be able to spend a month with them, now that I had also become an adult, as they both said half in fun, half serious, and as that summer Teresa was already engaged to Jorge and he could not move from his post, and the three of them (Edelmira, aunt Tomasa and Teresa) had decided to break with their summer routine and stay in the city, I would be without the in-laws and that part would also be a double rest for me. But those projects couldn't be carried out in any way... still giving thanks that at least our families were close by and all of them safe and well.

The year before the war ended Teresa and Jorge decided to get married. He was a very handsome fellow from Madrid and he had been destined to Turgalium the year I got married, a few months after my wedding. We got along very well because, although he had nothing more than what they paid him to work in the Telegraph offices, he was from a good family and it showed. His father had even been a painter to the last King we had, before the Republic, and despite never having had ranches or land possessions, he enjoyed everything in the countryside very much, he was very cultured, had a good voice and liked to sing zarzuelas and even operas, he was a great mathematician, and as I have always been lousy at numbers I liked that a lot, because whatever I asked him in this regard he explained it to me in a simple and clear way and without giving up. Anyway, although we didn't really know anything about the family he came from, and we couldn't find out because of the circumstances, we all welcomed him with affection seeing how in love they were with each other.

Because you could really tell: Teresa, who until she met him didn't really notice any of her suitors, when she met him fell like a teenager. And it was the same way with him. It was very nice to see them together but it was also when I realized more what I was missing.

Their wedding, although they had to celebrate it at home without many guests, and without even Jorge's family being able to accompany them, because they were trapped in Madrid, it was beautiful, I even liked it more than mine, all very intimate and simple, very endearing and without the burden of as many people as I had, kissing me and making me dizzy. The pity is that they could not even make a small trip because Jorge could not miss his post for a single day, and even my father offered them an hacienda so that they could go there to rest a little, but circumstances rule, and they had to accept what was.

Despite the fact that they had gone to live very close to the square, and after the wedding I continued to see Teresa every day, it was no longer the same: my mother-in-law stayed in the family home with her service and her cats on the main floor and out of the way as usual, and we upstairs and it all got a little more overwhelming for me.

In that family they had the custom of praying the Rosary together after tea-time, and there no way to skip it. Sometimes a visitor would join in, or Eusebia, my mother-in-law's sister, or one of the cousins, but usually, since my wedding, we were the family alone (that is, Edelmira, Aunt Tomasa, Teresa, Juan Carlos and I), who sat around the big round table, surrounded by all the service staff, including mine, who remained standing, but who were not allowed to miss it either. While Aunt Tomasa lived, that was the plan every day and when the old lady passed away, it continued, although we had one member missing, but then my sister-in-law's wedding came and there were only three of us in the family, because while Teresa was single, she and I, between our prayers and Hail Marys, spoke softly like two little school girls, we passed notes as if the nuns were still watching us, it was a respite, but since she got married sometimes she couldn't come in the afternoons and for me it was an ordeal, because Juan Carlos was good, he was terrific, but very devoted and a lover of prayers too, and the two of them enjoyed the long hour that the matter lasted, because after the litany other prayers would come: praying for the dead in the family, for the living, for the fallen in the war, for the dying, for peace to come... or for everyone that occurred to the one who led the rosary that afternoon, while I got bored and hid my yawns.

Every day that passed I was feeling more and more trapped. We did not have many diversions, or none, because of the damn war and it looked like the situation was not likely to end.

But in April of the year thirty-nine peace arrived and at last everything was all over, if what came later could be called the end.... Because the country was destroyed, many had died, too many on both sides, misery haunted everywhere, families had been split apart for political reasons, and under the new military and severe regime nothing was going to be the way it had been, and even for people like me, who had never been interested in politics, the situation affected me. All of a sudden we became adults in one fell swoop.

We celebrated the Victory with great parties, for certain, and in our close families, conservative and lovers of order, much more because we all ended up alive and due to geographical circumstances together. No one had died and that was already a good reason to celebrate.

My father, a latifundista landowner according to those on the Red side, who was getting older and who, with all the fighting, had finished quite fed up with dealing with the farm laborers and their demands, although not directly but through his administrator, a few months after everything was finished, in the 1940s, he decided to distribute most of his estates among his children, us. Perhaps it is that he did not want to see in what state his beloved possessions were after so long without setting foot on them, only reserving for himself some real estate and orchards near his home, enough, as he said, of an income to be able to live well, but without complications.

I got La Operetta, which was a beautiful hacienda, quite close to my town and not too far from Turgalium, a large property that had always been full of game, where great hunts had been held in the past, with beautiful cork oaks and centenary oaks, and in which despite the war the harvests and the gathering of fruits and cereals had not decreased as much as had happened in other places, although the flocks of sheep and goats had dwindled and had been reduced to a paltry pair of each species. They had stolen almost all the pigs from us, and of cows and bulls there were practically none left, but still it had enough for a start, and on that farm I had spent many happy hours in my childhood and youth. Perhaps that is why my father decided that I should keep it: that farm and I were his favorites.

The first time we went there, my soul fell to my feet. Of all the splendor of yesteryear, only the memories remained. But the house was solid and still whole, although it had been ransacked and was almost empty, dirty and sooty, and what little furniture it still had, had to go to the dump. What destruction, my God, how is it possible that people can behave like real animals? Is it necessary to go through a situation like the one we had had for those three years for all the bad things that we carry inside to come out? But after the first moment of shock, Juan Carlos and I did not stand still: from that first day we took charge, we both dedicated ourselves to trying to put everything as it had been before.

I, who love to decorate and who always, according to everyone, have had a very good hand and very good taste to turn something ugly into a beautiful, pleasant and cozy room - with that project of the house the boredom left since I did not have time to think about the big mistake I had made by getting married, and I dedicated many hours, many days and many weeks (which in the end turned into months), of my life and my energies until I managed to get everything beautiful, even better than it was before. The walls were thoroughly painted, and it was not an easy task because the dirt seemed to have embedded itself in the walls, new floors had to be laid, a new light installation installed, a kitchen prepared because the one that existed before was destroyed, the laborers installed a new main bathroom and another for the service, even the fireplace in the living room had to be redone, and when everything was ready came the great battle to get furniture, curtains and all the other elements to make the home pleasant. Because we had fully entered the era of rationing and black market.

Luckily my trousseau was huge and I was able to bring a little of everything to the farm to start.

While I was taking care of the house, my husband, together with my father's old administrator whom we had also "inherited" and who helped him a lot, worked hard so that the crops were regenerated, the trees were pruned, the cattle were increasing and production in general was reaching what it had been, a difficult task because it was to start practically from scratch.

In that period only the cork oaks gave us joy: we had more cork than ever before or since. He hired workers from neighboring towns and made new corrals, a pigsty, and little by little everything took the shape of a farm in operation.

During that period, Juan Carlos and I settled in to live in my father's house, much closer to La Operetta than our flat in Turgalium, in order to be able to monitor and control first-hand what was being done on the farm.

We were both excited about the project, because although it would take years for the fields and animals to get back to the way they were before, we knew we were going in the right direction and once the house arrangement was finished, we could enjoy it all a lot, and could spend long periods there, which I was excited about because living in open large spaces had always been my passion. And since my marriage overwhelmed me more and more, even if nothing was noticeable on the outside and I continued to look like a good wife, at least when I was there I would be enjoying the countryside in peace, having parties, being with the people who loved me again, and I liked to organize good huntings.

At that time we visited our apartment in the city very little and to tell the truth I did not miss it. Aunt Tomasa had died before the end of the war, my mother-in-law continued to live alone with the service and her cats, Teresa and Jorge had their lives and were already parents of a beautiful girl, Manuela, whom I loved as if she were already mine, the one that my husband (who was her godfather) doted upon, and as we didn't have any of our own, he was enchanted and totally in love with her since the day she was born, and his mouth would fill up with news and praises of every progress the child made, and although I had some friends there, they were not like the ones I have had all my life, I had not integrated myself totally, so to speak, and with most of them I was bored, because they were not interested in the same things that I was.

Juan Carlos was good, perhaps too good, always fine and polite, but boring and predictable, and our tastes and customs were totally opposite. He had grown up like me, being the center of everyone's attention, but instead of having become capricious as I sometimes did, all those attentions had only served to make him more responsible and more loving to his family. He never saw evil in anyone, he was not envious or stingy, he had no vices. His only madness was to love me and adore me and there was nothing that made him happier than when I smiled at him, held his hand or gave some small show of affection.

But the truth is that I still was not in love....

And it's not that I was foolish. Seeing what happened to others, I realized I had hit the jackpot.

But the truth is that I was still not in love....

Some of my acquaintances had made marriages that seemed very brilliant but that turned out to be a disaster, their husbands insulted, hit and made fun of them without the slightest shame. And they had already taken away the divorce law again, so they had no choice but to swallow and endure.

But, again, I was still not in love.....

Every day I told myself how lucky I had been, but all this was not an obstacle to my inner restlessness, even if I put on a good face on the outside. The six years that had passed since I got married could be summed up in one word:

Boredom.

The laborers finished with the work on the house and to celebrate it we had a beautiful party. Many friends came wanting to have a good time, and also all those who were younger in the family. As it was summer we set up tables in the garden with food and drink, and everything turned out wonderfully. Teresa and the girl stayed with us for a week afterwards, and it was a pleasure to be enjoying the little girl who was already about two years old and was in that wonderful time of discovering everything. As my sister-in-law and I, even though we were totally opposite in our conceptions of life, had always gotten along very well, those days only strengthened our ties. Juan Carlos was happy having the three of us under his roof. Her mother was missing there, but on that occasion we had organized the event excluding the elderly, there would be time for my father and my mother-in-law to come and see how everything had turned out.

My husband also finally had his long-awaited meeting with his boarding school friends, who were very fine gentlemen, but of the same style as Juan Carlos: they could spend hours talking about a detail in a painting or listen to the same music that they liked for days and hours, so I took the opportunity to go see my sisters and get rid of such boredom.

The farm was taking shape and we really liked being in it, but once things had been organized, my husband began to receive worrying news: the Maquis was around there and nothing good could be expected from them.

A certain "Maria la Balbotina" who had been working on the farm of some acquaintances at Alía, had joined the "Long Jacket" and "Miguelete"; and together with a few others, among them María's brother and sister, they were committing outrages throughout the area, so for us to be alone together at mercy of the service and the laborers did not seem safe. He decided we'd go back to Turgalium and he would come to La Operetta to spend a few days from time to time while things calmed down.

I was so happy there that I didn't like having to leave, but if we had come out of a war unscathed, it was not a good plan to expose ourselves now to the maquis, so I accepted it and we went back to our apartment.

The next time we went to the farm something happened that was going to change my life in the most extraordinary way. The administrator, who, as I said, we had also inherited from my father along with the hacienda, told us that he could not continue to carry out his duties because he was too old and with many health ailments, but if we wanted we could try his son Antonio, recently arrived from the north, where he had been fighting bravely with the national forces and had suffered serious injuries that kept him hospitalized for many months, although he warned us that as an administrator he had no experience, but that he was a smart boy and until the war started he had always been such a good student that he had even wanted to start studying at the university, and that he would teach him how to manage the farm and get him ready if we decided to hire him. Juan Carlos immediately said yes, urged him to come and we would talk to him.

And he came the next day.

I was practically speechless when I saw him: he was the most handsome guy I had ever seen. Tall, dark, thin, very active, with green eyes and a smile that illuminated his face, friendly, pleasant without being servile ... You couldn't quibble about him.

My husband immediately hired him, and since Antonio did not have his own home and told us that living on the farm would be very good for him to finish recovering, meet the laborers who usually work there and the day laborers, and get up to speed on everything, we agreed to rehabilitate a small house that was next to ours (and not in too bad condition), for him to settle there.

In a short time he was organized and happy in his little house.

The next time we went to the farm, my husband and he spent several hours together, talking about everything related to management and administration, and later Juan Carlos told me what good luck we had had finding him since he was indeed a smart and educated young man, and by living in situ it would free him from many burdens.

And very soon he had all under control without any problem.

Some acquaintances told us that the one who had been appointed ruler of the country (the Caudillo) when the war ended, liked hunting a lot, and Antonio proposed to organize a hunt and invite him, as well as many other big shots of the regime, with the confidence that he would accept, assuming that the contacts would be beneficial in the long run, which we agreed to immediately, knowing in addition that he would be the one who would take care of everything, and we also would be hosts but enjoying the parties like other guests, without the work that such a thing entails, especially when there are many personalities in the group.

The day of the hunt arrived, many good pieces were collected, the atmosphere was unbeatable, the outfits of the ladies who accompanied the hunters were beautiful, the delicacies we tasted were just right, everything was perfect and we received sincere congratulations from all those who participated.

When the last guests left, my husband decided to go with one of my brothers to my village to pick up more cartridges, since he had been left with few and I, who was a little tired, decided not to accompany him.

I sat in my living room, with a good cup of hot chocolate, with my eyes half closed recalling the past two days, happy with how they had turned out, when Antonio entered the room. I thought he would like to communicate something to me before retiring to rest so that I could tell Juan Carlos, but to my surprise he sat next to me, took me by the shoulders with his hands, strong but very soft and delicate, and kissed me on my mouth. There was not a word between the two of us. Just a deep kiss.

The same way as he had arrived he left. I was shocked because I had never felt anything like it. All my senses were suddenly awakened with that kiss and I doubted whether I had not fallen asleep and it had only been a dream.... But no, it had been real, the best thing I had experienced in my life, none of the kisses that had been given to me before my marriage or the many that my husband gave me could be compared to the one I had just received. I went crazy and wanted more.

When Juan Carlos came back I was still excited, but I managed to pretend a calm I did not have and the night continued without incident; my husband was very happy, and we both talked at length about the hunt and the good organization carried out by our administrator.

That night in bed, while my husband penetrated me, my thoughts were far from there, well, to tell the truth, not so far: a few steps from our house in the little house was the man I had fallen in love with.

Because with just one kiss I fell in love and denying that fact was silly.

We spent two days on the estate before returning to Turgalium.

In that time, every time I saw Antonio, I would look for something in his face or in his eyes that would reveal what he was thinking, or for some gesture that gave me a clue or indicated that what had happened was real and not a product of my imagination, but I could not find it.

And with great sorrow on my part, more than ever now because I was distancing myself from the man I already loved, we went to our apartment in Turgalium.

The following days were both a torture and a paradise: I was anguished at not being able to see him or know he was close by, but every time I remembered the intense kiss, his lips pressing on mine, the clash of our teeth and the tip of his tongue trying to find its way to the depths of my mouth, I went crazy with desire, and thus I went from a sad state to one of euphoria in a matter of seconds. Nobody noticed anything, or if they saw something strange there was always the explanation that I felt sad for not being in the hacienda.

Although winter was coming, an unpleasant time, and I didn't like it, I convinced Juan Carlos we should spend a fortnight at the farm. As it was the harvest season and he was thinking about the next crops, he agreed, and there came my happiness and my misery.

I did not know if for Antonio (much younger than me and fantastically handsome, so he could have any woman he wanted), the kiss he had given me was something fleeting and unimportant, or if it had also stirred something inside him. I had to be close to him and see how he reacted. The idea that he did not feel something similar to what I was experiencing tortured me and at night I woke up full of desires and fears. All I wanted was to see him again, to be able to touch him, even for a moment, hear his voice, to see him, to see him. That was the only thing that mattered to me. In those moments I would have given everything I had to be by his side, years of my life, possessions, everything ....

We arrived at the farm and he was not there. He had gone to a neighboring town to make some arrangements, and I contained my cravings knowing that soon he would be close, that we would breathe the same air, and I hoped that somehow the occasion would present itself and he would kiss me again.

He came back and if I remembered him handsome what I saw surpassed all my memories: with beige pants that fit where they had to fit, a green shirt that highlighted his eyes even more, if that was possible, and a smile that filled his face, he was the spitting image of youth and beauty, and at that time, although I was only seven years older than him, still looking very good, well cared for and impeccably dressed as usual, I felt old and worn out, not worthy of him wanting to have anything to do with me on a sentimental level. For the first time in my life I was afraid in case he wouldn't like me, of him not liking me, and that was a new feeling for me.

But they were only my speculations, as I learned later.

We settled in and our routine began. I had brought my maid and the cook as I always did when I went there, because even though there were women on the farm who could clean and cook for us, I preferred not to give up some of my servants, which were used to our tastes.

The day we arrived I suggested to Juan Carlos that he invite Antonio to dinner, as it was the first night and as an attention to him, to somehow thank him for how well he was working and how pleased we were with him, and my good husband agreed delightedly, so when the time came the three of us sat at a cozy round table instead of the one in the dining room, which was more formal and involved more apparatus, because I wanted to see Antonio in a relaxed and camaraderie atmosphere, although each one of us knew the difference and were in our place.

Towards the middle of the second course I noticed a brush of his leg against mine. I waited in case it had been something involuntary, but immediately I felt it again, this time with more urgency and I did not withdraw, but pressed my leg against his, trying to keep talking as if nothing was happening. We were like that throughout the dinner and that is how I would have continued until eternity, noticing his hot skin through his stockings and the fabric of his pants and wishing his hands would touch me.

But dinner ended, although I lengthened it as long as possible within the decorum that was imposed on me by my position, and when he said goodbye I felt as if a part of my heart and soul had been ripped from me.

Juan Carlos was delighted with him, so I was able to talk about Antonio freely and without raising any suspicions. I felt happy: I already knew that he wanted and desired me too and that it would be a matter of waiting until we could touch each other again.

The next two days there was no occasion; But on the third morning my husband had gone to see another farm with my father, the cook and the maid were with the watch-woman killing and preparing some chickens, while I was alone at home, thinking of him and eager to see him, when, when I least I expected, he appeared. He pinned me to a wall and without a word he kissed me again, this time pressing his body against mine. If the first kiss was good, this second was sublime. My whole body asked to be kissed by him, to notice his burning lips on my skin, to feel his hands caressing my breasts and my nipples.... Desire had never manifested itself to me like this, I had not experienced it before, those were things from novels or movies. But those moments were neither novels nor movies, they were real and they were happening to me, to me who could not have those feelings since I had a husband, and who was therefore not allowed to love another man....

When he separated a bit from me, with a voice broken by emotion and with almost no breath, he said to me: "I'm crazy about you, Margarita, I can't sleep or eat or live for thinking of kissing you, touching you, putting my tongue in all the openings that I can find on your face and on your body! Tell me that you want me too!"

I could only answer Yes! I didn't want to spend a second talking because that second deprived me of his contact, and I didn't know when I could be by his side again.

I don't even know how we were able to separate, but luckily we had just separated when the servants arrived, and later came

Juan Carlos with one of my brothers who had invited himself to lunch and to spend the afternoon with us.

From that meeting we both knew what we wanted: to kiss, touch, love each other, make tireless love and nothing else mattered. What we most wanted was to be together.

I went crazy with jealousy every time he was absent from the hacienda for any reason, even knowing that if he left while I was there it was for something very justified. And when he saw me from a distance, always with an arm of Juan Carlos on my shoulders according to my husband's custom, he later on confessed to me that the sight was a stab in his gut that hurt him more than all the wounds that he got in the war.

But the expected fifteen days of our stay passed and we had not been able to kiss again. Desire corroded me and my instinct told me that he was feeling the same but the opportunity did not present itself, although I was not willing to leave without achieving my goal, whatever the cost.

The night before we left I managed to get my husband to drink a lot; he was very sparing and austere with his drink, but if I encouraged him and pretended to drink, he would have a few glasses of wine at dinner. On that occasion I also insisted that he try a delicious liqueur that one of my brothers-in-law had given me and that I was saving for Christmas, knowing how strong it was and that added to the ingested wine it would knock him out, as it did.

We went to the bedroom, I was helping him to walk because he could hardly stand up, and we went to bed. In seconds he fell into a deep sleep; at that point I took the opportunity, I put on a robe and went out into the garden.

Everything was silent and it was a dark night. Nobody saw me.

I approached the administrator's house and before touching it the door was opened. There he was, waiting for me with outstretched arms to hug me, wearing only a long nightshirt and ready to give me all the love I needed. There were no words. We melted into a hug and his lips began to kiss not only mine but also my neck and shoulders, while his hands filled with my breasts, free under the nightgown and eager for his caresses. And right there, on the floor on a threadbare carpet, he possessed me and I gave myself.

Everything was fast, furious and joyous. For the first time in my life, after many years married and what they call making love to my husband so many times, I finally had an orgasm. What a pleasure and what a blessing, what a delight and what a joy.

I went back to my house and to my bedroom. Everything was just as I'd left it. The only one who had changed was me, who could never go back to being who I had been.

That night I was able to sleep as I had not done in months, perhaps as I had not done since I was a child, and I woke up feeling beautiful and complete, but as soon as I saw Antonio again, when we were already leaving, desire took hold of me again. The only thing I wanted was to feel my body in his arms, feel his hard member inside my body, breathe in his smell and feel his breath sticking to my skin.

For a month we did not see each other again and every day without his presence was torture. Our monotonous, boring and routine life continued as before; now I fully realized how insipid my existence had been, how long and how many years I had spent without knowing what is truly important: the joy of loving and being loved and the clash of bodies full of desire. I dreamed asleep and awake for the moment of reunion, but my fears that for him it had only been a little adventure, a momentary escape, persisted. He was so handsome and so young....

Before the Christmas holidays we returned to the farm for a short stay. It was my opportunity to see and touch him, since I knew that until spring came I would not be there again, only my husband would go to check everything and my presence would have no justification, because I had always said how little I liked the country in those months, and that not a soul would catch me there neither in January nor in February, and now that statement was working against me.

Our manager, my dear lover, was waiting for us. I felt an ineffable happiness: there he was, more handsome and virile than ever, at my fingertips.

We invited him to dinner again and I already knew that at least our legs would be together, but it was better than that: Antonio sat in front of me and when I began to think that he did not want even a furtive touch I was surprised to feel his foot, without shoe, sliding up towards my sex. I spread my legs as far as the skirt allowed me and he, with a skill that I don't know where he would have learned, stroked me with his toes until the pressure became so great that I thought I was going to scream in front of my husband. But Antonio, even though he spoke and explained things about the cattle to Juan Carlos as if nothing were happening under the round tablecloth, watched me and before reaching the climax he stopped, leaving me with the honey on my lips and eager to taste it.

When we got up from dinner, while we said goodbye and he shook my hand, he handed me a small piece of paper that only said "Touch yourself while you think of me."

Just that.

In bed, once my husband was sound asleep after having penetrated me so respectfully, as he liked, I followed the advice of the note and did something that I had never done before: I put my right hand on my sex and began to caress myself thinking about what had happened during dinner, remembering his lips and the green of his eyes, and a few minutes later my whole body convulsed with pleasure. With one end of the sheet I covered my mouth for fear that the sounds that escaped from it would wake up my husband. I felt not quite fulfilled, because I needed his body even after mine had lightened a bit. I needed more and more and I had to get it.

The next day a fortuitous circumstance made it possible for us to be alone. Two friends from nearby farms came to pick up Juan Carlos to go on a small hunt and shoot together. They invited the administrator to accompany them, but he pleaded some jobs that he could not leave and with great joy I saw how my husband and his companions, loaded with their shotguns and with their cartridge belts full of munition, left and went away for a few hours.

I entered his little house without anyone seeing me and this time we undressed and for almost three hours we loved each other, with a passion that led us to touch the sky. Every time our bodies had finished coupling and merging, it seemed to us that we could not do it again for hours; however, minutes later, it was enough to feel a finger of one on the skin of the other for the urgency of desire to fill us again and to melt, but with a trace of good sense, seeing the hours that had passed we got up and got dressed, and we were lucky to do so because not a quarter of an hour had passed when the hunters returned, so happy with the pieces they had collected and not suspecting what we had done in their absence.

I was full, my whole body exploded with beauty, and on the outside I think I have never been more beautiful or better. Inside I consumed myself thinking when the next meeting would be, which seemed difficult.

Once again luck was with me: the vet came because a cow that was about to give birth, had the calf crossed inside and we feared for its life, and for that reason, once everything was resolved favorably, my husband and the veterinarian went to a neighboring town to have some wines and continue talking about animals in a more relaxed atmosphere, a moment that Antonio and I took advantage of to melt and love each other as only we ourselves knew.

We were both aware that our relationship, the urgency of our desire was going to bring us problems, but we also knew that nothing and no one would come between us and our ultimate goal: to be always together no matter what.

Before returning to Turgalium, in a lucid moment, I wrote him a long letter with all the considerations and dangers we face, and as with his first note, when we said goodbye he slipped another small piece of paper into my hand, that just said "Don't worry, I'll fix everything."

The Christmas holidays came and went. I behaved on the outside as always: entertaining, witty and lively. Inside was another story. I had not seen him for weeks and each day that passed was a new thorn that pierced my depths. How long could I bear this torture from afar?

In January my mother-in-law had her annual appointment with Dr. Cifuentes and her loving son accompanied her to Madrid, but this time I stayed home, alleging some discomforts that I did not feel. I had always taken advantage of this trip to order my spring clothes from my dressmaker there, but nothing would have taken me to the capital if I lost the opportunity, even if it was remote, to see or touch my man.

Before the departure of the travelers, I made sure that Juan Carlos gave me precise instructions for what to do on the farm, because, although I was the owner, I had never had to take care of anything, and thus I had a reason to see him. As soon as I found out that they were already installed in Madrid, I sent him a message to come.

He did not know my apartment yet and he was amazed at how beautiful it was, but I wasn't in for unnecessary flattery; so I locked the parlor door and we mated right there, yes, because after so much time without seeing or touching each other, the first time it was as if we were animals hungry for sex and desire, and we had to satisfy it right away to be able to continue loving each other later.

The second time we made love it was a little less urgent: we had time to get to bed and in it we enjoyed our bodies to the point of paroxysm. And the following times; until he was totally dry and my body couldn't even move.

But we got up, got dressed, and for the first time since we'd met, we talked.

We talked about our future, the one we always wanted together.

There was no longer divorce in our country, and a separation from my husband was unthinkable. My husband would have to disappear and we had to study the way....

In order not to raise suspicions among the servants, Antonio left, leaving me the task to also think about how we would carry out our project. We did not know when we would meet again, but everything was decided: my husband would have to be killed.

The travelers returned, we went back to our normal life and I was sweeter, kinder and more affectionate than ever with my husband, because I knew that every day that passed I was closer to my happiness and that he would have to be an innocent but necessary victim for our projects.

In April we returned to the farm. I don't even know how, but Antonio and I managed and were able to resume our furtive encounters. We loved each other as always, or perhaps more than ever, now that the plan was drawn up: Antonio, taking advantage of the fact that the Maquis was prowling the area, would kill him and thus the murder could be blamed on strangers. I agreed. Years later, I felt a little sorry that things had to be like this, but at that time it was the only solution to solve our urgent need, and with the members of the maquis bearing the blame, in a reasonable time everything would be fixed and we could live together for ever.

May came.

Juan Carlos, prompted by Antonio who already had all the plans in place, told me that he would go to the farm for a few days to organize things with the administrator and then we would return together to spend part of the summer there: I did not resist the plan because I knew what would happen.

And what did happen.

At dawn on May 22, while he was sleeping, Antonio shot him three times in the head. According to what he told me later, he didn't even look, but after the crime was perpetrated in cold blood, I imagine that the scene must have been Dantean.

The Civil Guard notified me of what happened, and although they told me that he was seriously injured, I already knew that he was dead, and when they left I (though not devout) thanked heaven that everything had ended, because I knew that soon my life would begin. My real life.

Have I had sorrow or regrets for what my lover did, for what we did? Have I lost sleep over it? No — although later on things did not go as I would have liked.

The funeral, in which I had to play the grieving widow, passed; everyone was scared by what had happened, blaming the blessed maquis who were our salvation, but as soon as I was alone I could not help but laugh and rejoice, in a short time I would be with my lover forever. The rest did not matter.

In August Teresa had a boy and I took Manuela home for a few days. The girl was a delight and being with her was a respite. The two of us had a great time and I tried to indulge her in whatever she wanted, from eating what she wanted to not having schedules at night. In the afternoon we went to see her new little brother and her parents, but she was happy with me and didn't cry when she said goodbye to them.

The little boy had been born with problems, perhaps it was because my sister-in-law was so affected by the death of her brother, whom she missed terribly, because Teresa was very sensitive, and also was burdened by a heart condition since adolescence, and getting pregnant I don't think was a good thing for her, but since I'm not a doctor I can't be sure either, and in this case as I always say, and as the Americans are saying, in wars there must be collateral damage, and what was done could no longer be changed, because the most important thing for me was to be able to be forever with the one I loved, and that was not the one I had married.... Whatever the relatives of the deceased thought or felt was no longer my problem.

An unforeseen circumstance worked in my favor: in Alía, in mid-August, the Civil Guards caught and executed twenty-four members of the maquis, and thus the whole issue of the murder of Juan Carlos was settled. It would have been one of them who killed him and there was no evidence that pointed elsewhere.

As soon as a few months had passed, arguing that everything in the apartment and in the house reminded me of Juan Carlos and increased my sadness, I moved to live on the farm, where, as I explained, I could enjoy a peace and silence that I lacked in Turgalium. The atmosphere that was lived there was oppressive, between my mother-in-law, my sister-in-law and all their relatives who got together and spent hours singing the praises of the one who was my husband, and who sometimes made me have to get up and go to another room, according to them because of the immense grief I had, but actually because I could not stand them for another moment.

Only the girl Manuela somewhat mollified the environment, because the boy, who had also been called Juan Carlos in honor and memory of the one who was gone, had very precarious health and did not seem to be able to get ahead.

The farm was mine and I could do whatever I wanted with it. It produced enough to live well, and besides, Juan Carlos had provided me with enough cash and bonds and Treasury notes, which, when well administered, would allow me to lead the life I had always led, and since my plan was to spend most of the hours of the day and night with my lover, all the expenditures on suits, trips and trinkets that I had had until then would be drastically reduced. The truth is that none of those matters worried me.

Feigning great sorrow for leaving what had been my home for almost seven years, and my deceased's family, I finally left that house and that life. Everything started for me, although things did not go exactly as planned, since as soon as I settled in, my sisters came, first one and then the other, to keep me company. They did not want me to be alone for a moment and the love trysts with Antonio had to be postponed for a while. We just looked at each other when we could, but without any touch, and that made me crazy and nervous, which my sisters attributed to the tragic loss I had suffered. Better that way, because I didn't want to tell anyone I was in love, the time would come.

When I managed to get rid of them and it seemed to me that the time had finally come to fully enjoy myself, my father considered that it was not a good thing that I was left alone there, having a young man living so close by, because that would be enough to start gossip, and he planted himself in my home for another long season. It seemed I was not going to be able to get rid of any of them, although in my father's case it was not so bad since he went to bed very early, and as soon as I saw that he was completely asleep I slipped into Antonio's house, and there we both enjoyed our bodies, until satiated I went back to my house. There was always an urgency and the first moments were especially intense: we could not articulate words, only kiss, caress and love each other. Feeling his extremely hard member inside my body was what I wanted and for him to slide it among my juices was the greatest pleasure. When, after we were satisfied twice, we could begin to breathe, the softest caresses began and the love game increased until he penetrated me again. We did not get tired and so we would have continued for hours if we could have, but since we had managed to make almost everything go well according to our plans, we were not about to spoil things, so we reluctantly parted, hoping that the hours would pass soon and the next night come so we could return to our lust.

Months passed. Teresa and Jorge's son had died before Christmas, plunging them into more pain if that was possible. When I went to the funeral I took the opportunity to dismantle what had been my home, I took the furniture and everything of greater value to the farm, I gave away many things and told my mother-in-law that she could have the apartment for whatever she wanted; that I was never going to live there again.

I closed that phase of my life without any regrets, although I performed some comic theater for the sake of others. I have always liked to keep up appearances.

The farm was already in full swing. My father was still with me and Antonio wanted us to get married, which I fully agreed with, and little by little I put that idea into my father's head, presenting it as something very beneficial for me, telling him that I wouldn't be alone and he could rest and be calm, without having to take care of me, and for me at the same time besides having a sentimental partner, he would also continue with his administrator functions, and since my father on the one hand was unable to deny me anything, and on the other he liked the boy (as he called him) a lot, like everyone who knew him, after a reasonable time to show respect before others about widowhood, we got married.

It was a low-key ceremony, without guests or anything unnecessary. Only my father, his father, and my brothers with their wives. We celebrated it on the hacienda without any fuss and we didn't even go on a honeymoon. We didn't need to go anywhere because we had what we needed right there: each other.

And another stage in my life began.

The first few months were wonderful, better than that. During the day, when we passed each other there were always caresses, little kisses, rubbing touches that seemed naive but we both knew what they meant. And the nights? The nights were simply dreamy, although we slept little. I do not want to stop to describe them because it would take me months and even now, after everything that happened later, they are in my memory as something that is difficult to live more than once in a lifetime and that only if you are one of the lucky ones....

But from the beginning of our life together, in our nights together, I had observed that Antonio suffered from frightening nightmares: he raised his arms, convulsed and twisted in bed, punched the pillow.... Later he began to scream in his dreams, and his screams were so loud and terrible that they woke me up. Then, when I looked at him I saw him bathed in sweat, his face contorted with pain, and more than once I wanted to wake him up to get him out of his anguish, but I didn't. I would roll over and continue sleeping.

One day I asked him why he did not tell me about his dreams (not to mention nightmares) and he replied that he never dreamed, that when he fell asleep he was not aware of anything again until dawn the next day. I attributed the night terrors to images of war, and we got on with our lives.

But almost without realizing it, over time our lives had become very lonely, just he and I, and I and he. We had practically no contact with anyone. Even my family seemed to have forgotten that we existed, and only on rare occasions was there a minimum of communication, and always through third parties.

I didn't know anything about Teresa, Jorge and Edelmira, even though the geographical distance was not great, but they, so formal and proper, had not liked my new marriage, although I didn't care, and I expected it; when I put my money on Antonio, I already knew that a lot of people were not going to love that decision, he much younger than I, my paid employee, and all the etceteras they found, and least of all, in pure logic, my former in-laws, but at that time nothing and nobody was going to dissuade me from my intentions, although now I missed Teresa, her serenity and sympathy and our entertaining and interesting conversations, in which we did not even have to talk about others, and also little Manuela whom I loved so much, even Edelmira with her cats and her monetary dealings.

Antonio was changing. It's not that his love and ardor had diminished, on the contrary, with each passing day he desired me more and more and couldn't get enough of me, but at the same time his nightmares came almost daily, his character darkened, he didn't only stop laughing, he never even smiled, he became possessive, and the simple fact that I spoke to any laborer on the farm, put him in a hellish mood. Everyone who lived there began to fear him, and I was no exception, because there was not a trace of the guy I had fallen in love with, even his physique had changed: large wrinkles crossed his forehead, his mouth always had a bitter expression, his once pretty green eyes were sunken. Only his body kept something of what it was, it was still flexible and thin.

As far as conversation goes, talking together, we had never done much, nor was there much that united us in that respect, and he (unlike Juan Carlos) was not a cultured or cultivated man. I had never seen him pick up a book, much less read it, and he had not the slightest interest in anything other than being in bed with me, which had seemed very good to me, but that suddenly began to bore me a bit, because I also needed to cover other areas of my life.

Thanks to pampering and caresses, I convinced him to go visit my father, and when he saw us, just by looking at his face I realized that not only Antonio was horrible, I must have seemed terrible to him, but he didn't say anything, always so polite and gentle, and at one point when the two of us were alone he told me that he thought the isolation we lived in was not good or healthy for me, and that he was going to try to change it.

He talked to my husband about organizing a hunt, and he presented everything in such a way that Antonio agreed. Because the funny thing about the whole thing is that I, who had always been independent and free in my actions, in recent times felt like I had no will of my own, perhaps what we had done was beginning to leave a mark on my mind. I cannot say that it was regret, I have never regretted being if not the executor, the inducer of that crime, but I often remembered Juan Carlos, his exquisite education, his tender love for me, his patience, how peaceful and cultured he was.... I spent hours wondering how good it would have been to put them in a bag and mix them up together with a magic wand, and that gives an idea of how bad off I was, even if I didn't realize it.

A few days later my brothers came and had everything programmed: the date, those who would participate in the hunt, the area that was going to be covered, the meals that were going to be served.... It was like a ray of hope in the middle of my so lonely life.

I started to make all the preparations, fixed myself up again and took care of myself, something that I had not done in our time of isolation, since my husband did not care exactly how I was since all he wanted was to be with me in bed, have me naked by his side, kiss me, touch me and hug me to finally penetrate me, and that not once or twice a night, but for hours and hours, so when I managed to get up in the morning I didn't even have the strength to put on a dress; most days I left on the robe and slippers, even to eat.

Since I didn't need my maid at that time, I had fired her, and shortly after I did the same with the cook. The housekeeper made us meals, which although they were not as refined as the ones I was used to, my husband liked them better, he had enough with some good soups and some fried food, and little by little our daily habits had gone on changing without my even realizing it, or to tell the truth it had been I who changed mine, since Antonio's family were good people, but simple and of very humble extraction, and what we were doing now was what he had seen done in his house always, and before I knew it, we were eating our meals in the kitchen, I clad in a dressing gown and sometimes even without combing my hair, without speaking, and I am not talking about something exciting or interesting, but simply about anything at all, with nothing to say since we had nothing in common...

It was difficult for me to be presentable again, but I managed to do it. I hired my old maid again, who luckily had returned to my village, although I had to double her salary, I got a good cook and two women to clean, and together they got the house ready.

As my clothes were outdated and it had been so long since I had bought any, I wrote to my sisters, giving them my measurements, which fortunately were almost the same as before my marriage, with precise instructions for my old dressmaker to prepare a few outfits for me. Simple, as my style had always been, but elegant and discreet and good for a country party. Because my plan was to have parties the three nights that the hunt lasted. During the day they would do whatever they wanted to do, but at night we would have dinners, drinks, music and dances, and that's where Antonio and I had the first bad row of our lives.

My husband had agreed to the hunt, thinking that in the remaining two months something would happen and that it would not be carried out, but since everything was going smoothly, he saw that the date was inevitable and his character soured more and more as the days days went by and the event was getting closer. In addition, the house had been overturned: we no longer ate in the kitchen, I got dressed and shod since morning, we had forgotten about the caretaker catch-as-catch-can meals and we again ate with tablecloths and dishes. Anyway, I had recovered my old self and as the date approached my joy was reborn, and that seems to be what Antonio did not like too much.

One afternoon, while I was looking through some fashion magazines that my sisters had sent me, he approached me and, taking me by the shoulders violently, almost dragged me to the bedroom saying: "We have to talk, Margarita." That in itself was a novelty since we never did it, so I started to listen and what I heard I did not like at all, since he intended to cancel everything, and he threatened that if we did not cancel it for good, neither he nor I would be present, he would take care of that matter. At that moment my passion for him disappeared the same as it had come, and he appeared to me as a dangerous being, capable of anything to achieve his wishes. I replied that the hunt would be done, and that he could go for a walk or wherever he wanted, that the farm was mine and I was in charge there, he must never forget it, and we got into an ugly argument where we both said more things than we should have; he even accused me of making him a murderer, that it would be he who would have to render accounts, if not before the justice of men, before the divine.

Despite that at night, in bed, he looked for me as always, but something in me had broken and although my body let him do it, my mind was already elsewhere. I no longer wanted him to be by my side. He would have to disappear.

The atmosphere between the two of us was not good while we were out of bed, but I continued with all the preparations, the days passed and the day of the get together arrived.

It was divine to have the house and the hacienda full of people again, wanting to have fun and spend some super days. The hunters were happy because they got many deer and wild boar, the lunches in the field were liked by everyone, the dinners and suppers were memorable. We all sang and enjoyed ourselves very much.

Everyone except Antonio, who, citing terrible back pain, did not even come out of the bedroom to greet the guests, about which I was happy because the tensions that existed between us would have been noticed, and when the last guest said goodbye, my decision was taken: I'd get rid of him.

And this time I would do it alone. I didn't want to have to endure some kind of unwanted emotional or verbal blackmail afterwards. On my own.

I needed to plan everything in detail, I couldn't leave a single loose end, I had to think of the best method, the simplest and most effective, that would not leave visible traces. Nor did I want blood because, although they had tried to avoid describing how they found Juan Carlos, I was not so stupid as not to imagine his condition after Antonio had shot him three times in the head, and I schemed and ruminated about all this while I tried to lead a normal life. I thought that the best thing for the moment was to redirect Antonio towards a less tense state, and to achieve that I dedicated all my tricks towards that goal. I became cuddly, affectionate, soft and charming, not only in our love making, but every hour and minute of the day, and he succumbed to manipulation. He began to smile a little, perked up and believed that everything would be as it had been.

But no.

I was already decided and it was a matter of finding the moment. It would be when he least expected it, because I already had the weapon: poison.

On the farm we had various kinds, and for various things, but in this case after thoroughly reviewing all the labels and finding out about the effects, I decided on a powerful rat killer with lethal effects; my plan was to use it in several sessions so that the event seemed more natural.

We went back to eating first-class soups at noon and in the evening, and when that routine was already established my attack began.

The first time I put a small amount in his darling soups, I had to see what happened.

Not an hour later Antonio writhed in pain, he could hardly speak a word, and I insisted on sending for a doctor, something which he flatly refused, blaming the pain on something that must have disagreed with him. Since I had eaten the same thing and I was fine, then he thought perhaps he had caught cold, and he was thinking about all the possibilities while I, surrounded by almost all the farm staff "cried and cried" and appeared anguished. I wanted witnesses and the more the merrier.

But my husband escaped that time, which was also part of my plan. He was young and healthy, and I was interested in him not dying the first time, because it would have given rise to suspicions.

I let a couple of days go by and repeated the operation. Again the pains returned; this time extremely acute, and despite his protests I sent for the doctor: he would be another witness without knowing it, and on that occasion I knew who would come.

When the doctor came, a young and inexperienced boy, he suggested to me that it could be an attack of appendicitis and he was so concerned when he saw the state in which I was, that he insisted that I have a cup of linden in front of him, lie down a while while he was with the patient and I relax a little. The plan was working and everything was working in my favor.

Antonio came out of that attack again, although he was very weakened. From then on and since I already knew the necessary amount that I would have to use for the poison to do its job, I dedicated myself to being a loving wife, worried to the point that I did not even want to go to bed so there would be no possibility of my falling asleep, and to be able to monitor his sleep at all times, with everyone who worked for me watching my performance. I did a good job. I embroidered it and everyone felt sorry for me.

Came the day.

He did not want to eat much, but they made him a bowl of chocolate, thick and sweet the way he liked it and he agreed to take a few spoonfuls.... The last of his life, because there was the lethal dose. Not even half an hour had passed when the death throes made him almost jump out of bed; I hastily sent for the doctor, because in that situation I was interested in his dying in front of him: when he arrived, my husband was in the final agony, and shortly afterwards all he had to do was sign the death certificate. I was free and unattached again.

Once again I had to go through the heavy routine of funeral, burial and comments. What a bore: "Another tragic death... A man in the prime of his life... As much as he loved her... A life cut short... Maybe it could have been avoided if he had been in a hospital... Poor Margarita, how unlucky she is...." My head ached listening to the gossips of my town and their litanies, but it was done and that was what mattered.

My sisters insisted on taking me with them to Madrid, and although I played the comedy for a few days, then "I gave up"; and not four weeks had passed since we had buried Antonio when I finally settled in with my oldest sister: another stage of my life was beginning .

Although I was officially in mourning, I kept coming and going, and my usual dressmaker made me some gorgeous black outfits. Little by little, everything that had stuck to me in those years of isolation was peeling away from me, I don't even know how I endured, with how sociable I am and how I love partying, but that guy had me subjugated, and without realizing it I fell into laziness.

One of my brothers-in-law suggested that I move permanently to Madrid, and I wondered why it had not occurred to me before. Going back to live at La Operetta made no sense, now that I was alone, going back to town or to Turgalium even less, and in the capital I had almost all my family, friends, and a good atmosphere, so I started looking for a suitable apartment, because I didn't have financial problems, and being at my sister's house for a while was fine, but for something longer I preferred my own independence, and that although everyone went out of their way for me and fulfilled all my wishes.

Did I remember Antonio? Some nights. But the memories were not of the last unbearable Antonio, but of the young boy I met when I was still married to Juan Carlos and who fell madly in love with me.

Was I sorry for what I had done? Of course not. It was the best solution for everyone: I was not happy, he was not happy, what point was there in prolonging a state of unhappiness? None. Regretting it would have meant that I thought what I had done was wrong, and I was convinced it was right.

So I forgot the details of his death, as I had done in the case of Juan Carlos, and I took care of my affairs, which had many things to be resolved.

I got a really nice apartment on Serrano street, very close to the Archaeological Museum, with good communications, beautiful shops and some very fine neighbors, elegant and friendly people. It was very close to the Plaza de la Independencia, where my sisters lived in luxury apartments. They would have liked the three of us to be together in the same building, but at that time there was no flat free, and to tell the truth, Serrano's was better for me because we were very close, but I could escape their over protection.

The first thing I did was bring my maid and the farm cook, as well as some furniture to which I had a special attachment, and with the help of my sisters and a friend from the coming out party, we looted the stores until I found everything that I wanted to make it precious; the result could not have been better: the living room was spacious, welcoming, comfortable and elegant; the entrance (which had no direct light), they draped in a golden silk and we put in two large mirrors and a very nice ceiling lamp and the result could not have been more perfect; I organized an intimate and secluded parlor where I could spend time listening to the radio or reading quietly when I was alone. The bedrooms had balconies facing the street, and the two bathrooms did not lack a detail in terms of modernity. The kitchen and the service area were also spacious and pleasant, so as soon as everything was ready, the three of us moved there.

I started some routines. I would go for a walk in the mornings, visit a museum, have an aperitif in a nice place, eat at home or at my sisters', rest and go out again at night, to the movies, to a show, to the home of friends.... Life was once again wonderful and Madrid had a lot to offer me.

I went into half mourning in a short time, my hairdresser gave me a great cut, which took years off me, the house worked without me having to take care of anything, since I had brought another maid from the town who was in charge of cleaning, scrubbing and washing, unloading the cook and my maid of these tasks and everything hummed along. Also, my father, although he was getting older, still had his head in place and found me a good administrator, a mature and sensible man who took care of everything and was accountable to me on time.

When I was settled, one of my sisters gave a small party in my honor at her home, and told the attendees that they could bring some of their single friends, if they saw fit; that everyone would be welcome.

My friend Lolin, whom I saw a lot, showed up with her husband and a very elegant boy named Rodolfo. Others also brought more guests, but from the first moment Rodolfo and I fit together as two symmetrical parts of a whole, and we spent all the time that my work as honoree left me talking, telling jokes and anecdotes and laughing at everything imaginable.

It was a fun night and when he said goodbye, while he gave me a kiss on my right hand, he looked at me and asked if I would be so kind and good as to allow him to invite me to the aperitif and lunch the next day, which I agreed to immediately.

And that's how my new romance began,

Rodolfo was a charming boy, and when I say boy it is because he was: I was eleven years older, although you wouldn't notice the difference from my appearance.

He was Spanish, although he had an Italian mother. His father, who was a diplomat, had met her at one of his destinations. They immediately fell in love, got married and had born to them this offspring, who was an only child and very close to them, as he told me.

The mother was a countess and when she passed away the title passed to him. He had lived in several countries and at the end of the second great war he settled permanently in Spain, a country that he adored and where he had many contacts and friends, like my friend Lolin, who was the one who introduced us.

From our first date we became inseparable.

He seemed like a cultured boy, although no comparison with Juan Carlos, and certainly much less ardent than Antonio, but going out with him was very pleasant. We spent hours talking about trifles, while we went for a walk or had a cocktail. We went to dances, to shows, to dine in small inns in the towns around the capital.... We did not stop, and since he had a beautiful luxury car, an Hispano Suiza, the trips were very easy. I did not know what he lived on or what profession he had, but it seemed that money was not lacking and he had an incredible wardrobe. He was always dressed with great taste and elegance, his tailor on Savile Road in London made him from suits to shirts (with the county crown embroidered in colors contrasting with the fabric), he had the largest collection of shoes I had ever seen, silk socks, the handkerchiefs in the top pocket of the jacket always matched the ties.... In short, he was a dandy in every sense of the word.

Our relationship was chaste. We spent several months in which the only thing we did was give each other a few kisses and a few hugs, and in some moments I even wondered if it was not an invert, a fagot, (although it did not seem like it) because, although I displayed all my arts, and flirted at all times and pouted at him with my lips in a way that drove Antonio crazy, and that even Juan Carlos was not indifferent to, making his member grow, even if we were in public, with Rodolfo those tricks had no effect.

I asked Lolin to tell me about his profession and she said "Business." I also inquired if she knew anything about his previous love life and she told me that she did not know anything, but assumed that in France (where he had resided before returning to Spain) he would have wreaked havoc among the women, but she did not know the particulars.

I spoke to Rodolfo a bit about my life, within the limits that circumstances imposed on me, although logically I spared many details, not to mention all the annoying ones, and when he learned that I was twice a widow he felt great empathy for me, who had had to go through those unpleasant circumstances, he squeezed my hands and caressed my face wiping a timely tear that I had shed.

I also told him about La Operetta and a little about my finances, because if he was in business he could advise me.

I hadn't inherited anything from Antonio since the poor thing had nothing, well I had good sex with him, everything must be said, unbeatable, but not a tittle of money or possessions, but Juan Carlos had left me well supplied. He thought about everything and liked to have his finances well organized, so when the poor man died, so young, and in such a tragic way, I found a good amount of money not only in cash but also in bonds and stocks, which gave me good returns and freed me from the uncertainties of harvests or inclement weather, though actually with the farm I had no problems because it worked like a charm: the harvests and the cork provided me more money than I could spend, I sold the animals to a company that brokered them, and besides, I paid all those who worked in La Operetta a pittance, although I allowed them to have their vegetable gardens and chickens and to those who wanted them even a pig for their slaughter. In other words, everything was in my favor and I had no financial problems, thank goodness because at my age and with two deceased husbands it was enough.

Rodolfo was very interested in the farm and wanted to get to know it, and even more so when I told him about the hunts and parties that we had celebrated there in the past, and Lolin told me that he had also asked her and suggested that she convince me that with her husband, the four of us spend a few days there, which seemed marvelous to me, and I started to prepare everything.

I notified the steward that the house be prepared for this purpose, the kitchen stocked and no detail missing, and three days before our departure I sent my maid and the cook in the route bus to prepare good meals, because while Lolin and her husband had come to my house countless times, and had eaten and dined with me on many occasions, Rodolfo had never passed the entrance when he came to pick me up and I wanted to impress him, since even without a noble title I had always had a good upbringing too, and I was not going to shrink before counts or marquises.

It was spring and we had a delicious trip, albeit a long one because we stopped at various places to sample things, and the curves of the Puerto de Miravete instead of making us dizzy filled us with joy when we saw Rodolfo's astonishment, which was the first time he passed through our region, and how he marveled at everything.

When we arrived at the farm, the cook had prepared us a snack on the terrace with local products, accompanied by good Cañamero wine, and we all ate it before we even went to refresh ourselves and change for dinner. I assigned Lolin and

Eduardo the furthest bedroom, but I put Rodolfo in one that was attached to mine, and that in reality had hardly ever been used, in case the effect of the countryside and the proximity encouraged him to take some action.

But no, this ruse did not help much.

We spent some great days, with abundant food and drink, walks in the countryside so that Rodolfo could see everything, excursions to the Monastery and surrounding towns and everything turned out perfect.

Actually, not everything: my new friend, although delicious and witty at all times, gave no sign of being sexually attracted to me, despite my hints or more than hints....

I was in my usual bedroom, in the same one where my two husbands had died, the poor ones so young, and in that strange way, but alone and I didn't like that too much, especially knowing that it was only a partition that separated me from the object of my desires. He was the first who had not succumbed to my charms, although that was not entirely true either, for since we had met we had seen each other very often and, as far as my knowledge went, he was not seeing others, but there was a great age difference between us and that worried me a little....

The night before our return to Madrid I decided to make a frontal attack, and already at dinner I did the same thing that Antonio had done with me that memorable night: I brought my leg to his and to my surprise he withdrew. I did it again, in case he hadn't realized my intentions, and got the same answer: rejection. But I'm not one to be put off by so little, so I tried it a third time and with the same result. I would have to use another tactic.

That night, while the house was now quiet and everyone was sleeping, dressed (or to be more exact undressed) in my best transparent negligee and with nothing underneath, I knocked on Rodolfo's door in case he wanted a glass of milk or any other drink and he, very fine and correctly, told me that no, that he only wanted to sleep after the sumptuous dinner, so I went back to my room with my tail between my legs, to use an expression, although between my legs I had the same as when I left my room, that is to say, nothing. My frustration increased.

When we returned to Madrid I decided to stop seeing him for a season, to see if that would work. I went out in a group again, I resumed my readings, and when Rodolfo wanted to meet with me, I always had an excuse ready for not seeing him, while I was sweeter and more affectionate than ever with him and I "regretted" that due to this or that commitment we could not even have a snack together.

And it worked, you bet it worked.

One morning, while my maid was finishing my hair, Rodolfo came to my flat: he wanted to see me because he urgently needed to talk to me.

They showed him into the living room, a room that he hadn't known before, and there I found him admiring my signature paintings and my Sevres porcelains.

I came in smiling, relaxed and pretty, and right away he began with his speech, telling me that he was crazy about me, that he had tried to resist but couldn't take it anymore, that the days gone by without seeing me had been hell, that all he wanted was to marry me, and spend the rest of his life by my side.

I let him elaborate since in so many months knowing each other, his behavior had always been lukewarm, polite, correct and witty, but very poor in sexual matters, and when he finished, instead of words, what I did was approach him and give him a kiss on the mouth.

That kiss, which for my part was trying to be intense, was not like the kisses that I exchanged with Antonio, it did not even reach those that Juan Carlos gave me, but I blamed his response on the unexpectedness of my action, nothing more.

And we got engaged.

I did not care what type of wedding we had, I had already had two versions, and whatever the third was, it was no big deal, as the Madrid folk say, but Rodolfo wanted a ceremony in style: in the Church of Los Jerónimos, with cocktail and dinner at the Ritz and later our honeymoon in Venice. I let him do it because I understood that it was his first time and for him it was something very important. I would be a countess and even if it were an Italian title, I liked the idea.

So again I saw myself preparing everything: sets of clothes for the trip, wedding invitations, ordering flowers for the ceremony, talking to some, sending others, they were a few days of whirlwind, because Rodolfo did not want to wait long, and after going months and months without any indication he suddenly had an urgent need, but fine, I wanted to have a young and attractive husband, with a good figure, educated and with good contacts, and a count as well.

My sisters and their husbands were delighted with the engagement, but when I told my father the first thing he asked me was "How does he make his living?" and I could not answer him. I told him with business, but he insisted on asking what kind of business and things like that, and as I was getting bored I told him not to worry, that he would be delighted when he met him, because he was a fine and educated boy. All this time our relationship was chaste and pure. We were so busy that we couldn't think of anything other than a simple kiss when we met or said goodbye. They were very intense weeks.

Rodolfo suggested the convenience of settling in my apartment once we were married, since it was spacious, the location was perfect, I was used to the neighborhood and he wanted to respect my habits above all else, among other reasons, and it seemed fine to me. I didn't even know where he lived, but I supposed he would have a bachelor's apartment, and the truth is that I loved the place where I lived and I was very comfortable in my house. Lately a couple of times they had offered it to me for sale, but following his advice I had decided to wait in order to get a better price. There would be time for everything.

We celebrated the petition for my hand with my family and some friends. His mother was long dead as I already knew. His father suffered from senile dementia, as he told me, and despite being alive he was in very poor health, confined in a sanatorium in a town in Andalusia, where he was originally from, and he had no siblings or relatives, so the formality was performed by a friend of his who asked my brother-in-law Emilio for my hand. We had a most delightful afternoon.

I gave him a watch with diamonds around it and he gave me a small tiara that he told me had been in his family for many years. Cute yes, although to tell the truth, nothing spectacular.

Finally the wedding day arrived. My father was going to give me away for the third time.

He had arrived the day before the ceremony, and he would stay at my house for several days afterward, while we spent our wedding night at the Ritz, and would leave for Italy the next morning. Although he was very polite as always, I immediately saw that my father did not like my future husband, they didn't click from the beginning, but my father had had a special relationship with Juan Carlos, whom he adored, and even with Antonio on another level, he also got along, but that's the way things are sometimes. We fit in better with some people than with others, but since they both had good manners, nobody noticed anything except me, who regarding relationships have always been very insightful.

My suit this time was white, guipure, without a train, but down to the ankles, and on my head I wore the small diadem with diamonds that his mother had also worn when she married, of more sentimental value than real, holding a small tulle veil that reached down to my shoulders.

Rodolfo was gorgeous, in a pearl gray suit, black patent leather shoes, and a shirt so white it seemed to sparkle. It was a simple ceremony, very emotional and I almost had a tear, for I am deep down a sentimentalist. Besides, the priest did not give us a big spiel of the kind that those of his trade are used to, which I appreciated. The church was beautiful, full of white orchids, which are my favorite flowers, and all the very elegant guests, with the latest suits, and the men with formal attire, so we finished that process soon.

From there we all went to the Ritz banquet and, as the appetizer trays began to be passed, my new husband and I went up to the room where we would spend our first night together, so that I could change. In my mind I was doing something else, but Rodolfo limited himself to giving me a couple of kisses, claiming that the guests were waiting for us and that it was in bad taste to leave them alone; so I put on a beautiful green dress that my dressmaker had made for the occasion, and we went downstairs and joined the group.

They were all very animated and when we sat down to dinner the smiles, jokes and conversations flowed relaxed, although no one paused in the great orchestra that he had hired to entertain while we ate, and that would then continue with more lively rhythms for the dance. That was also one of the things that Rodolfo insisted on: a good orchestra.

We two opened the dance and immediately many joined. Everything was going wonderfully and they congratulated me profusely for the organization that I had done.

At two o'clock in the morning we bid farewell to the last guests.

I had eaten little and drank less, but my husband could scarcely stand, so, holding on to my arm, leaning on me so as not to fall and almost crawling, I managed to get us to the room where, dressed and even with shoes on, he collapsed, leaving me without a wedding night. How different from the previous two! But life is so.

When we woke up, and it is a way of talking since I had not slept all night and was afraid that it would give me dark circles or bad color, Rodolfo apologized for having drunk so much, assuring me that he was not used to it, that is why he got knocked out, and a lot of other things, but he had a terrible hangover that did not disappear even with the help of several coffees or a special brew that was brought up to the room.

Time was pressing for the departure of the train by which after several transfers we would arrive in Rome, to later transfer by bus to Venice, our final destination, so we collected our suitcases and went to the North Station, where my sisters were already waiting for us to say goodbye and wish us a good holiday. I pretended a happiness that I did not feel, and after many kisses and hugs we left.

We had a very hard trip and when we finally got to Rome the truth is that it we were pulverized. When we settled in a hotel on the Appian Way to spend a couple of days, we both fell into a deep sleep, or rather stupor, from which we didn't wake up until fourteen hours later, and my great surprise when I opened my eyes was to see Rodolfo very close to me, with a very sad and worried face.

To make a short story shorter, the summary of what he told me, after giving me a chaste kiss on the forehead, was that as a result of poorly cured mumps that he had in his childhood, he had been powerless to procreate and even to have erections. I was open-mouthed and he, seeing my embarrassment, could not do anything else than to cry like a child. Seeing him like this struck a chord with me and I told him not to worry, that I would take care of fixing him, that with a little time everything would be as it should be and his sighs of relief confirmed that I had spoken to him in the right way.

We saw Palaces and ruins in Rome, we went to Venice, we walked along its canals, and the city disappointed me with how dirty and smelly it was, and the sadness that was reflected on the faces of the people we saw. They had not yet recovered from the ravages of the war, although many years had passed since it ended. We ate pasta and seafood, and during those days we were just two good travel companions. The whole thing was a bit frustrating, but I put my mind to it and thought about Rodolfo from our first meetings and so I endured everything without problems; I had no other option for the moment.

We returned to Madrid full of gifts and stories to tell, although the juiciest had not taken place and I had to invent some for my sisters, and we resumed our activities.

My husband had a valet for a long time, who took care of all his clothes and his comfort and wanted me to take him on in the service. At home we had enough space to accommodate him and I did not raise any objections, quite the contrary, because my own women already had enough, taking care of the house, preparing our meals and looking after me.

Pedro was a very young, handsome, educated boy and, judging by how impeccable Rodolfo was always, I understood that I didn't want to get rid of him, and I welcomed him into my house without problems. And all those who made up the service were delighted with him, since he was friendly and witty, according to my maid.

We returned to our activities and an intense social life. Every night we went to dance, to have dinner at the fashionable places with my sisters or with other friends, to shows.... Life was a whirlwind, but shortly after, when we were fully installed in certain routines, the surprises. Lots of bills came in every day: from the hotel where we celebrated the wedding and spent the first night, to the florist who had so beautifully adorned the church, to restaurants where we had eaten or dined, this and that, some from his tailor and shoemaker in London, and even a very threatening letter demanding payment of an amount with so many zeros that I had to reread in case I was wrong the first time. The truth is that I did not know what explanation to give to everything, and before paying anything I asked my husband, because we already know the confusion that some companies bring, and I did not want to pay double.

Rodolfo told me that his businesses were going through a rough patch, that his stock trades had taken a beating, and that he had no choice but to go to moneylenders to get out of the hole, that I should pay everything and he would reimburse me as soon as things had stabilized. I did not like the matter at all, not because of the money, I had money to spare, and although the final amount of all the payments amounted to a very considerable amount, it was not going to make a big dent in my economy, but because he had not warned me of his situation; but my husband told me that he had done it so as not to worry me, thinking that by the time the payments had to be made all his finances would have returned to normal, so I believed him, paid, and we continued with our life.

We entered the summer and that year it was time to strip the cork oaks, so we all went to the farm, the two of us in Rodolfo's car, and the service the day before our departure in the line bus.

My sisters also went to their farms, which were close to mine, so we had guaranteed days of entertainment.

When I arrived at La Operetta, I was reminded of my two previous husbands and the sexual life I had with them.... What a great difference with the current drought! I had not had any luck so far, and although I spent hours thinking up tricks for the member to get up, these did not help me much since it stayed a worm just like it began. I was beginning to wonder if a doctor could fix the dysfunction, but I still didn't want to bring it up with my husband. I would wait for the right occasion to present itself.

And being back in my bed, where I had enjoyed so much with Antonio, put me in such a state that I had to relieve myself several times during the night. It was nonsense to have a young, strong and healthy boy by my side and not be able to feel him inside me, but no attempt would work, and I had no choice but to caress myself, put my fingers where his virility should have been, and think of Antonio's skill. In the morning, after my night touches, I would wake up happy and relaxed and that was what mattered to me.

Rodolfo had never seen a decorking and for him it was quite an adventure.

My farm was populated by thousands of cork oaks and once every nine years the cork they produced was harvested. The first and second strippings did not provide high quality cork, but when you got to the third you got some great plates.

When I inherited the farm, or more properly when my father donated it to me, most of the trees were over fifty years old, the optimum age to produce quality cork, since, although they can be produced from the age of twenty-five, the plates are thin and not very good for making stoppers.

The manager had hired a magnificent team of harvesters, who, assisted by the rest of the permanent staff of the farm, would do everything necessary to produce a large harvest in less than a month.

The beginning of summer is the ideal time for this operation since the tree contracts, the wood expands and the plates come out practically clean. Three types of product are extracted from the tree: the "plates" (with which wine bottle stoppers will be made, mainly), the borizo, of inferior quality, which is dedicated to other uses, and the "claws," which are the irregular edges of the plates, and from which more uses are being found every day.

Extracting the cork, although it may seem simple to laymen, is a complex and delicate operation: usually a team of three or four men is assigned to each tree under the command of a foreman called a *manijero*. He first observes each tree individually to see the conditions in which the cork is found, and armed with an ax in the shape of a crescent, with the point sharp like a knife, and at the other end instead of a normal handle a wedge of wood that will serve as a lever, he commences the decorking process: once the tree has been analyzed, they decide on which side they are going to start. With the tip of the ax they take off the cork and with the lever they lift the plates little by little. If they see that it is very stuck, they stop so as not to drag what they call the mother (or let's say the soul of the tree) along with the plate, since if they damage it, the cork oak will not produce cork again. Once the plate is detached, they place it on the ground next to the already extracted ones, one on top of the other forming a circle that allows air to pass through and the cork to dry a little, and then proceed to send it to its final destination.

On the first day, Rodolfo asked me how long it took to decork each tree, and it was the manijero who explained that it depended on each tree, since if it was healthy the cork came out the first time, and it also depended on how experienced were the cork crews, but sometimes they encountered beetle infestations and had to forget about that tree, so the duration of the process could not be estimated.

It was the third time I had harvested that crop since the farm became mine in 1940, and it could not have been better: the sale had been previously agreed and I received an impressive amount of money.

And since my husband's financial situation apparently hadn't improved since the wedding, and it was completely up to me, when I received the money from the sale of the cork, I gave him the entire amount, so that he wouldn't feel humiliated having to ask for even the simplest things, which he liked very much but it did not improve the state of his flaccid member.

We had a magnificent season. I have always enjoyed the country and in the afternoons we would go to the farms of one or the other of my sisters, or they and their husbands would come to mine; we had cocktails and great dinners and on many occasions other friends joined us so the evenings were very enjoyable.

The decorking was finished, we returned to our Madrid residence and continued with our normal lives after the country period. That year we had decided to spend a season in San Sebastián, meet friends there and have a good time, enjoying the sea and the environment. We took a very large house so that we could all share it: we three sisters, their children, our respective husbands and all the service, who between them formed a battalion, and we got ready to prepare our outfits for the season.

My dressmaker, as always, made me some beautiful costumes, which enhanced my figure while allowing me to move with ease, because what I liked most of all was dancing, and according to the opinions of my acquaintances, and also of those who were not so intimate, it was a pleasure to watch me on the floor and as I always told them, half kidding half serious, dancing also served me as gymnastic exercises and helped me keep in shape.

One afternoon when the service had the afternoon off and I was out shopping with one of my sisters, suddenly one of those terrible summer storms broke out; in a few minutes it started to rain heavily so I took a taxi and went home.

Everything was still and in total silence, only a few sounds came from my bedroom, and thinking that something was happening to Rodolfo, very carefully I opened the door. How did it occur to me?... the scene I saw surpassed anything I had ever seen: standing in front of the large mirror that almost covered one of the walls, my husband was naked, but he was not alone. Pedro accompanied him, also naked, with his back to Rodolfo's body, who had his member inserted while both of them writhed with pleasure. They were so absorbed in the act that they were not even aware of my presence, so with great stealth I closed the door again, and went to the other side of the house to calm myself a bit.

When my heart stopped beating like a runaway horse, just like when I was young when I was running with my friends, I quietly left home and went to a cafeteria, giving enough time for the two lovers to finish their games and the maids and the cook to return from their afternoon off, and when more than three hours had passed I went back up to my apartment as if what I had seen had not happened, and my shopping afternoon had been simply perfect.

But I had seen and it had happened.

When I arrived Rodolfo was reading the newspaper, happy and relaxed, like many other afternoons that I found him like that. And I acted with the utmost naturalness.

From then on I dedicated myself to noticing their behavior, but there was nothing to give them away: no furtive glances, no apparently involuntary touch, nothing; absolutely nothing that was not a normal relationship between a man and his servant, so I redoubled my attention thinking of catching them, but no.

Since when was that happening? It was a question that I constantly repeated and my only answer was always the same: surely since the day they met, long before Rodolfo even met me.

I hired a very discreet private detective, of whom I'd heard good reports, to investigate my husband, his business, his life before our marriage and everything else he could find out, although I already knew the most important thing: I had been made a fool of. Thank goodness I had never been in love with him so I was able to act coldly.

The reports that reached me before leaving for our summer vacation were devastating: the only truth in all his stories was his age and that he was indeed a count, but from one of those Italian noble titles without lands and possessions, and where the title held on more by inertia than by anything else. The rest was a lie. Neither was his father (whom in all those years he had never gotten to know) a diplomat, nor did he have or had ever had a stock brokerage business, nor had he lived in any bachelor's apartment as we assumed, but in a terrible guest house in Cava Baja where all the dregs of the capital gathered, and where even then he shared a room with his "servant" Pedro. And I was wondering where did he get his wardrobe from? I also learned that detail. An authentic gentleman who had fallen on hard times, and whom he met by chance, sold most of his clothes for a handful of change, and from them he had the details to be able to get in touch with the tailors in the British capital, which he did immediately, emphasizing his title of Count, with which the others, without further ado, prepared to serve him without problems. An old embroiderer, also in decline, who settled in the same den where the couple lived, embroidered the famous county crowns of which he was so proud.

The report went on and on.... What I paid the investigator was the best money I had ever spent in my life, and even though at the time I hit the ceiling for having succumbed and fallen into the clutches of a scoundrel, I held back and continued acting as always: loving and friendly, and still trying at night to give a little life to that flaccid part of him, knowing that there was no dysfunction, that what there was was vice and deceit on his part. That person had to disappear from my life.

The day before our trip I sent the service to San Sebastián. Only Pedro stayed in the house, since he would be in charge of closing everything and going later.

Adducing some last minute purchases, I left home in the morning and left him alone with my husband, in case they happened to do something and give confirmation of what I already knew, and indeed I had it: I returned not an hour later, I entered by the service door, and the first things I heard were laughter and conversations in the servant's room, and immediately the voice of Rodolfo saying "Let's get to our business before the old cow comes back.... Turn around so that I can gore you, on the beach it's not going to be like on the farm, where we had the other husband's house to touch and enjoy each other...." I went out again, I gave them plenty of time to do their dirty work and when I got home, I found again the family scene of my husband sitting and casually reading the newspaper.

That night I redoubled my attempts, I wanted my husband to have no idea that I suspected something, but I got the same as always, that is to say nothing, so I turned around and fell asleep. Not exactly: I pretended to be asleep. After a while, Rodolfo got up, went back to Pedro's room and there they coupled again, not even bothering to close the door in an orgy of bodies, kisses and touching like I had never imagined. They didn't even see me.

In the morning we went to San Sebastián as planned.

It was there, in a relaxed and serene atmosphere, that I would organize my plan.

The holidays were being good for everyone, even for me, on the exterior, since I continued to behave as always, being the soul of parties and dinners, but I began to comment that I was not sleeping well lately, so a friend recommended a good doctor there to me.

I put this doctor in my pocket five minutes into our interview, and he immediately prescribed a few drops for me before going to bed, warning me that it was a very strong narcotic, that I should only take one drop every day and not leave the bottle out, not within reach of anyone. As I was not going to take it, I did not care how much he told me. I already had what I wanted. Of course, I didn't tell anything about that interview, not even to my sisters.

We finished the maritime stay after a month, and the autumn season in Madrid was looking fantastic, you couldn't ask for more. Movie premieres, new variety shows, theaters, dinners and dances awaited us, and we threw ourselves into enjoying ourselves like the rich landowners that we were.

To make sure the drops worked, I did a test: one night that had been great and where the whole group had really enjoyed it, when we got home I insisted that we have a last glass of a mild liqueur, and while my husband was changing I added three drops to his drink that we would take already lying in bed.... In a few minutes he fell into a deep sleep that lasted until the afternoon of the next day. The narcotic was effective. With this knowledge, I just had to wait. I "worried" a lot about the episode, I discussed the matter with my sisters and friends because nothing like it had ever happened, but my husband played down the importance of it, attributing his long hours of sleep to accumulated fatigue, non-stop parties, and assured me that he was perfectly fine, I should not give it the slightest importance.

We always left the room unlocked and after that we did it with more reason, and I gave strict orders to the service, that if we hadn't gotten up at nine in the morning, they come in to wake us up.

Two weeks later I repeated the dose, but this time with only two drops and, just as I expected when nine o'clock passed, my maid and Pedro entered our bedroom. I was pretending to be asleep, but when they shook me a bit I "woke up", although it took a lot longer to get Rodolfo to do it.

We both downplayed the matter by saying that the night before we had eaten and drunk too much, and that from then on we would be more prudent and sensible.

I waited three more weeks, and with the help of the steward I organized a hunt that would take place at La Operetta, coinciding with the feast days of All Saints and All Souls. My husband was excited, and all our friends made plans to have a wonderful time and be able to take good pieces, but I was the one who got the best.

On the day I would carry out my plan, in the evening on one of the rare occasions when we stayed home, I put ten drops in his drink. I didn't want failures.

Rodolfo, as expected, fell into a very deep sleep. I locked the door, cleaned his glass, and refilled it. I put a cushion over his mouth, squeezed and waited until he stopped breathing. I opened the door and since I had nothing better to do then I went to sleep.

In the morning it was the screams of the two servants that woke me up, reminding me of a scene that Aunt Tomasa had told me about when my father-in-law died: my husband was lying next to me, cold as an icicle and with a huge erection! The damned scoundrel, after having denied me it all the time he lived.

My doctor came, who limited himself to signing the death certificate due to cardiac arrest, without further questions. I got back to taking out my widow's clothes and going through all the funeral formalities, condolences and crying. I fired Pedro because he no longer had to do anything, although I gave him some of my deceased's suits, thus giving him the option to scam another sucker. I canceled the hunting, and when all the mess was over, I went to rest for a while at the farm and continued with my life, yes, swearing and vowing that I would never marry again, as I have not, because as I tell my sisters and my friends, it was enough for me, losing three husbands, so young and in the prime of life, than to repeat....

A few days ago my usual doctor gave me bad news: my bowels are invaded with cancer and nothing can be done anymore, so he advised me to put all my affairs in order and, half kidding half serious, to confess and repent of my sins if I had them, but I have never liked confessions, I do not trust them, that is the truth, so I am writing these paragraphs in case any of my nieces ever want to know more details about my life.

Have I regretted what I did with my three husbands? Absolutely not, but it is true that I have missed Juan Carlos many times, so gentlemanly and always generous with me, and with age I have often wondered if his death was not a mistake, or if with time (if Antonio had not crossed my path), I would not have fallen in love with him and we could have grown old together, as they say happens in novels.... But the reality has been different and I am not complaining.

Who I would have liked to continue seeing is Teresa. She was my sister-in-law, but she was also my friend and we never had any friction. It was a shame that life separated us, but things got like that and I understand that her brother was more to her than I was, and that she cut off relations when I married Antonio, but deep down, I have always wished her the best, just as for my dear Manuela, who will be around eighteen years old, and I hope she is still as precious as she was when I knew her.

I say goodbye to everyone, and as the poet said "Goodbye cruel world," although I do not complain how life has treated me.

THE END

ABOUT THE AUTHOR

Victoria F. Leffingwell is a young writer with almost three-quarters of a century behind her. She defines herself as a "storyteller", understanding that qualifier as someone who likes to tell stories. She has written crime stories, children's stories, haiku poems, and essays.

This novel, as if it were a snake, travels a meandering journey. Although it begins in the year of the protagonist's last burial, its chapters go winding back and forth through various decades, and in that sinuous course we learn about his murder, his life and the lives of some of those who surrounded him.

But who killed him? Was it really the Maquis? Because at that time, only three years after the end of the Spanish civil war, under the umbrella of the name of that organization, some people who belonged to the winning side took the opportunity to commit misdeeds and go unpunished.

With an ending that will not leave any reader indifferent, its pages take us to El Escorial, to Madrid in the 1920s, to the extensive farms of Extremadura, and to many other parts of Spanish geography, with a stylistic skill and flowing narrative that captures us from the first lines.

As she is a nomad, she does not live more than four months in any one place, although she has fulfilled her dream of living, when she is in Turgalium, where live the villeins, in the walled promontory called La Villa.

But you can always find her at: shuinero@icloud.com, where she will be happy to communicate with you.

BIBLIOGRAPHY

Her series of stories "**Memories of America**" is a fun collection that spans several decades in that country, with a vision that is sometimes a bit acid, sometimes ironic, but always friendly.

"**Childhood with A-ma-ling**" tells us the experiences of two little girls from a Spanish province, in the 1950s.

The stories "**Escritos y Tontunas**" ("Writings and Nonsense") are also a series of experiences, but this time they are memories of her childhood.

"**Tales for Ariel**" are filled with wonderful imaginary animals that are already a part of many children's memories, and that continue to grow every month as Ari changes interests.

"**A Serpent in the House**" is a novel based on real events: a murder attributed to the post-civil war Spanish guerrilla band called "Maquis," but which was simply a crime of passion.

Now she is working on a novel about the experiences of five cousins, a novel that will span four generations and that she hopes will see the light before the end of the year.